08-568

the elevator

**Center Point
Large Print**

**This Large Print Book carries the
Seal of Approval of N.A.V.H.**

the elevator

ANGELA HUNT

CENTER POINT PUBLISHING
THORNDIKE, MAINE

This Center Point Large Print edition
is published in the year 2008 by arrangement with
Harlequin Books S.A.

The text of this Large Print edition is unabridged. In other
aspects, this book may vary from the original edition.
Printed in the United States of America.
Set in 16-point Times New Roman type.

ISBN: 978-1-60285-064-4

Library of Congress Cataloging-in-Publication Data

Hunt, Angela Elwell, 1957-
    The Elevator / Angela Hunt.--Center Point large print ed.
        p. cm.
    ISBN 978-1-60285-064-4 (lib. bdg. : alk. paper)
    1. Elevators--Fiction. 2. Women--Fiction. 3. Family secrets--Fiction. 4. Hurricanes--Fiction.
    5. Large type books. I. Title.

PS3558.U46747E44 2008
813'.54--dc22

2007037503

"Deception is not as creative as truth.
We do best in life if we look at it with clear eyes,
And I think that applies to coming up to death as well."
—Cicely Saunders

"We can believe what we choose.
We are answerable for what we choose to believe."
—John Henry Newman

the elevator

SATURDAY, SEPTEMBER 15
7:00 A.M.

~⊁⚡~

CHAPTER 1

Wrapped in the remnants of a dream, Michelle Tilson opens her eyes and smiles at the ceiling until she remembers the monster looming in the Gulf. She reaches for Parker, but the spot where he should be lying is empty and cold. She pushes herself up, the satin sheets puddling at her waist, and looks into the bathroom, which is empty.

But a single red rose lies on Parker's pillow.

Of course—he's gone to the office. He said he might not be here when she woke.

Groaning, Michelle falls onto his pillow and breathes in the sweet scent of the flower. Typical Parker, the disappearing man. Here for a night, gone for a week. Most women would resent his inconsistency, but she's become accustomed to his vanishing act.

She props her pillow against the headboard and leans back, surprised she can feel so relaxed on a Saturday morning. Weekends usually depress her, but despite the hurricane warning she floats in a curious contentment, as though the previous night's love and laughter have splashed over a levee and flooded the normally arid weekend.

Parker is good for her. The man knows when it's time

to work and when it's time to play, a lesson she's been struggling to learn.

She reaches for the remote on the nightstand and powers on the television, still tuned to the Weather Channel. A somber-faced young man appears before a map on which a swirling bull's-eye is moving straight toward Florida's west coast. Hurricane Felix, already a category four, has left Mexico and is churning toward Tampa Bay.

Michelle squints as her mind stamps the map with an icon representing her condo at Century Towers. Nothing changed overnight; she's still in the hurricane's path.

At least she's well insured. Parker's made sure of that.

She turns down the volume on the television, then drops the remote and considers closing her heavy eyelids. She could easily sleep another hour, but Parker might call and she wants to be alert if he does. He's already told her he plans to ride out the hurricane at his house, but who knows? This could be the weekend he'll realize she ought to meet his children. . . .

She eases out from under the comforter and reaches for the computer on her nightstand. The laptop is always online, maintaining a quiet vigil as it files incoming e-mail and prowls the Web for prospective clients.

Michelle slides her glasses on, then clicks on her e-mail program and checks the inbox: three inquiries from her Web site, www.Tilsonheadhunter.com, a note from her administrative assistant, four ads for fake Rolex watches, three for cheap (and undoubtedly illegal) pharmaceuticals.

The spam gets deleted without a second look, but Michelle smiles as she opens the Web mail. The first inquiry is from Don Moss, a Houston CFO who has recently lost his job with an oil company. He's looking for a management position in the four hundred thousand to five hundred thousand dollar range and he's willing to relocate.

The second is from a local woman with a newly minted MBA and "a strong desire to succeed."

The third e-mail is from a school principal who needs to move west due to his wife's severe allergies. Can Tilson Corporate Careers help him find a university position?

Michelle clicks her nails against the keyboard as she considers the requests. The CFO will get her full attention; he's probably good for a fifteen-thousand-dollar fee. One of her associates can coach the girl with the MBA on how to create a résumé and urge her to attend industry conferences. She'll not bring in much money, but she should find a job within a few months. The principal might be tough to place, but since he's probably been in education a few years, he's bound to know someone who knows someone in Arizona or New Mexico. He'll land a job . . . eventually. Tilson Corporate will simply have to make sure he exhausts all his resources.

She moves all three messages into her Action folder,

then opens the message from Reggie. She sighs when she reads that he's taking his wife and new baby to Georgia to escape the storm.

I'll keep an eye on the news, he promises, *and you can call if you need me. I'll be at my sister's house in Marietta.*

BTW—last week one of the counselors took an application from a young guy who's looking for a management position. Nothing unusual in the app, but I saw him through the window and recognized him—he's a columnist for the Tampa Tribune *and he belongs to the gym where my wife works. Long story short, Marcy chatted him up and found out he's doing a story on employment agencies who don't meet their contractual obligations. Looks like we're at the top of his hit list.*

I pulled his file and left it on my desk—he's using the name Marshall Owens, but he writes his column under a Greg Owens byline. You might want to look him up.

Michelle swallows hard as her stomach tightens. Her agency does find jobs for clients, though not as often as their brochure claims. And while their advertising states that they typically place people in positions with salaries ranging from seventy thousand dollars to seven hundred and fifty thousand dollars, she can't remember the last time they referred a prospect to a situation worth more than eighty grand.

If she doesn't find an appropriate position for this columnist, he'll be all over Tilson Corporate Careers.

If any of their procedures arouse his suspicions, he might dig deeper and investigate *her.*

Reporters ask questions; they verify facts and check entries on résumés. If she doesn't find Owens a job, he could crucify her.

She presses her hands to her eyes as dread whirls inside her stomach. Only one thing to do, then—find the fake applicant a real job, and pretend to be surprised when he doesn't take it.

That part, at least, will be easy. She's been pretending all her life.

Isabel Suarez drives the vacuum across the carpet, her hips working to a disco beat as Donna Summer sings in her ears. She maneuvers the machine around a desk chair that has rolled off its plastic mat, then stops to flip the power switch. A candy wrapper has drifted beneath the file drawer, out of the vacuum's reach.

Unlike the others in this tidy office, this employee—Waveney Forester, according to the nameplate—obviously enjoys eating on the job.

Isabel crouches and pulls the crinkled wrapper from its hiding place, then yelps when someone yanks the earbuds from her ears. Her forearms pebble in the sudden silence, but when she peers over the edge of the desk, she finds she is still alone.

The speaker cord has caught on a drawer handle.

Exhaling, Isabel releases the cord, then dumps the employee's trash into the receptacle attached to her cleaning cart. A load of printed forms, typed pages and soft-drink cans tumble into the bin, followed by a rainbow of cellophane squares—the secretary's guilty secret. Every Tuesday and Friday night Isabel finds dozens of candy wrappers shoved to the bottom of Waveney Forester's trash. The sight never fails to make her smile.

Isabel returns the trash can to its hiding place in the desk's kneehole, then lifts her gaze to the wide windows along the east wall. A sprinkling of lights still sparkles in the skyscrapers of Tampa's downtown district, a waste of electricity no one seems to mind. The sun has begun to rise, but only a glimmer of light penetrates the cloudy eastern horizon. Carlos warned her to be careful on the way home because a storm is on its way, a *huracán*.

Because her fellow custodians like to complain about the weather, Isabel knows Florida has suffered many hurricanes in the last few years, along with states called Mis-sis-sip-pi and Lou-i-si-ana. She doesn't know anyone in those places, but the people she knows in Florida are rich beyond imagining. They complain if their roof leaks—*¿por qué?* At least they have a roof. And homes. And a government that hands out money and food to anyone who asks for it.

She presses her hand to the cool window and feels a shiver run down her spine. America. Home of the blessed and the free. Home to runaways and castoffs and so full of people a girl could get lost forever . . . if she has reason to hide.

14

A flag on a nearby rooftop snaps in the rising wind, but Isabel can't feel even a breeze in this fortress of steel and glass. At this daybreak hour, in this towering perch, she can't help feeling safe. No one from *México* can touch her here. Even if her enemy manages to track her to Tampa, she will not surrender. She has Carlos and Rafael now, and she would rather die than lose them.

She catches sight of her mirrored reflection, gives herself a relieved smile, and nudges the earbuds back into her ears. Leaving the vista of Tampa behind, she powers on the machine and hums along with Donna Summer as she vacuums her way toward the executive's inner office.

Tucked into the corner of a wing chair, Gina Rossman lifts her swollen eyelids and stares at her unrumpled bed. The report, in a manila envelope, still rests on Sonny's pillow. She spent the night in this chair for nothing.

So much for dramatic gestures.

She lifts her head and glances at the clock, then frowns at the view outside the bedroom window. The sun is usually brighter by seven-twenty . . . but how could she forget Felix? Destructive hurricanes are nothing new for Florida; in the past three months Hillsborough County residents have anxiously monitored the paths of Alberto, Chris and Debby. The local weathercasters, who would probably lash themselves to a wavering flagpole if the stunt would get them national airtime, are positively giddy about the latest patch of weather heading directly toward Florida's central west coast.

Sonny will blame his absence on the storm, of course. He'll claim he didn't come home because he had to single-handedly prepare for the hurricane. He sent his employees home Thursday afternoon, he'd remind her, because he wanted to give them time to leave the state. His act of generosity left him with a stack of declaration pages that had to be faxed to frantic clients who needed to know the limits of their coverage. Besides—and at this point he would give her an easy, relaxed smile with a great deal of confidence behind it—he hadn't built a Fortune 500 company by limiting himself to a forty-hour workweek.

She used to accept his excuses, used to be proud of him for putting in more hours than the average husband. But no longer.

Now she knows where he's been working overtime.

She pulls herself out of the comfortable depths of the wing chair and smoothes her slacks. She wanted Sonny to find her awake and still dressed when he came through the door, but if he didn't come home last night, he won't show up this morning. He'll be at the office, feeding papers into the fax machine.

An alarming thought skitters across her brain. What if he doesn't come home at all? He might want to protect that woman, so he could be planning to ride out the hurricane in whatever rathole she calls home. Later, when the weather has passed, he'll claim he was slaving at the office until the power went out and he had to evacuate to the nearest shelter.

Last year, she might have believed his lies. This year, she has rebuttal evidence waiting in the manila envelope, along with a private investigator's report. A list of places, dates and times; eyewitness accounts of intimate dinners and lunches; even a receipt Sonny dropped outside Foster's Jewelers.

The amount on the receipt nearly buckled Gina's knees: forty-three thousand dollars for a diamond bracelet. Forty-three thousand that must have been siphoned off the company books. Forty-three thousand—money that should be part of her children's inheritance—has been wasted on baubles for some tart's wrist.

How much of his children's future has Sonny squandered?

A flash of grief rips through her, one of many that has seared her heart in the last twenty-four hours. How could her husband turn his back on the wife who's loved him faithfully for more than two decades? How could he neglect his precious children? Matthew is supposed to take over the business in a few years, but at the rate Sonny is spending, how much of the business will remain? These are lean days for insurance companies, especially in Florida. The bad weather of the past has devastated the industry.

The investigator included a photograph of Sonny walking down Ashley Street with the woman on his arm, her head brushing his shoulder. Sonny's face, visible at an angle, is marked by an expression of extraordinary tenderness. The object of his inappropriate attention is not facing the camera, but the photo reveals a tall, lean creature with a striking sense of style, a floppy hat, and a youthful body that has not borne three children and invested its best years in Sonny's dreams.

Gina moves to the bed, plucks the envelope from her husband's pillow and stares out the window while she taps the package against her fingertips. A maelstrom is swirling in the Gulf beyond; a killer storm. Before the sun rises tomorrow, its merciless winds and rain will sweep over Tampa and destroy anything that hasn't been properly secured.

Her husband's office is in the Lark Tower, Tampa's oldest skyscraper. His suite is on the uppermost floor, where the intense wind and rain will have unfettered freedom to do their worst. Downtown Tampa is under an evacuation order, but everyone knows Sonny Rossman is a stubborn workaholic.

What might happen if he decides to remain in his office as the hurricane blows in?

CHAPTER 2

Michelle returns the laptop to her dresser, then curls back under the covers to think. So—Marshall Owens is a plant, a test of her company's legitimacy. Owens has probably noticed the ads she places in the employment section of every Sunday newspaper, ads that suggest her expert counselors will market clients through exclusive insider channels and help applicants obtain interviews with top executives at major firms.

She pounds her pillow, then slides her hand under her cheek. Her agency won't be the first vetted by an ambitious reporter. She's read articles that condemn companies like hers, using words like *fraudulent* and *scam*. They promise to network and investigate for you, the typical exposé reports, and charge thousands of dollars for services you can perform yourself using free materials and the Internet.

If finding an executive position is so easy, why does she have so many clients? So what if on occasion she does little more than polish a CEO's résumé? Most administrators haven't evaluated their biographical materials in years. They wouldn't begin to know how to portray their skills in the light of an ever-changing employment market. They care only about the bottom line: salary and benefits. They want a job that offers a corner office, a savvy staff and a generous paycheck, but they don't want to do the legwork it takes to land such a position.

That's why they come to Tilson Corporate Careers. Michelle and her associates spend hours, if necessary, prying important details from clients and taking copious notes about the applicant's past employment, skills and responsibilities. They ask for address books, references from previous employers, even Christmas-card lists. Somewhere amid all that paperwork, Michelle and her staff usually find the opportunity that will result in a new position.

She is trying to think of the best way to approach the *Tribune* reporter when Roy Orbison begins to warble "Pretty Woman" from the depths of her purse. She groans, then reaches for the leather bag on the floor.

A digital photo of Lauren Cameron, her workout partner and best friend, lights the cover of her cell phone. "Hello?"

"Good morning!" Lauren's voice, as bright and vibrant as a new whistle, hurts Michelle's ears. "Did I wake you?"

Michelle nestles the phone between her shoulder and chin. "I've been up a while."

"I thought you might be. I've been watching the Weather Channel since five. But hey, I wanted to be sure you didn't forget our date tomorrow. You and me at Lord & Taylor, right? I'll meet you outside the bridal salon at one."

Michelle resists the urge to groan. In a weak moment she promised to serve as maid of honor at Lauren's second wedding, but the thought of standing alongside the bride's young nieces now seems ridiculous. "Are you sure about this? Your sister's oldest daughter might be hurt if you don't ask her to be your maid of honor."

Lauren makes a small *pffing* sound. "She's a child. You're my best friend."

"She's sixteen, I'm thirty-three. The thought of standing with all those little girls and holding a nosegay—"

"I won't ask you to wear a prom dress. We'll pick out

something sophisticated and you'll look wonderful."

Lauren's lying, of course, the way one girlfriend will always fib when she wants to neutralize the other's feelings. She'll probably dress her attendants in yellow, a color that will make the little girls glow like sunbeams while it tints Michelle with shades of cirrhosis. At the wedding, Lauren's relatives will elbow each other and someone will whisper that the really tall attendant is Michelle Tilson, and yes, the program's correct. She's really a *maid* of honor, because the poor woman has never been able to snag a husband.

Michelle rests her head on her hand as Lauren chatters about her preparations. So much to do, because even in cosmopolitan Tampa, marriage is a sacred estate and must be celebrated with every appropriate ritual. Prevailing attitudes assume that any woman who's over thirty and still single must be a little odd, while a woman who's over thirty, single and not looking to be married—well, that scenario is just plain unnatural.

Funny how Michelle never feels like a spinster in the office or at a club. At Lauren's church, though, with a half-dozen preteens clustered around her elbows, she'll feel like somebody's withered maiden aunt.

". . . I'm thinking yellow chrysanthemums will be perfect for November. You agree?"

The direct question hits Michelle like a thump between the eyes. "Mums? You don't mean those plate-size things, do you?"

"You're exaggerating, as always. But yes, I want this

wedding to be bright and colorful. I want to hold the reception outdoors and I thought big yellow mums would be gorgeous against the deep shade of those oaks on the property"

Michelle rolls onto her back and studies the ceiling. "I don't know if you should count on those old oaks. We do have a hurricane headed our way."

Lauren *pfffs* again. "It's going to blow right by us. They always do."

"This one might not. Parker's really concerned. He's up in his office now, checking on—"

"They said Charley was going to hit us, but that one turned at the last minute. Besides, my neighbor says the Native Americans who used to live here performed ritual sacrifices or something and swore no major storm would ever hit this area. So far, they've been right."

Michelle can't stop a wry smile. "Well, if you promise to sacrifice a chicken—"

"The weather wouldn't dare interfere with my plans. So don't forget—tomorrow, one o'clock, Lord & Taylor. We're going to find my maid of honor something scrumptious to wear and soon you can ask me to return the favor."

A sudden surge of adrenaline sparks Michelle's blood. "Why do you say that? Did Parker say something the other night?"

"Not to me, he didn't. But I'm sure he's getting ready to make his move. He's got that smitten look."

Michelle closes her eyes, glad that Lauren can't see

22

her face. "He's not in a hurry . . . and neither am I."

"Good grief, why are you waiting? Haven't you been dating over a year?"

"He has kids, Lauren, and the youngest is still seeing a shrink. Parker doesn't want to rush things."

"So you're going to let him keep you hanging indefinitely?" Lauren sighs. "Out of all the available men we've met, why'd you have to fall for a widower with teenagers?"

Michelle turns her head and spots the single red rose Parker left on the bureau. "Because I was tired of dating boys," she whispers, "and Parker's the most honest man I've ever met."

Her comment hangs in the silence, then Lauren clicks her tongue. "Whatever you say, girlfriend. Stay dry today, okay? And don't stand me up tomorrow."

"I won't."

Michelle snaps the phone shut, then sets it on the pillow that still bears the imprint of Parker's head. She misses him already. If he doesn't call and invite her to his house, it's going to be a long, lonely weekend.

She rolls out of bed and plants her feet on the carpet, then hunches forward as an unexpected wave of nausea rises from somewhere near her center. Last night's pasta primavera must not have agreed with her . . . but she didn't eat that much. They slipped out of the restaurant after only a few bites because that gleam entered Parker's eye. She has never been able to talk to him when he looks at her like a starving dog yearning for a steak.

At the thought of food, her stomach lurches again. She places her hand over her belly, where some sort of gastric disturbance is doing its best to emulate the hurricane. Deep breaths. If she can convince her gut she will never look at another calorie-laden pasta dish, she might make it to the medicine cabinet and that bottle of chalky pink stuff. . . .

Another deep breath. When the gurgling beneath her palm subsides, she lifts her head and straightens to an almost-vertical posture. She can't be sick today. She needs to get to the office before the weather worsens; she has to pick up the Owens file.

The third-floor window, flanked by accordion storm shutters she has not yet closed, reveals a slate-blue sky and the swaying tendrils of a tall palm. The live oak shading the rear of the condominium stands like a silent sentinel, its thick canopy too stubborn to shift for only a probing, preliminary wind.

A sudden urge catches her by surprise. Forgetting the weather, she flies into the bathroom and crouches by the toilet.

When her ravaged stomach has emptied itself, she leans against the wall and pulls a towel from the rack, then presses it to her mouth. A sheen of perspiration coats her arms and neck, but she is beginning to feel better. What lousy luck, to suffer a bout of food poisoning today—

Her breath catches in her throat as a niggling thought rises from the back of her brain. What if this nausea has nothing to do with food?

Like a child who can't stop picking at a scab, Gina spreads the investigator's report on the bed and reviews the list of dates and places.

8/21: Subject dines with young woman at Bern's steak house

8/23: Subject and same woman eat dinner at the Columbia

8/25: Subject and woman have lunch at International Plaza, followed by afternoon of shopping. Subject delivers young woman to residence on Bayshore Boulevard, departs 1:30 a.m.

9/08: Subject and young woman register as Mr. and Mrs. Rossman at the Don CeSar Hotel on St. Petersburg Beach.

The last entry sounds like a perfectly idyllic getaway, but Gina has never stayed with Sonny at the Don CeSar, and she would have remembered staying there as recently as last weekend. Sonny was supposed to be at a convention. In Orlando.

The corner of her mouth twists when she remembers a wedding reception she and Sonny attended at the Don CeSar. The place must have impressed him if he decided it was worthy of his mistress.

She shudders as a cold coil of misery tightens beneath her breastbone. Why is she torturing herself? Bad enough to learn of Sonny's infidelity; she doesn't need to know details.

Unless there's a logical reason for all these meetings. The truth might lie in some arcane bit of information the investigator missed. Sonny could have purchased the diamond bracelet as an investment or a Christmas gift for his wife. The young girl on Sonny's arm could be an overfriendly secretary; perhaps the lunches and dinners are innocent business appointments. He might have a hard time explaining the Don CeSar rendezvous, but one night does not have to destroy a marriage.

Gina moves to the heavy mahogany armoire in the corner of the room, Sonny's private domain. Because the housekeeper folds and puts away laundry, Gina hasn't opened these doors since they moved in three years ago.

If Sonny is saving the diamond bracelet for her, it's likely to be hidden here.

She lifts stacks of folded underwear, rifles through a mound of socks and slides her hands beneath several cotton handkerchiefs. Nothing. She opens the lowest drawer on the right, scoops up a collection of cuff links and watches, and sets the jewelry on the edge of a shelf After running her thumbnail along the side of the drawer, she removes the velvet-lined false bottom and exposes the digital keypad.

If she hadn't been home alone when the deliverymen brought the armoire, she wouldn't know about this secret safe. In an effort to be helpful—and undoubtedly to secure a bigger tip—the deliveryman had pointed out the safe's location and given her a sealed envelope containing the combination Sonny had chosen: six, five, eighty-five. Their wedding anniversary.

She had never mentioned the safe to Sonny; she wasn't sure if he even used it. But now her breath solidifies in her throat as she presses the appropriate keys. The keypad beeps, releasing the lock on the hinged cover. She opens the safe she hasn't thought about in years.

No bracelet. Nothing but papers: the deed to the house, their passports, a card with bank and mutual-fund account numbers. Nothing unusual, nothing incriminating, except—

Despite the bands of tightness around her lungs, Gina snatches a breath and picks up an unfamiliar bankbook. The plastic cover is shiny, the opening date less than four months ago. The bank is located in the Cayman Islands, and the account is in Sonny's name alone. Opening balance: one hundred fifty thousand dollars.

Her heart turns to stone within her chest. He's already begun to bleed his family dry.

She sinks to the edge of the bed. At various moments since receiving the private investigator's report, she's wanted to deny everything, strangle her husband and kill herself. At one point she was certain she deserved Sonny's betrayal because she hadn't been a better wife.

But those were emotional responses; she should have expected them. Now she needs to put her feelings aside and think about what to do. She needs a plan . . . and the courage to see it through.

Her thoughts drift toward a book on her night table: *Courage* by Amelia Earhart. "Courage," the aviatrix wrote, "is the price that Life exacts for granting peace."

If Gina is to have peace, she must move forward with confidence and determination. At long last her questions have been answered, her suspicions confirmed. Now she has evidence in black, white and full color. The P.I.'s package has provided everything she needs to divorce Sonny, but no one cares much about culpability these days. No-fault divorce has simplified procedures for cheating spouses and the sheer frequency of cases has made the division of a couple's estate a matter of routine. A judge will look over their assets, draw a line to divide his from hers and send them on their way. Of course, with the wrinkle of this other bank account, perhaps it's not going to be that easy.

Gina turns to the investigator's report and runs her finger over the notation about Bern's. How could Sonny think he had the right to take that woman to their favorite place? And how could Francis, the maître d', seat Sonny with an imposter hanging on his arm?

Maybe Francis didn't know about the affair. . . . Then again, it's more likely that Sonny bought Francis's silence with generous tips and sly smiles. Despite the camaraderie Gina and Francis have shared within the walls of the restaurant, the man is a servant, not a friend.

Only a close friend would be honest and courageous enough to reveal that your husband has a mistress, a sad truth that underscores an unexpected revelation: Gina has no close friends. No one told her about Sonny's affair; no one at the office, the country club or the church they faithfully attend at Christmas and Easter.

Surely someone has seen him with that woman. Gina can't shop at any mall for more than an hour without encountering someone she knows through the business or the club. Sonny is far more extroverted than she is, so people have to have seen him with his little chit.

Perhaps people *have* seen him . . . and traded knowing looks, clucking in sympathy for the deceived wife and the poor children. Maybe they've wondered aloud how long the marriage will last . . . and what she's done to make Sonny wander.

What has she done? Nothing but give him the best years of her life, raise his children, decorate his house and stand by his side through dozens of boring conventions, holiday parties and client dinners. She's reined in her instincts and bitten her tongue so many times it's a wonder she can still speak, and for what? A man who would betray her and squander his children's future on a tramp.

Sonny hasn't mentioned a divorce, but his girlfriend won't wait forever. She'll press for marriage one of these days, but before he hits Gina with the news, he'll make sure his assets are hidden and his business protected . . . just as he's already doing.

Gina will be ambushed.

Her children are being bankrupted.

She places the bankbook back in the safe and returns the jewelry to the drawer. She folds the investigator's report and slides it back into the manila envelope. The man has written a note on his business card—*If you'd like me to spend a few more hours on the case, I could identify the woman in question.*

Gina snorts softly. She's not spending another penny on Sonny. He can exchange his forty-something wife for two twenties, for all she cares. But he cannot steal from his children.

Ending this marriage will crush the kids, of course. They will be loyal to her, but they love their father and won't want to hurt him. She could tell them everything, let them see the proof of his infidelity, but teenagers don't always accept the truth. Most of the time they end up resenting the messenger who brings bad news.

She won't let them resent her because she's done nothing wrong. Sonny is the guilty party, he's the gangrene. And like an infected limb, he deserves to be chopped off.

Being teenagers, the kids have been so wrapped up in their individual worlds they haven't noticed Sonny's absences, his odd lapses into silence or his indifference on the rare occasions he's come home for dinner. He has already impoverished them emotionally; he will not ruin them financially, too.

If Gina says nothing and keeps Sonny's failings private, the kids will split their loyalties and try to make the best of a bad situation. They might even accept the other woman, whomever she is. Like characters in one of those Lifetime movies, every weekend they'll kiss Gina goodbye and head off for picnics and football games with Sonny's replacement wife.

That would be altogether unacceptable.

Michelle crouches on the tile floor and opens the cabinet beneath the sink, searching among bottles of hair spray, lotion and nail polish remover until she spies the blue box. How many years has it been sitting there—one or two? Has it expired?

She pushes aside a bag of cotton balls, then pulls out the box and searches for the expiration date—the kit is still good, so she skims the instructions. The test kit promises quick results and ninety-nine percent accuracy. After five seconds in the urine stream, the stick will turn pink; after two more minutes the result window will reveal an easy-to-read plus or minus.

Pregnant or not?

She sinks to the cold tile as the significance of the question hits home. She's tried to be responsible, but life is like a baseball game; you can't score every time you step up to the plate. Some homes aren't happy, some girls don't go to the prom, and sometimes your birth control fails.

But nobody should have to strike out on all three counts.

Pregnant. Or not.

She presses her hand to her forehead and tries to picture herself as a parent. Parker already has three kids, so she doesn't have to worry about his ability to cope with children. Matt, Amanda and Sam are practically grown, but their father adores them. He'll adore this new baby, too—if her nausea isn't the result of a virus or pasta gone bad.

On the other hand—she swallows as the gall of envy burns the back of her throat—Parker has been surprisingly protective of his children. Though she's boldly hinted that she'd like to get to know them, she's never met his sons and daughter. She's shopped for their birthday presents, dispensed advice about Christmas gifts and helped him understand the emotional complexities of teenage girlhood. But when she mentions meeting his kids, he insists they are not ready to accept another woman in his life. They're still torn up about losing their mother. . . .

After five years, shouldn't those children be ready to move on?

She straightens to relieve the ache in her shoulders, then shakes her head. Technically, Parker's opinion doesn't matter. She could have a baby and raise it alone. But a child deserves a father's love, and Parker would want to know if he has created a new life.

He'd be surprised, of course, maybe even stunned, but she'd assure him she didn't intend to get pregnant. Their relationship has been stable for over a year and until now she's felt no need to change things. She hasn't pressed for marriage and isn't even sure she believes in it. Matrimony might be fine for women who need to belong to a man, but Michelle has always valued her independence too much to surrender it.

Yet perhaps it's time to reconsider. Greg Owens's name keeps slipping through her thoughts, reminding her that investigation is only days away. If she can't convince Owens that her agency fulfills its promises, he may start digging into her past.

How nice it would be to surrender her responsibilities and walk away. To wake up in the morning and have no appointments. How liberating, to trade the support of a dozen employees for the care of one child. Parker wouldn't need her income. And he's so protective of his kids—if she had a baby, he'd probably want her to stay home and spoil the kid rotten.

She's never visualized herself as a parent, but she could learn to appreciate motherhood. Hard not to think about having a child when her employees are reproducing like rabbits and every other month some celebrity is showing off an infant Apple, Coco or Kumquat. . . .

Since her thirtieth birthday she's become increasingly aware that every menstrual cycle represents an irreversible loss of fertility. She's thirty-three, old enough to know herself and settled enough to sacrifice for a child.

Michelle stands on wobbly legs and opens the test kit. Inside the box, a sheaf of printed instructions and a white plastic stick nestle in a molded shell. She plucks the stick from its resting place and holds it up to the light. This little gadget will tell her if she's pregnant or not. If today will be just another day or the start of a new life. If her next strong emotion will be alarm or relief.

No . . . not relief. Maybe happiness.

Staring at the stick, for the first time Michelle realizes how much she'd like to be pregnant. If not now, then next month or next year.

She wants a baby . . . a cooing bundle of hope for which she could correct life's mistakes and build the home she's always wanted. Most people do live in happy homes; most girls do go to the prom; most women do want to be mothers.

She's tired of pretending otherwise.

Pregnant or not, she's going to tell Parker she wants a family. If he won't let her be part of his, she will create a family of her own.

CHAPTER 3

With her hair still wet from the shower, Michelle wraps her robe more closely about her, then sits on the edge of her bed and picks up the phone. Though she is determined to reach Parker, she hesitates before dialing his number.

Odd. Though she has no trouble telling people at her office what to do, she wouldn't dare try to order Parker's day. Strength and independence are two of his most attractive qualities, and he is one of the few men she has never been able to intimidate.

Still . . . she needs to talk to him.

She dials his office number, punches in the extension for the executive suite and holds her breath until he picks up. As always, her heart does a double-beat when his voice rumbles over the line.

"It's me, Parker." She lowers her head and plucks a dark thread from her white cotton robe. "Am I interrupting anything important?"

His voice, which had been toneless when he answered, warms with huskiness. "You are a delightful surprise. I almost didn't pick up—I've heard from too many clients who would like to fry my hide for their mistakes."

She chuckles. "That'd be a terrible waste of a perfectly good hide."

"Listen to you—you always know how to make me feel better." He laughs. "What are you doing up so early? I thought you'd sleep in."

"You're not the only one with responsibilities. I have things to do, too."

"Like what?"

"Well . . . I have to close the storm shutters, fill the bathtub with water and backup all my computer files. You know, the usual prehurricane preparations."

"Didn't you buy bottled water?"

"Sure."

"Then why are you filling the tub?"

She smiles at the teasing note in his voice. "Because Lauren told me to, okay? She's a native. She knows about these things." Silence rolls over the line, then he says, "I loved last night."

35

"I loved the rose you left for me."

"My pleasure."

Michelle wraps the telephone cord around her wrist. "Parker . . ."

"Hmm?"

"What are you doing now?"

He laughs again. "I'm cleaning up. Thought I'd take a shower and shave this stubble before I frighten someone."

"I like your stubble. I've always thought a salt-and-pepper beard is attractive."

In the background she can hear the sound of running water, so he must be talking on the extension in his private bathroom. Closing her eyes, she can almost see him, phone in one hand, razor in the other.

"Have you heard the latest on the weather?" he asks.

"Yeah. Felix's still on a northwestern track."

"Coming straight for us?"

"Looks like it."

"Then you need to lock those shutters. Make sure—"

"Listen," she interrupts, unable to wait a moment more, "I was thinking about driving in. I need to pick up a file at the office."

"Can't it wait? They issued an evacuation order for all of the downtown area. They'll be closing the interstates soon."

"But you're downtown."

"Well . . . I have connections. But you should stay put. It could get dangerous out there."

"Not for a while. They say we have at least twelve hours before Felix arrives."

"Things can get wicked in a hurry if tornadoes form in front of the storm. You ought to stay put."

"Lauren says there's nothing to worry about. Something about the Native Americans killing a chicken and making predictions—"

"What?"

"Never mind. Please, Parker, will you wait for me? I can get my file and we can leave together. We could even evacuate, maybe drive someplace north of here."

He lets out a long, audible breath, then speaks in a voice heavy with apology. "I'll wait if you promise to come right away. I don't want to hang around much longer because I need to get home. The kids, you know."

She draws a breath, about to ask why they don't pick up his kids and drive to Ocala or Gainesville, but Parker is no fool. If he wanted to knit her into his family life, this would be the perfect opportunity.

Obviously, he's not ready. Yet.

She swipes at a tear with the sleeve of her robe. "I suppose—" she steadies her voice "—you need to stay in the area for your clients. If Felix comes ashore here—"

"I'll be as busy as a dentist in Hershey, Pennsylvania. That's why I can't leave, sweetheart. I need to stick around. For my business and my kids."

She lowers her gaze, grateful he can't see the hurt welling in her eyes. Any man might have said the same thing, but she has a feeling his refusal has more to do with his children than his client list. "I'll be there in twenty minutes."

"Be careful. And, by the way, your timing's perfect. I ordered something special for you and it arrived late yesterday. I was going to save it for your birthday—"

"Good grief, Parker, that's two months from now."

"—then I thought maybe you could wear the surprise when I take you out for dinner next week. I mean, why wait?"

Michelle smiles as a blush heats her cheeks. Is he really ready to commit?

"Parker," she breathes, "what have you done?"

"You'll have to see, love. Come on up, I'll be waiting."

As Donna Summer continues to warble from the CD player, Isabel raps on the inner-office door, then uses her master key to enter. A quick glance assures her the space is empty, but she hesitates at the sight of a burning lamp. Though the computer behind the desk whirrs continually, the lamp is usually dark when she cleans this suite.

She shakes her head. More waste. Americans are always complaining about the high cost of gasoline, but still they burn lamps in empty rooms and run their computers all night and keep their air-conditioning so low she has to wear a sweater while she works. Maybe Americans just like to complain.

She blows a stray hank of hair from her forehead,

then walks over to the executive's waste can. Wadded papers and soda cans spill from the edge of the container, so she tamps down the trash before carrying it to the cart outside the door. No candy wrappers lie at the bottom of this bin; no cigarette butts, either. This boss, whoever he is, has few obvious bad habits.

She frowns as she returns the trash can to the side of the desk. An unusual amount of clutter covers the work area, so perhaps she shouldn't try to dust. A pile of papers litters the blotter, an uncapped fountain pen atop the stack as if the man—Mr. Rossman, according to an envelope on the desk—has just stepped out of the office.

But no one comes here on Saturday, and no one would come with a hurricane spinning in the Gulf of Mexico . . . would they?

Maybe she shouldn't have come downtown. Carlos did not want her to come to work. When she insisted they needed the money, he told her to hurry home because Rafael will want his *mamá* if the weather gets ugly. So she promised to work quickly, even though her paycheck will be short if she doesn't put in her full eight hours. There will be little money for groceries in the week ahead, but Carlos will put in extra hours at the gas station if he has to. If the storm doesn't come and the gas station stays open.

Somehow, they will—how does Carlos say it? Make the nickels stretch.

She smiles as she runs her feather duster over the edge of the credenza and skims the letters on the computer keyboard. When the monitor flashes to life after she touches the egg-shaped thing they call a mouse, she backs away.

She has been warned about American *tecnología.* The government here has hidden wires in the walls to listen to phone calls and read e-mail messages. Cameras sit atop traffic lights and snap *fotografías* of passing cars; computers at the grocery know what she buys and when she buys it.

Computers make Isabel nervous. So many Americans depend on them, especially the people in this building. Sometimes she feels as if the sleeping computers watch her as she dusts, ready to spill her secrets if she touches them in the wrong way.

Florida's attorney general has offices in this building—six floors of desks with computers—and his office terrifies her more than the others. She doesn't know who the attorney general is or exactly what he does, but with such a title and so many employees, he must know everything about everyone in the state. Which means he might know about her . . . but doesn't yet know he knows.

She must never give him a reason to search for any of her names on his computers.

She runs her duster over the back of Rossman's chair, then peers out the wide window behind his desk. More color has filled the sky since her last look, but the sun is glowering behind a cloud. After giving the glass a quick spritz of cleaner, she swipes at nonexistent fingerprints. Apparently Mr. Rossman never stands at this window, never touches the glass out of appreciation for the view. Perhaps he takes the scene for granted.

She pauses as she looks toward the west. A series of darker clouds hovers in the distance, swallowing up the horizon's light. The street lamps far below remain lit, but few vehicles move over the roads. Here and there, police cars hold a vigil at intersections, their lights flashing blue and red. Tampa appears quiet, almost deserted.

Donna Summer is singing "Any Way at All" when Isabel crosses the office. She is about to haul in the vacuum cleaner when she spies a large gold box resting on the arms of one of the visitor's chairs. An extravagant bow adorns the lid, but the top of the box is askew and merely resting on the bottom. Someone has examined whatever lies inside and left the box open . . . almost.

What could be inside a box so beautiful?

She stands by the chair, wavering, then tosses her feather duster onto the cleaning cart outside the door. What would it matter if she takes a peek? She will not hurt a thing. She only wants to see what kind of present a rich American boss buys his *esposa* or *novia*.

She dislodges the fancy lid with a fingertip, then pushes it out of the way. A white softness lies inside the box, and on closer examination Isabel discovers a gloriously lush fur jacket.

"*¡Está maravillosa!*"

Oh, what she would give to have such a *chaqueta*. A man buys a coat like this, only if his woman needs

41

nothing else, for why would any woman need a fur coat in Florida? Owning a coat like this would mean the bills were paid, the baby had clothes and they owned a home of their own. No one in her hometown ever owned such a jacket, but on television she's seen snowy landscapes populated by beautiful red-cheeked ladies in furs as white and lush as the snow surrounding them.

Isabel runs her hand over the garment, its softness like air beneath her palm. After glancing toward the door, she lifts the jacket out of the box and holds it up. The sleeves might be too long and the buttons a little tight, but what does that matter?

She turns to the mirror on the wall, then presses the jacket against her shoulders. The light color complements her dark hair and eyes, and the belt might make her look slender. She bites her lip, suffering a momentary jealousy of the woman who will claim this—why should she be so *afortunada?*

Isabel lowers her gaze as a wave of guilt slaps at her. What is she thinking? She has Carlos and Rafael and she is safe in wide, anonymous America. She might never own a fur like this, but she will never need one.

Still . . . maybe she could wear it for a minute?

Through the earbuds, Donna Summer urges her to follow her dreams.

Ingrained caution falls away as Isabel slips her arms into the coat. The silk lining, dyed to resemble a leopard pelt, feels glorious against her skin, and the fur collar softly tickles her throat. She wraps herself in the luxurious creation and ties the belt at her waist, then moves to the mirror to see if the *chaqueta* lives up to its unspoken promises.

A pale oval of apprehension stares out from the glass, then eases into a smile. Isabel relaxes with the stranger in the mirror, recognizing the fur-clad lady as a woman who could walk into any store in the country and not feel anxious. In this coat Isabel could shop at Nordstrom or Lord & Taylor; she could examine a fancy dress without some clerk rushing over to suggest that she would be better off looking . . . somewhere else.

She presses her hand to the soft collar and lifts her chin, determined to enjoy the moment. Even if by some miracle Carlos earns a raise and a promotion, they will always need money for Rafael's food and clothes and medicine and school. One day her son will go to college; later he will become a doctor. He is an American, so he will speak good English and feel free to shop in any store. His wife might own a coat like this, and she will wear it with pride.

Isabel slips her hand into the pockets and flashes a movie-star smile at the mirror, then realizes one pocket is not empty. It contains a thin blue box, hinged on one side.

She gasps when she lifts the lid. On a bed of midnight velvet, dozens of diamonds have been strung together, more than she can count. It's a *pulsera,* a bracelet, but unlike any bracelet Isabel has ever seen.

"What do you think you're doing?"

The masculine voice rips through the music in

Isabel's ears. She whirls and sees a man—¿*Senor Rossman?*—coming out of the bathroom at the back of the suite, his hair wet and his shirtsleeves unbuttoned.

Terror lodges in her throat, making it impossible for her to reply.

CHAPTER 4

Gina fastens the clasp of the manila envelope, then stiffens at the sound of movement in the house. Is one of the children awake? Not likely this early on a Saturday morning, but Matthew might have decided to get up and turn on the Weather Channel. Of all the children, he alone seems to realize the danger Felix poses. The girls have grown inured to the threat of hurricanes; Samantha actually complained when she heard the malls would be closed today.

Gina tiptoes to her bedroom door, opens it a crack and listens. No sound comes from the upstairs bedrooms, so she must have heard the wind moving over the attic vents. She steps out and looks through the wide living-room windows, guaranteed to withstand hurricane-force winds. The curling fronds of the palms around the pool are swaying toward the sunrise, which means the wind is coming from the unsettled west.

Dangerous weather may be on its way, but she has plenty of time. The sky is cloudy, but not sagging; the wind is brisk, but not yet dangerous.

She inhales a deep breath to bolster her courage. She can proceed with her plan. She'll freshen her makeup, pull on casual slacks and a light sweater. She needs to look like a devoted wife running upstairs to lend her husband a helping hand.

Few people, if any, will be in the building this morning. The first-floor deli, bank and florist are certain to be closed. She'll speak to anyone she meets and make it clear that while Sonny may be workaholic enough to risk his neck, she's not going to stick around. Maybe on the way out she should ask the security guard if the Pierpoint restaurant will open at all, implying that Sonny might need an afternoon snack.

She should be home before the kids wake up. Even if the wind rouses them, they'll get breakfast and settle in front of the TV. A couple of hours could pass before they notice she's gone.

Her family may not be perfect, but they are predictable. Sonny may not have come home last night, but the hurricane will force him to the office this morning, where he'll be scurrying like a squirrel before an oncoming Mack truck. At the last possible moment, he'll either run home or go to that woman's place.

He has no right to that choice.

Gina slides the P.I.'s report under her mattress, then pauses before the dresser to run a brush through her hair. She can't look unkempt or nervous today; she's a dutiful wife on a mission of mercy.

She presses two fingers to her right temple as a baby migraine drums a faint rhythm on a nerve. Wait . . . what about the private investigator? If the police call

45

him in, he'll tell them that Gina knew about Sonny's adultery.

Well . . . fine. She could say she's suspected that Sonny had other women through the years. That he's always been a scamp, and she hired the investigator to get hard proof of her husband's infidelity so she could beg Sonny to stay for the sake of their children.

Knowledge might be a key to motive, but it's not proof of murder. To find her guilty, they'll have to send crime-scene investigators, the coroner and detectives.

Hard to do when a hurricane has paralyzed a city's law-enforcement infrastructure.

She steps into her walk-in closet and selects a yellow sweater and black slacks from the cedar shelves. As she changes her clothing, grainy images rise on a surge of memory. During the news coverage of Hurricane Katrina, she couldn't help thinking that a person could disappear without a trace in the midst of such confusion.

Bodies washed up everywhere in the aftermath of that storm. For weeks, police and rescue workers found corpses in attics, under debris, in swimming pools and ditches. The levees of New Orleans hemmed in the dead of that city, but there are no levees in Tampa. The rains will fall, the tides will surge and the water will retreat, taking many of the dead along with it. Those who aren't washed out to sea will quickly and quietly decompose where they fell, adding yet another layer of stress to an overburdened police department.

Gina checks her reflection in the full-length mirror,

then pulls her trench coat from a hanger. She will need its deep pockets.

Before leaving the bedroom, she walks to Sonny's night-stand. The small gun waits inside the drawer, a Rohrbaugh R9 her husband insisted on buying "to protect the family."

Exactly what she intends to do with it.

She shrugs her way into the trench coat, drops the weapon into one of the pockets, then pulls her keys from her purse. Her shoulder feels empty without her handbag, but today she will travel without it. If she's stopped at an intersection, she doesn't want to be able to produce identification or a wallet. A policeman is likely to forget a flustered face, but he might remember the name on a driver's license.

She looks in the mirror and practices her lines: "I'm here only for a minute. I have to run upstairs."

A guileless face smiles back at her.

In the great room, she listens to the rising wind and swats at an insistent gnat of worry. Downtown Tampa may be at Felix's mercy, but the suburbs are braced for the worst. This three-year-old house meets the tough new building codes and Sonny has stocked the garage with water, batteries, flashlights and packaged snack foods.

Before leaving, she tiptoes up the thickly carpeted stairs to check on her children. Matthew's door is ajar; she gives it a gentle push and sees him sprawled over his bed, arms and legs akimbo. A handsome auburn-haired nineteen-year-old with amazing potential, according to his high school counselor, Matthew represents the best of her and Sonny. He has taken a year off to work and gather what he calls "life experience." While Gina admires his practicality, she suspects he's postponed college because he knows his leaving will break his mother's heart.

Seventeen-year-old Mandi has fallen asleep with her television still flickering in the corner. While one of the Three Stooges snorts and wheezes into the depths of an enormous handkerchief, Mandi snores like a lumberjack, her head back and mouth open. In the room next door, Samantha, Gina's youngest, is curled under a puffy pink comforter, her head sharing the pillow with a bedraggled stuffed animal.

Gina lingers in the doorway and smiles at her baby. Samantha would die if she knew Gina was seeing her like this; at fifteen, she pretends to be past caring for the sentimental treasures of her childhood. Gina knows better, though. A mother always knows.

She closes Samantha's door and blows a kiss toward each of her sleeping offspring. If she's delayed, Matthew will watch out for his younger sisters until she returns home.

After the initial shock, her kids will be fine. She and the children only have to weather this one storm.

Michelle checks her reflection in the mirror, wipes a smudge of gloss from the edge of her lower lip and hopes Parker will look up from his paperwork long enough to appreciate her efforts to look nice on a blustery Saturday morning. The man has a tendency to be testy when under pressure, and he definitely didn't get much sleep last night.

But he has a surprise for her. If all goes well, his surprise and her decision will complement each other.

She leaves the bathroom and moves through the living room, picking up drink glasses and napkins left behind on the coffee table. After setting the dishes in the kitchen sink, she returns to the living room and stops to press the power switch on the television remote. Several channels of kids' cartoons flash in a blur until she finds a weather map. The fresh-faced newscaster holds a rain-coated toy poodle on one arm while he points to what looks like a frosted doughnut spinning toward Florida's central west coast.

"Pressed by a descending cold front, Felix is taking a more northwesterly track than initially predicted," the weathercaster says. "The hurricane is now expected to come ashore near Madeira Beach in less than twelve hours. If you haven't evacuated and you live on the water, forget about leaving the county The interstates are congested and you don't want to be trapped on the highway. Instead, get to a shelter right away."

Michelle glances at the clock on the wall—the storm won't arrive until day's end, but the winds could become dangerous long before Felix makes landfall. Then again, the hurricane could veer north or south and barely ripple the air, making fools of the people who have spent the last week slapping plywood on their windows and loading their pantry with toaster pastries. Over the years she's done that herself, stockpiling bottled water she eventually uses to mist the ferns on her front porch.

But at this moment she has something more important to think about. Whether or not Felix reaches Tampa Bay, Parker will soon finish up at the office and head home to be with his kids. If she's going to talk to him alone, she has to leave now. She could wait, but she doesn't want to lose her nerve. . . .

The television camera shifts to a reporter standing in front of a pile of rubble. "Bob Ruffalo here," he says, squinting into a spotlight, "in Puerto Juarez on the Yucatan Peninsula. Twenty-six hours ago Hurricane Felix blew through this place with winds of one hundred forty miles per hour. What you see behind me was once a thriving village—now the village has all but disappeared beneath a mountain of debris. Forty-four people are dead, scores of men, women and children are missing—"

Michelle clicks off the power and drops the remote onto the sofa. She moves toward the door, but the image of the ruined village lingers on the back of her retinas. When she tries to imagine what sort of diamond Parker may have picked out, the only picture her mind supplies is that of a big-eyed Mexican girl in a torn and muddy dress—

She stops at the door and rakes her hand through her hair. Okay, she'll admit it. This may not be the most appropriate day for personal ultimatums, but what can she do about hurricane victims in Mexico?

"Get a grip, Tilson," she says, her voice echoing in the empty foyer. "The Yucatan is in a different country. Rural villages like that don't even have building codes, but we do and they're tough. You need to be tough, too."

Maybe Lauren is right and Felix won't come here . . . but if it does, she'll be ready.

Michelle walks to the large front window that overlooks Tampa Bay, tests the lock with her thumb, and is reassured to find the frame sealed tight. The accordion shutters wait at the right and left, ready for her to secure them. Nothing short of a Learjet, the installer assured her, could blast through those shutters when they are locked and loaded.

In an hour, two at the most, she'll be back, ready to button up the condo and ride out the storm . . . unless Parker convinces her he is finally ready to get serious about their future. If so, she'll come home only long enough to close the shutters and pack a bag.

Elated by her renewed determination, she pulls her keys from her purse, opens her front door and strides toward the elevator.

She's thirty-three years old and she wants a family. If Parker doesn't want to join her, then she'll find someone else, but she will not be kept dangling.

If all goes well, she will spend this night with Parker's children by her side and his ring on her finger.

And she will not have yellow mums at her wedding.

8:00 A.M.

CHAPTER 5

As the wind fires sharp pellets of rain at his windshield, Eddie Vaughn turns up the volume on his radio. On the seat beside him, Sadie, his golden retriever, shifts her weight and gives him a beseeching look.

"Almost home, girl." He slows to ease the pickup across a stream gushing through an intersection, then tears his gaze from the pavement to grin at the dog. "You ready to settle in and watch some TV? If the power goes out, I figured we could play a few rounds of Go Fish or do a crossword."

Sadie makes a *rhrrrumph* sound deep in her throat, then lowers her chin to the top of the seatback and stares out the truck's rear window.

Eddie forces himself to whistle a bar of "Singing in the Rain," then gives up the effort. The dog is worried, and no amount of grinning or whistling is going to relieve her anxiety. He's heard that animals can sense impending natural disasters—whether or not the rumor is true, Sadie has been antsy for the last couple of days.

Felix has been swirling around in the Caribbean for almost a week, but only in the last twelve hours has the storm drawn a bead on Tampa Bay.

When the cell phone on the seat buzzes, Eddie turns down the volume on the radio, then scoops up the phone with his free hand. " 'Lo?"

"Hey, doll." Charlene's voice, crusty from chain-smoking, fills his ear. "Are they all squared away up there at Freedom Home?"

"You can scratch that one off your list, ma'am. Those folks aren't going to be using the elevators anytime soon. The nurses have moved all the residents into the common room—the poor people who didn't have anyone to pick them up, anyway."

"Thanks for running up there, Eddie. I hated to call you out so early."

"No big deal. I can go power 'em up after the storm passes, if you want."

She croaks out a laugh as another phone rings in the background. "You must have gotten a look at my friend's daughter. Did you meet Emily? She'd be the blonde, the one that looks like Pamela Anderson."

Eddie brakes for a stop sign. "Yeah, I saw her. Pretty package. Nothing inside."

"You're too picky, Ed. Here I go out of my way to hook you up with a girl—"

"Give it a rest, Charlene, I'm doin' fine."

"But you're too nice a guy to be livin' all alone—"

"I'd rather live alone than try to talk to a woman who's as shallow as a pie pan." He catches a quick breath. "Don't you have to answer that phone?"

Thankfully, the question derails the dispatcher's train of thought. "Yeah, I'd better. Well, doll, you take care.

Batten down the hatches and all that. Check in when you can."

"You take care, too, Charlene. I'll talk to you when it's all over."

He disconnects the call and tosses the phone back onto the seat. Sadie lowers her head to sniff at it as Eddie slants into the left lane, where the water isn't as deep.

"Almost home, girl."

Charlene's well-intentioned meddling has turned his thoughts toward Alabama . . . and Heather. His memories of her are hazy now, blurred by time and the receding fog of pain.

Yet thoughts of Alabama still tighten his throat.

He turns up the volume on the radio. No music yet; the newscaster remains focused on the threatening weather: "Experts are saying Felix could wreak the kind of damage Charley did to Punta Gorda three years ago. The tidal surge could rise as high as twenty-two feet, enough to flood the downtown area, Tampa International Airport and MacDill Air Force Base."

"Good thing we don't live in Tampa, huh, Sades?"

Eddie clucks his tongue as he turns into his subdivision and peers through the pouring rain. His neighborhood seems deserted, which means people have either heeded the evacuation warnings or hunkered down inside their homes. Sheets of plywood or corrugated aluminum cover most of the windows and the seven dwarfs have disappeared from Mrs. Jackson's flower bed. Jack Tomlinson has parked his wife's minivan on the open lawn, away from the heavy oak tree that shades the south side of their house. Though the Tomlinson family's garage is crowded with old newspapers, paint cans, sports equipment and tools (several of them on loan from Eddie), apparently Jack has found room for his Corvette.

"I'd like to repeat," the radio announcer says, "that the governor has ordered the mandatory evacuation of ten coastal counties, warning that those who stay behind face certain injury or death. If you're not in a shelter and you live on the beach, you need to evacuate immediately to protect your own life."

Eddie's house, located on high ground in unincorporated Pinellas County, is part of a thirty-year-old subdivision built when contractors cared more for utility than aesthetics. The rainwater is draining properly on his street, a road lined by three-bedroom, two-bath structures of concrete block. Like its neighbors, his house isn't fancy, but it has a fenced yard for Sadie, a small pool and a half-dozen shade trees to protect it from the sweltering summer sun.

Eddie hopes those leafy canopies survive the approaching hurricane. Last year even the storms that merely swiped at Pinellas County toppled hundreds of trees, which damaged cars and homes as they fell. Not even a house of concrete block can withstand a direct hit from a sprawling two-hundred-year-old live oak.

"Officials estimate that 487,000 people in Hillsborough County alone have had to seek shelter," the newscaster continues, "and over 550,000 have filled shelters in Pinellas County. They're fortunate—the Florida Highway Patrol has halted access to the interstate system, and those who haven't made it across Pinellas County's two bridges and single causeway are out of luck. Wherever you are, I hope you're safely tucked away and not on the road."

"You and me both, bud," Eddie says, turning into his driveway. He pulls the pickup under the carport, then steps out of the truck. He doesn't have to call Sadie— she leaps out behind him, a graceful golden blur on a beeline for the back door.

He laughs as he looks for his house key. "Ready to go inside, are you? Me, too. Let's eat while we still have power to the microwave."

Sadie scratches at the threshold, then sits back and waits for Eddie to slip the key into the lock. After opening the door, he takes one last look around before following the dog into the house. The garbage cans have been hauled into the utility room, the bird feeders tucked into a sheltered corner of the carport. He has covered his windows with plywood, turned the glass-topped patio table upside down on a mat of old towels and tossed his aluminum lawn chairs into the pool. He and Sadie have bottled water, a battery-powered radio, canned foods, a manual can opener, a stash of cash and a full gas can—enough supplies to get them through a couple of weeks, if necessary.

Satisfied with his preparations, he steps into the utility room and locks the door, securing the dead bolt, as well. The dead bolt would stop a human intruder, but he's not sure it will hold against a category-four wind.

A year ago, when he left Alabama to escape an emotional storm, he never dreamed he'd be exchanging one kind of disaster for another. All things considered, though, the literal storms are easier to handle.

"God, help us," he murmurs, one hand on the doorknob. Then he turns and whistles for the dog.

Because a man on the radio keeps insisting the police have blocked the downtown exits off I-275, Gina avoids the interstate and drives toward Sonny's office along a less-traveled route. Several ominous clouds have swept in from the bay by the time she reaches the edge of the downtown district; a gray curtain of rain hangs beneath them, obscuring her view of the river.

On her approach to the Platt Street Bridge, she spots a policeman sitting in his cruiser. The brim of his hat shifts toward the rearview mirror, so he's seen her.

Well . . . Sonny always says it's easier to beg forgiveness than permission. She could almost believe he was counting on her forgiveness for the affair . . . if she hadn't found the bankbook.

Rage rises in her cheeks as she stomps on the gas and steers around the police officer.

On the far side of the bridge, she looks in her mirror and sees the cop stepping out of his car. He might be frustrated, but he won't stop her. He's needed at his post.

Sonny is needed at home, but where has he been

lately? With his mistress. With a young, pretty trophy tartlet.

She turns north and heads up Ashley Drive, then brakes at an intersection. No one else moves on this riverside street, not even the police. She glances at the wet road, where the traffic light shivers in red reflection beside her car, then turns the asphalt green.

She drives on. The haze of gasoline and diesel fumes that usually hovers over the downtown streets has been replaced by a thick humidity. She can almost feel the skin of the storm swelling like an overripe grapefruit. Soon it will burst.

Just as she will burst if she fails to act.

She is overcome with a memory, unshakable and vivid, of a character in a Flannery O'Connor short story. The woman's thin skin is described as "tight as the skin on an onion" and her gray eyes are "sharp like the points of two ice picks."

Today Tampa wears the look of O. E. Parker's cold-hearted wife.

After passing the light at Jackson, she spots the flashing bubble of another police vehicle. To avoid it, she heads the wrong direction down Kennedy, a one-way street, then breaks the law again as she drives north on southbound Tampa. After a quick turn, she pulls into the whitewashed entrance of the Lark Tower's parking garage and guides her car up the slanted driveway.

At the entry gate, she presses the red button, then takes a ticket. She looks to her left, where the parking attendant's booth stands empty. The garage, in fact, is as quiet as a ghost town.

The black-and-white striped arm lifts, allowing her to enter. She turns and glances in the rearview mirror. No lights flash behind her; no siren breaks the stillness. She glories briefly in her accomplishment, then follows the curving arrows past the visitors' parking to the third level, reserved for tenants.

She smiles after rounding the corner. Her instincts about her husband were spot-on, as usual: Sonny's silver BMW is snuggled into its reserved space. He must have been in a hurry when he arrived, for he pulled in at an angle, carelessly trespassing on another tenant's parking place.

"How rude, darling." Purposely remaining between the painted lines, Gina pulls into the space next to the BMW and crinkles her nose as the front of her Mercedes just misses her husband's back bumper.

She would have liked to hit his precious car, but she can't afford to indulge a childish whim. She needs to get in and out of the building with as little fuss as possible.

Gina kills the engine, then pulls her keys from the ignition. Pistol in the right pocket, keys in the left. She steps out of the car, gives Sonny's unblemished bumper a regretful smile and strides toward the elevators on legs that tremble despite the dead calm in her heart.

The designers of the Lark Tower have done their part to ease Tampa's traffic congestion by reserving the six lowest floors for parking. On an ordinary day all six levels would be filled by tenants and visitors, but most of the spaces are vacant now.

The garage is heavy with after-hours quiet, broken only by the echo of Gina's footsteps and the tick of her cooling engine. She glances over her shoulder to be sure she's alone, but no one has driven in or out since her arrival. Most everyone, apparently, has gone home.

Sonny should have gone home, too. If he hadn't been playing around with his girlfriend last night, he wouldn't need to come to the office this morning.

Twelve elevators at the center of the building provide access to the Lark Tower's thirty-six floors. Six of the elevators are express, stopping only at levels one through seven and office levels twenty-five through thirty-six. A second bank of six elevators serves the first through twenty-fifth floors. A special plaque announces the eighth-floor location of the renowned Pierpoint Restaurant, home to one of Tampa's finest chefs.

Since Sonny's office is on the uppermost level, Gina steps into the air-conditioned space at the express landing and presses the call button. While she waits, she checks her reflection in the polished bronze doors. In order to surprise her cheating husband, she needs one more thing.

With Florida's attorney general occupying five and a half floors of office space at the top of the building, the Lark Tower's uppermost levels aren't accessible to the public. Every visitor has to obtain an access card before the elevator will rise to the thirty-sixth floor, and Sonny believes the extra layer of security lends the offices of Rossman Life and Liability a certain cachet.

A bell dings to signal an elevator's arrival. Gina steps into the car, then turns and presses the button for the lowest level. The polished doors slide together, then the car lowers her to the marble-tiled lobby.

Gina moves into the open area and strides toward the security station, where a tubby older man in a blue uniform blinks at her approach. She doesn't recognize him, nor, apparently, does he know her. Not surprising, since she hasn't visited Sonny's office in months.

Behind a granite-topped counter, the guard slides off his stool. "I'm sorry, ma'am," he calls, his voice ringing against the marble walls, "but the building is closed. We're under an evacuation order."

Something in his appearance—perhaps the stun gun attached to his belt—sends a wave of reality crashing over her, as hard as the terrazzo beneath her loafers. She is about to do something that cannot be undone. She has planned a heinous act, a deed that would cause her children to gasp in revulsion if they knew what she had in mind.

Can she really go through with this?

How easy it would be to smile at the security guard, profess ignorance of the evacuation and take the elevator back to the parking garage. She could drive home to her sleeping children. They would never know what she'd planned or how far she'd gone—

But they need not know anything. She won't tell

them about this, or the bankbook, or the forty-three-thousand-dollar bracelet Sonny gave to his Don CeSar date. She'll keep everything from them, just as Sonny has kept secrets from her for who knows how many years.

Yet some secrets refuse to stay buried. Matthew might find something in the office or Samantha might run into someone at the club who knows that woman. Idle gossip is a powerful force, and even if her plan goes off without a hitch, someone might guess at the truth. . . .

She sways on her feet as the walls blur and only half hears the security guard's alarmed question: "Ma'am? Are you all right?"

She puts out a hand and grips the edge of the counter. "Just give me . . . a minute."

Can she continue to ignore Sonny's late hours? Can she pretend she doesn't notice another woman's perfume on his shirts? When the inevitable occurs and he comes in to ask for a divorce, can she look her children in the eye and say she didn't see it coming?

She can't. She sees, she knows, and she has to stop Sonny from ripping her family apart.

She blinks at the guard and forces her lips to bend in a curved, still smile. "Sorry about that," she says, realizing that this man could be called to testify at her trial. "I should have stopped to grab a bite of breakfast."

The guard's brow wrinkles with concern. "Should I call a doctor? Get you something to eat?"

"I'm fine now, thanks." She broadens her smile. "My

husband is tending to some last-minute details in his office. I thought I'd help him out—you know, speed things along so he can come home."

The man's look of unease deepens. "I'm not supposed to let any visitors go up. We've been experiencing blackouts and I wouldn't want to be responsible—"

"Don't worry." She flattens her hands against the countertop and softens her smile. "I'm sure I can talk him into leaving the building eventually. But I need an access card."

The man crosses his arms and folds his hands into his armpits. "No can do, ma'am. Why don't you call him? There's a phone around the corner—"

The ding of the elevator interrupts. Gina pivots, half expecting to see Sonny, but the man who steps into the lobby is a stranger. He comes forward, drops a sealed envelope onto the security desk, then returns to the elevator. An instant later he reappears, pushing a cart loaded with cardboard file boxes.

Gina transfers her gaze from the stranger to the wealth of silver hair on the guard's forearms. "You let that man go up."

The tip of the guard's nose goes pink as he shoves the envelope into a drawer. "I—I can't stop anybody with a pass key. They come straight from the garage and go up, nothing I can do about that. But I've been told to clear the building by ten o'clock, so that's what I aim to do."

"The thing is," Gina says, lowering her voice, "I

haven't been able to reach my husband by phone. I'm worried and I need to see him."

"I'm sorry, but I can't give you a card." Despite his concerned expression, the guard is proving to be about as flexible as a brick wall. "I didn't even program any visitor's cards this morning, on account of the evacuation order. So you can sit and wait or you can call your husband, but I can't give you an access card."

Maybe she can sweet talk him into going upstairs with her. Once she's on the thirty-sixth floor, he ought to let her walk to Sonny's office alone.

"I'm worried," she repeats, meeting the man's gaze. "Sonny doesn't answer his phone. Could you—could we go up together and see if he's okay?"

The man frowns, glances at the elevators, then shakes his buzz-cut head. "Can't leave my post. The other guards didn't come in today, on account of the hurricane. I'm supposed to leave in a couple of hours. The entire building's gotta be evacuated."

Sonny used to say she could charm the sting out of a bee, but she must be losing her touch.

Sighing, Gina scans the desk behind the counter. No access cards in sight, but they're probably in a drawer. She has no idea how to program one, but if Deputy Dawg can do it, surely she can figure it out.

She smiles, then lowers her arms and slips her right hand into her pocket. Reluctantly, she grips the gun. "I suppose you've left me with only one choice."

CHAPTER 6

After dodging traffic cops, gyrating stoplights and barricades, Michelle pulls onto North Tampa and squints through the blurred arc made by her windshield wipers. Is that a perfect line of empty parking spaces on the street? She's been renting office space in the Lark Tower for two years, but until now she's never been able to park on the curb.

She whips her car into a prime spot, then pushes the car door into the steady rain. Flurries of paper and leaves fly past her in a pirouetting whirlwind that tugs at the canopies of the neatly trimmed live oaks. The radio weathercaster has been predicting intermittent rain for the next several hours, with increasing wind speeds until well after sunset.

Michelle grabs an empty Applebee's take-out bag and holds it over her head as she dashes toward the lobby entrance, her raincoat rippling and snapping in the wind.

Maybe she's crazy for coming here. Lauren would certainly think so, but Lauren has a ring on her finger and a date on the caterer's books. More to the point, Lauren's biological clock is running at least five years behind Michelle's.

Though she's almost positive Parker is preparing to propose, she can't let this opportunity for action slip away. The threat of an imminent hurricane ought to make it easy for him to get serious about drawing his loved ones close, but the man might need a nudge toward matrimony. If this wild weather isn't enough to make him think about his responsibility to her as well as his children, her ultimatum should be.

The rising wind whooshes past her, clawing at the Applebee's bag and whipping her raincoat around her frame. She nearly falls on the rain-slicked pavement near the building entrance, but catches the brass bar on a lobby door. The door seems heavier today, and she struggles against it until the wind pries the Applebee's bag from her fingers and whips it across the street, then releases it like a free-floating parachute. With both hands she pushes against the door until it moves, but a gust of wind follows her into the building, rattling the leaves of two potted ficus trees standing guard at the perimeter of the lobby.

Flustered, she shakes water from her hair and looks around. The sandwich shop, florist, bank and office center are all locked and closed, their interiors dark. No one sits in the lounge chairs scattered among the massive bowls of bromeliads, but she glimpses movement at the security station beyond the reception area.

Good to know she's not alone in the building.

After wiping raindrops from her face, she settles her wet purse on her shoulder and strides toward the security guard, who is talking to a woman in a tan trench coat. She calls out a greeting as she heads toward the elevator landing. "Surprised to see you this morning, Gus."

"Miss Tilson, wait." Stepping away from the woman in the trench coat, the guard lifts his arm to hold her attention. "We're urging all tenants to evacuate immediately. Haven't you seen the news?"

She gestures toward the elevators. "I'll only be a few minutes. I need to run upstairs and pick up a file."

"Come on, now." Gus hikes up his belt and gives her a look of paternal disapproval. "You shouldn't even be downtown in this weather. We're locking the building at ten and I'm not supposed to let any visitors into the office areas."

Her mouth twists in an expression that's not quite a smile. When will he realize she doesn't need his protection? "I'm not a visitor, Gus, I'm a paying tenant and I need to go to my office."

"But, Miss Tilson—"

"That storm is hours away and I'll only be a few minutes. Thanks for your concern, but I'm going upstairs."

Gus's features crumple with frustration, but he retreats to his stool.

Michelle walks to the express elevators and presses the call button, then crosses her arms. According to the lit panels above the doors, one car is on the second level of the parking garage; the others are scattered among floors twenty-five through thirty-six.

The woman in the trench coat steps onto the carpet at the landing and catches Michelle's eye. "Tilson?" she asks. "Tilson Corporate Careers?"

Michelle gives her a perfunctory smile. "Yes."

"Ah." The woman nods and looks away. "I've seen your name on the registry."

Michelle frowns, wondering if she should know this woman, but then the light above the middle car shifts from thirty-six to thirty-five.

Could Parker be on his way down?

After pressing the button that will take her to the maintenance department, Isabel turns and drops her forehead to the elevator's back wall. What is she going to do? If the authorities find out what happened, they might arrest her, maybe even put her in prison. She has tried her best to avoid trouble, but trouble seems to find her at every turn, even in *los Estados Unidos.*

Ernesto said she wouldn't be able to run forever, but she has to try. Again. She and Carlos and Rafael must go someplace where they will never be found.

As the elevator descends with a smooth whoosh, Isabel feels a rush of gratitude for its speed. If this were a weekday morning, the building would be so crowded it would take forever for the express to travel from the top of the building to the custodial office on the seventh floor. Today, however, the elevator escorts her to the lower level without interruption.

The bronze doors slide open, revealing a concrete hallway, scraped walls, dented lockers and another cleaning cart—

No.

Isabel's hand flies to her mouth. She left her cart in Rossman's outer office. Anyone who sees it will know she was there . . . and might guess why she left in a panic.

As the elevator door begins to close, she thrusts out her arm and stops it.

What should she do? She could clock out, go to her car and drive home. She'd have to beg Carlos to leave the area because he wouldn't want to go, not with the hurricane coming. Driving on old tires in a storm would be dangerous.

But how can they escape when *la policía* are positioned throughout the city? They will stop the car and they will want to know why Carlos waited so long to leave. Carlos is a good man; he will not lie and Isabel will not allow him to lie for her. So she will tell the truth, and they will put her in jail and tell the attorney general that a criminal has been working under his nose all these many months. . . .

She can't run, not today. She will have to wait, talk to Carlos, pray that the authorities never learn that she was in Rossman's office this morning.

So she must go back upstairs and get her cart.

When the elevator buzzes to protest the prolonged stop, Isabel takes a half step back and allows the doors to close. As the car begins to move, she returns to the back wall and presses her hand to her chest, where a bulky, cold lump is scraping against her breastbone. Things will be all right. She can get her cart, return it to the seventh floor, clock out and go home. Her secret will keep; no one will know for hours, maybe days.

A chill shivers her skin when the car stops on the ground floor. The lobby.

¿Qué pasa? Her thoughts whirl in a rush, then she remembers: she forgot to push the button. Someone in the lobby must have called the elevator, and this was the closest car.

Though it hurts to draw breath, Isabel reminds herself to stay calm and keep her head down. She can't let anyone see the distress in her eyes or her trembling hands. Fortunately, few people in this place ever really see her. They pass in an office or hallway and notice her no more than they notice the potted plants or the exit signs above every stairwell doorway.

She steps to the far right corner of the car as the bronze doors open. *Mi querido Dios,* let me remain alone a little longer. . . .

God must not be listening. The sweet scent of perfume reaches her nostrils as *dos gringas* enter the car.

Isabel holds her breath as the first woman, a slim brunette, pulls out her access card, slips it into the security slot and presses the button for thirty-six.

The other woman stands silent against the left wall, her hands shoved into the pockets of her tan coat. The lump in Isabel's chest grows heavier when the second woman does not move to press any of the elevator's many buttons.

Are they all riding to the thirty-sixth floor?

Michelle smiles at the woman who followed her into the car. "Can I press a button for you?"

The woman shifts her gaze from the elevator panel to Michelle's face. "No, thank you." Her shoulder-length hair, a vibrant shade of red, is far drier than Michelle's, so she must have parked in the garage.

Smart lady.

Out in the lobby, Gus has left his station and is rocking toward them on stiff hips. "Ladies, I have to close this building and leave by ten, so I really must advise—"

Michelle is about to ratchet the argument up a notch when the redhead steps forward and jabs the Door Close button. The doors slide together before the security guard can reach them.

Michelle laughs. "He really doesn't want us to go upstairs."

The other woman shrugs. "I really don't care what he wants."

"I think we're all a little on edge today." Michelle glances at the cleaning woman at the back of the car, but she seems to be studying the floor. A pink portable CD player is clipped to her sweater pocket, and from it a gray wire snakes toward her head and ends in a pair of earbuds.

Michelle snorts softly and turns back toward the front of the car. No wonder the housekeeper is oblivious. She probably hasn't heard a word they've said.

She pulls the edges of her raincoat together as the express elevator begins its ascent. Time to focus on Parker. In a moment she'll be face-to-face with the man who could be the love of her life. She'll hear what he has to say and he'll listen to her.

After he hears her challenge, he'll either react with joy, indifference or irritation. Maybe he's been waiting for her to state her willingness to start a family; maybe he's never guessed that a successful career woman might want a husband and children.

On the other hand . . . maybe he thinks three children are enough. Maybe he's done a little digging in her past and he doesn't want her to play any role in his kids' lives. Maybe he doesn't want a wife because he's content with a part-time lover.

If he's that narrow-minded, she'll either win him over or she'll move on. But she will not worry about the future. Since becoming independent, she's never encountered an obstacle she couldn't overcome . . . one way or another.

Gina stares at the bronze elevator panel and struggles to corral her racing thoughts. *The best-laid plans of mice and men often go awry. . . .*

Who said that, Shakespeare? No. Burns, but not in those exact words. Saikaku, that Japanese poet, phrased it another way: *there is always something to upset the most careful of human calculations.*

She should have allowed for Murphy's law, chaos theory, whatever they're calling it these days. She should have realized the security guard might give her a hard time. She should have considered the possibility that other people might share a ride in the elevator.

She had been certain the thirty-sixth floor would be

deserted by the time she arrived, but these two women are on their way to that same landing.

In this situation, three is definitely a crowd.

Gathering up the pearls at her throat, Gina cuts a glance to the woman across the car. The tall and slender stranger holds herself like a model or a dancer. Miss Tilson, the guard called her, and Gina recognized the name from an office on the thirty-sixth floor. What else had she said? She'd come to pick up a file?

Must be a terribly important client.

The brunette, who has closed her eyes and is leaning against the wall, doesn't notice Gina's scrutiny. She's wearing jeans, but they're adorned with a designer logo and the blouse beneath the raincoat has the soft sheen of silk. Her nails are short and neatly trimmed, her glasses tortoiseshell, her hair a chic brown cap. Even in denim and sneakers, the woman radiates success. She's the type to notice things . . . so she's one to avoid.

When the maid coughs, the brunette lifts her head and Gina hastily looks away. She'd give anything to be invisible at this moment, but she'll settle for remaining anonymous.

She leans against the wall and peers over her shoulder at the thick Hispanic woman in the pink uniform. The maid is studying the floor—maybe she resents the water dripping off the brunette's raincoat. Gina lifts a brow at the sight of the earbuds—what's she listening to, mariachi music? In any case, she must be doing well. The managers of the Lark Tower take good care of their employees, even the foreigners.

She shifts her gaze as she thinks of the Hispanic families Sonny has insured over the years. Many of the Cubans in Tampa's Ybor City are quite prosperous; she's lost count of the *quinceañeras* she and Sonny have attended to celebrate the fifteenth birthdays of clients' daughters. Those people spare no expense to honor their blossoming young women; they spend buckets of money on food, bands and party dresses.

If only they spent as much insuring their belongings and their loved ones. How many will be adequately covered if Felix rips their homes apart?

Gina folds her arms. Ordinarily she wouldn't be aware of the other passengers in an elevator, but today she needs to notice everything. If the police ever launch an investigation into Sonny's death, they'll try to track down anyone who was in the building today.

The maid is not likely to be a threat. Many of Tampa's Hispanics are transient; this woman may not even be around by the time Sonny's case is investigated.

No need to worry about the maid, then. The brunette is a different story. With her, Gina should be polite, but detached. She should stay calm and try not to do anything that might stick in the woman's memory.

She slides her right hand back into her pocket and curls her fingers around the pistol. She will warm it with her flesh, prepare it for the task ahead.

She must be patient and courageous. In less than five minutes she'll be facing her husband; in less than ten minutes he'll be dead.

She frowns at a sudden thought. How thick are the walls in this building? If either of these women hears the shot, will they assume they are hearing some noise associated with the approaching storm or will they run for help? Gina has never heard a live gunshot, but she's read that distant gunfire often sounds like firecrackers. Surely no one would think it remarkable to hear a vague pop or two amid the howling of the wind.

She tilts her head and looks at the two women—neither of them look like the hero type, but maybe she ought to sit and chat Sonny up while these ladies do whatever they've come up here to do. Fifteen minutes of polite talk about the kids ought to be enough time. . . . Or maybe she should let Sonny know she found his secrets in the safe. After he's had a chance to rattle off his excuses and protestations, she can give him the bullet he deserves.

A wry smile tugs at the corner of her mouth. Letting Sonny have a last word . . . why, that'd be more than fair. That'd be absolutely honorable.

After the deed is done, she might linger in Sonny's office, giving the hurricane time to move closer. The police are already so strained it's unlikely anyone will be dispatched if a shot is reported, but she shouldn't take any chances.

While she waits, she'll wipe her prints off the pistol and drop it on the floor. No one will think it strange that a successful downtown businessman was carrying his legal, registered weapon on a day like this. The scenario will make perfect sense—looters caught her workaholic husband in his office after the building had been evacuated. Sonny pulled out his gun; a trespasser wrested it away from him; Sonny caught a bullet. The murderer wiped the weapon clean and dropped it before leaving the office suite.

What could be more logical?

So she will proceed with her plan . . . even if it means spending an extra hour with a dead husband. Sonny's been dead to her these last few months, anyway. When he does come home, he spends his time in his den, watching TV and reading the paper. . . .

She can't remember the last time he looked into her eyes and asked her opinion about anything.

Like that mother who drowned her children and then lined them up on the bed, Gina might pull Sonny into his executive chair, adjust his tie and roll him closer to the vulnerable windows. The windows might break in the storm, and water would do its part to eradicate any trace evidence she might leave—

She blinks as the overhead lights flicker and the elevator shudders to a stop. She looks at the panel—the thirty-six has gone dark. The seven is still lit, but they've been traveling far too long to be near the seventh floor. Because the twenty-five has not yet lit, she can only assume they have stopped somewhere between the seventh and twenty-fifth floors.

The brunette looks up and catches her eye. "This can't be good."

Gina doesn't answer. As long as the lights remain on,

they have power. As long as they have power, surely the elevator can move.

Without speaking, she steps in front of the brunette and presses the button for the thirty-sixth floor. The button won't light and the car doesn't budge.

"Let's try this." The brunette pulls her access card from the pocket of her jeans and slips it into the slot, then presses the thirty-six with a manicured fingertip. As some unseen power source hums, the car begins to rise.

Gina exhales the breath she didn't realize she'd been holding. The brunette leans against the far wall and grimaces. "That'd be just what we need, wouldn't it?"

Gina watches the elevator panel. They're still rising in the concrete shaft, but the twenty-five has not yet lit.

Behind her, the cleaning woman barks another cough. Gina grimaces and hopes the maid doesn't have avian flu or some other awful disease. Ventilation is terrible in elevators; what one person exhales, another inhales.

She stares at the twenty-five on the elevator panel, willing the button to light.

The brunette lifts her head, doubtless about to utter some other scintillating bon mot, then the lights flicker again; the elevator stops and darkness swallows the car.

9:00 A.M.

~✴~

CHAPTER 7

Cold terror sprouts between Michelle's shoulder blades and prickles down her backbone. Not even a glimmer of light remains in the enclosed space.

She presses her hand to her chest, which has begun to suffer short, stabbing pains. She hasn't felt these invisible arrows in years, but she knows the paralyzing pricks of panic all too well.

Get a grip, count to ten, breathe deeply. You're a grown woman and everything's fine; this is an elevator, not the trailer.

Sounds trickle into the car, a faint buzz followed by a steady tick. When a small bulb on the elevator panel blooms into light, Michelle inhales an unsteady breath and looks at the others. The housekeeper's fear is visible in her trembling chin and wide eyes, but the redhead's face is as blank as a mask. Something about the woman ignites a spark from Michelle's memory cells, but after an instant the ember burns out.

When she is certain she can speak in a steady voice, she asks, "Are we all right?"

The redhead doesn't respond, but the cleaning woman pulls the earbuds from her ears and dips her chin in a solemn nod. "Then let me see if I can get us out of here."

All the buttons on the elevator panel remain dark. Michelle presses the thirty-six, but the car doesn't respond. She tries again with her access card in the security slot, but none of the buttons light at her touch, not even the *L* for *Lobby*. Finally she punches the Door Open button with her knuckle and holds it while she counts to five.

Nothing.

She slowly exhales a breath. She will not panic. There's a light; she can see; she is no longer a child. No one here wants to hurt her.

She turns to the others. "Gus mentioned occasional blackouts—" she forces a smile "—so I'll bet that's what this is. As soon as the power kicks on, we'll start moving again."

She glances from Ms. Trench Coat to the house-keeper, but her companions are as unresponsive as the elevator controls.

"This same thing happened to me a few months ago." In an effort to ease the tension, she locks her hands behind her back and leans against the wall. "I was stuck with a group of lawyers for about fifteen minutes. No big deal, except they kept arguing about who they should bill for their lost time."

Neither woman smiles, leaving Michelle to wonder if they belong to some legal eagles' anti-defamation league. The redhead stares at the control panel as if she could diagnose the dead circuits with X-ray vision. The cleaning woman takes a tissue from her sweater pocket and blots pearls of perspiration from her forehead.

"Excuse, please?" The housekeeper lifts her hand and points to the light fixture on the panel. "We have light, no? So we have *electricidad?*"

"We have some power," Michelle says, relieved that she is no longer talking to herself "When I moved into my office, the building manager said something about the emergency systems being powered by a backup generator. We'll be fine. We just have to wait for the main system to come back on. Of course—" she raps the plastic dome over the light with her knuckle "—for all I know, this thing might be powered by batteries."

The woman nods, but a worry line has crept between her brows. "When power comes back—we will go down?"

Michelle shrugs. "I would imagine we'll keep going up, since we were heading in that direction. But what does it matter? As long as we make it to any floor, we can open the doors and get to the staircase. So we're fine. Maybe we should even be grateful. At least we're not falling to the bottom of the shaft."

She chuckles at her feeble joke, but the sound dies in her throat when the cleaning woman's round face ripples with anguish.

"Don't worry," Michelle hastens to add. "This elevator is not going to fall. That only happens in bad movies."

The housekeeper acknowledges Michelle's comment with a slight nod, but Ms. Trench Coat either doesn't appreciate Michelle's attempt at humor or she's not listening.

Michelle crosses her arms and leans against the wall, not certain where to rest her gaze. The little lamp is now glowing at maximum wattage, a token effort that doesn't eliminate the shadows at the back of the car.

Michelle faces the doors and clenches her hand until her nails slice into her palm. Shadows and closed spaces elicit far too many painful memories.

"Michelle Louise Tills! Where are you, girl?"

The girl wriggled forward, digging her elbows into the soft earth, pulling her body through the narrow space. Dust and dirt rose with every movement, tickling her nose, but she would not sneeze. She wouldn't make a sound, not as long as Momma waited out there.

"Where are you, Shelly? You'd better come out before I have to come lookin' for you."

Shelly moved deeper into the shadows, the raspy voice scraping like a razor's edge against the back of her neck. Beyond the lattice apron, a blue warbler perched in the tall pine at the edge of the lot, calling *Zhee zhee zizizizi zzzzeeet.*

Shh, bird. Don't tell.

"Shel-leeeeey! I'd better not find you messin' around with those boys!"

Past the fraying lawn chairs, the sun warmed the asphalt drive where the Smith boys were playing keep-away. The girl could hear Job Smith's voice ricocheting among the trailers as he teased his younger brother, calling him *noodle arms* and *stork legs. . . .*

"Shelly Louise! You get out here this minute or

I'll—well, you get out here. I'm losin' my patience!"

Her mother's words, pitched to reach the edge of the lot and no farther, were already softly slurred and she hadn't even begun what she called "serious drinkin'." In a while, if the girl was lucky, the woman would give up and go inside the trailer, forgetting about her child while she focused on the tall bottle of amber-colored liquid that demanded every drop of a worshipper's devotion.

Shelly dropped her arms onto the soft dirt, then rested her cheek on her hands. If she could lie perfectly, soundlessly still, maybe she could become invisible. Maybe she could go away and wake up as someone else's little girl.

Her mother's slippers shuffled from the last porch step to the lawn chairs, her pale legs casting twin shadows that stretched toward Shelly like tongs. Instinctively, the girl recoiled, lifting her head so quickly that it clunked against the bottom of the trailer.

She squinched her eyes shut as the top of her head throbbed. *Pretty, pretty please, don't let her hear.*

When Shelly lifted one eyelid, her mother was crouched on all fours, eyes hard and shining through the lattice at the bottom of the trailer. "Young lady, get yourself out here right now."

Shelly put her hands over her eyes and wished the image away. A minute passed, maybe two. She breathed in the scents of earth and dust while the Smith boys laughed and the warbler sang so maybe everything was all right—

When she lifted her gaze, her mother was sucking at

the inside of her cheek while her thin brows rose and fell like a pair of seesaws. "Shelly! You don't want me to have to come in there after you."

Dread gave the girl courage. "Go away!"

"Michelle Louise! I'm gonna count to three and you'd better be out here! You don't want to test me, girlie. One! Two! Three!"

Though a warning voice whispered in her head, Shelly didn't move. She waited, shivering from a chill that had nothing to do with the mountain air, until her mother straightened up and moved away.

Could winning be that easy? Momma was a proud woman, in those days as protective of her reputation as she was of her liquor bottles. A good woman never drank in public, she often assured Shelly, and a good woman took care of her man and her kid before she took care of herself.

The girl looked toward the gravel driveway, where her father's pickup wasn't. Daddy was still at the mine; he wouldn't be home until after dark.

She'd come out if he were here. She'd climb into his arms and ride his bony hip into the house. She'd be happy to see him, even if they found Momma passed out on the sofa. Her daddy loved her, but he was rarely home.

She had just buried her face in her folded arms when new sounds reached her ear—the steady swish of tall grass and the heavy *heh, heh, heh* of a panting animal. Shelly spun on her belly, turning toward the gap in the lattice where she had wormed her way in.

She saw her mother's legs scissoring through the grass, accompanied by four brown-and-white paws, a small head, a snarling muzzle and two rows of jagged teeth.

"I've got Harley," her mother called, a victorious edge to her voice. "And I'm gonna let him go if you don't come out this instant. What's it gonna be, Michelle Louise? Shall I send Harley in after you?"

For an instant the girl couldn't speak. The neighbor's pit bull haunted her nightmares and often drove her from peaceful sleep into her father's arms. Harley had never actually threatened her, but he bore an unfortunate resemblance to a dog that had attacked her once, pinning her to the ground while it ripped at her upper lip.

A thin scar still marked the spot.

"No, Momma." Torn between her desire to surrender and her fear of the waiting beast, Shelly rose as high as she could. "I'll come, Momma, but get rid of the dog."

"He's stayin' right by my side until you walk yourself through that front door."

"Momma, I'll come, but I don't like that dog."

"I'm not gonna argue with you, Shelly. Get your fanny out from under there and get in the house."

Shelly gulped down a sob and crawled forward, then froze when the dog lifted his head, ears pricked to attention. When he growled deep in his throat, she knew he could see her . . . or he smelled her fear.

Dogs know, the Smith boys had told her. Dogs know when you're scared of 'em. When they smell your fear, they'll attack 'cause they know they can take you down.

"Momma?" She bit the inside of her lip and looked toward the pale legs. She could see the edge of the housecoat, a blue fabric scattered with white daisies. "Momma, take Harley away and I'll come out."

A fly, drawn by her sweat, hit her face and bounced away, then circled and landed on her cheek.

"Momma?"

"I'm still here." Her mother's voice had gone flat, almost pleasant. Anyone passing by might have thought she was waiting to give her daughter a welcome-home hug.

Harley growled and pulled at the leash. Shelly rocked back on her haunches, one hand pressed to her mouth as a cry bubbled up from someplace in her chest. She tried to choke off the sound, but she failed and began to sob in a high, pitiful, coughing hack. "Ma-ma! I—can't—come—with—"

"Stop your cryin', Shel, I didn't raise no coward. I'll hold the dumb dog—you get yourself out here right now."

"But—I—can't—"

"If you don't, I'm letting Harley go. Wonder how long it'll take him to wiggle under there and tear you up? I saw him get a possum the other day. Even though the critter played dead, he tore that thing to pieces. Not a pretty sight, not a'tall."

Shelly fell forward and began to creep toward the lattice on shaking limbs. No sense in talking now; her mother had won . . . again.

She crawled over the dirt, every atom of her being cringing in revulsion, and trembled as she approached the gap in the lattice. Her mother stood ten feet away, one hand on her hip, one arm extended as Harley strained at the leash.

Squatting in the opening, Shelly swiped at her wet cheeks with grimy hands, then launched herself upward and ran for the front porch as if her feet were afire. When she reached the bottom step she heard the thrum of the pit bull's pounding paws; by the time she passed the threshold the dog was on the porch and snapping at the screen door while her mother watched from the grass and . . . laughed.

Shelly ran into the bathroom, hiccupping as she washed her hands. She tried her best to clean up, but she couldn't get the muddy streaks off the counter or the towels.

Maybe it was the mud that did it, or maybe Momma was past caring about anything but being mad. Without a word, she grabbed Shelly by the arm, pulled her through the living room and thrust her into the linen closet. At the bottom, beneath the shelf where they kept the good sheets, was a space just big enough for Shelly to sit with her knees bent up and her head bent low.

That space—and its darkness—were as terrifying as the dog. "Momma—"

"Hush, Shelly. Get in there."

"Momma, no." She knew she shouldn't touch Momma with damp hands, muddy arms and dirty clothes, but in a desperate plea for mercy she threw herself onto her mother's frame, shaping herself to the woman's body, clinging like a shadow. "Momma, Momma, I don't like the dark—"

"Don't be a baby." Her mother's iron fingers pulled and pried while her feet pushed Shelly into the closet.

"Momma, no!"

"And stop that screamin'. The more you scream, the longer I'm leavin' you in here."

Because Momma did not issue idle threats, Shelly clamped her trembling lips, imprisoning the cries that scratched at her throat. She thrust out her hands in silent entreaty, but Momma pushed her firmly into a sitting position and closed the door.

"Momma," Shelly whispered into her hands, "please don't."

She uttered the words without meaning to; long ago she'd learned that protests made no difference. Momma liked having her child put away before she started serious drinking; she liked knowing the shades were drawn, the oven was turned off, everything was in its proper place.

Good women made an effort to keep up appearances. They didn't let outsiders see things that might get a little messy.

Shelly lowered her head onto her bent knees when she heard the thunk of the padlock against the hasp. She'd stay in the closet, silent and folded up, until Daddy got home . . . if he came home. All she had to do was keep quiet and try to think of happy things when her muscles began to complain.

She opened her eyes, but creatures swirled and danced in the darkness, slinking gray shapes that squeezed beneath the thin crack at the bottom of the door and buzzed in circles, darting around her arms and bouncing off her face until icy fear twisted around her heart and her breath came in short gasps.

Shelly Tills closed her eyes as tightly as she could and begged God to send her daddy home.

Gina stares across the gloomy car and struggles to retain her composure. One of her professors used to quote Christopher Smart in frustrating situations—what was he always saying?

The words ruffle through her mind like wind on water: *determination is the key to success in any venture.*

If she is going to succeed in this venture, she can't falter or risk reacting to this mechanical malfunction. In a moment the power will come back on and they will continue moving upward as if nothing had happened—

Unless this is more than a temporary blackout. What if they are stuck in this car for hours?

At the sound of sniffling she glances to her right, where the maid is cowering against the back wall. What is wrong with that one? The cleaning woman is a Nervous Nelly, but the brunette seems to have at least a measure of self-control.

Gina lowers her gaze and counts to ten, trying to maintain her focus while a hundred worries needle her nerves. Why doesn't Ms. Tilson use the emergency phone? Gina would press the button herself, but then she'd have to interact with these women, maybe even take charge. An anonymous woman would stare at the wall, remain silent, maybe clench her hands in her pockets—

All the things she's already doing. She exhales in a rush and turns her head to stare at the circular speaker beneath the emergency light. Look at the panel, Ms. Corporate Careers. See the light? Right beneath it, did you notice the speaker and the button labeled Phone? Push it. Push the button and speak into the little microphone. Come on, look up, *look at the stupid panel!*

Michelle brings the edge of her thumbnail to her front teeth and bites down. How did she manage to get trapped in an elevator with pod people? She glances at the redhead, who still won't meet her gaze. The cleaning woman has crossed one arm in a nonchalant pose, but her shoulders are visibly trembling.

Hoping that the housekeeper has inside information about building maintenance, she gives the woman a smile. "Do you know if anyone has been working on this elevator?"

The woman cringes under Michelle's gaze. "No, *no se.* I don't know."

Michelle averts her eyes. "I knew they'd been having problems with the lower elevators, but the express cars have always been reliable."

She moves toward the panel and presses the Door Open button again. Nothing happens.

Vaguely aware that she is trespassing on the redhead's personal space, Michelle steps to the center of the car and presses her palms against the cool surface of the bronze doors. With an effort, she wedges her fingers between the rubber bumpers, then gasps when the doors move.

"I think I've got it!"

The doors slide apart, but move no more than a few inches when they stop, revealing a solid expanse of concrete wall. Though Michelle strains and tugs, the doors refuse to open farther.

When she releases the doors, the bronze panels slowly slide back to their closed position. Michelle straightens and rakes her hand through her hair. "I don't get it. It's almost as if there's something blocking—"

She groans as a memory surfaces: last year, a memo from the building manager mentioned a new device for the elevators, a gadget that would prevent a passenger from opening an elevator door and falling down the shaft.

"The HatchLatch," she says, looking at the housekeeper. "I remember the name because it rhymes. The doors can only be opened from the roof of the car."

The cleaning woman shakes her head. "It does not matter. Is nothing to see out there."

"I know, but if we could open the doors, we might at

least be able to get some fresh air into this place—"

The redhead finally meets Michelle's gaze head-on: "Would you please press the button for the blasted phone?"

CHAPTER 8

Gina looks away and grimaces. She shouldn't have blurted out a command like that, but she simply could not endure one more minute of useless talk.

"Getting upset is not going to help anything," the brunette says, a truculent note in her voice. "I'm sure Gus knows we're trapped. There's a panel on the security desk that's supposed to alert him to problems with the elevators."

Gina ignores the woman and flexes her fingers within her pockets. Her nerves are strung as tight as a violin string; no wonder she snapped. But all is not lost. Ms. Tilson may finally do something useful.

She flinches when a hand falls upon her arm. The younger woman has moved to her side; her long fingers now rest on Gina's sleeve.

"It's okay," the brunette says, her eyes soft with understanding. "I used to suffer from claustrophobia myself. You should take deep breaths and try to think of a happy place."

Gina blinks, unable to believe what she's hearing.

"While you calm down—" the brunette releases Gina's arm and moves toward the elevator panel "—I'll try to get someone on the line."

Gina sighs in grim satisfaction when Ms. Tilson squares her shoulders and steps up to the receiver.

About time.

Isabel's stomach tightens as the younger *gringa* pushes the button for the *teléfono*. But who will answer the call: *la seguridad o la policía?*

She presses her lips together in an effort to stifle the quivering of her chin. She had been relieved when the elevator stopped. She cannot help but hope that when it starts again the two *gringas* will be so frightened they will get off at the nearest landing and take the stairs down to the lobby. She will have time to go upstairs and retrieve her cart.

But if the power comes back on and these women continue to the thirty-sixth floor, she'll still be in trouble. If either of these ladies goes into Mr. Rossman's office, they are sure to call the police. If the police come, they will look Isabel up on their computers and her life will be over.

Everything she and Carlos have accomplished—their new jobs, new lives and new home—will be finished. If the attorney general learns what happened in Rossman's office, she will be put on trial, her *fotografía* will appear in the newspapers, and her life will be worthless. A fluid stream of communication flows between *los Estados Unidos* and Monterrey; people will recognize her. Ernesto swore he would see her dead if she did not follow his instructions, so *muerta* is what she will be, probably before her trial comes to an end.

Ernesto has friends everywhere, so he will find her and kill her. If he learns where she has been living, he will come after Carlos and Rafael.

Because he knows her son is *his* son.

She gulps hard and swipes at her cheek, grateful that the *gringas* are too busy concentrating on the *teléfono* to notice her tears.

If God is merciful and gets her out of this elevator, perhaps she can take Rafael and disappear. But though running might save Carlos's life, her departure would destroy him. He is a good man; he loves her.

Most important, he loves her son.

She rubs her neck as her throat aches with regret. How can she take Rafael away from this place? He is an American citizen. He deserves to experience fine schools, good doctors and opportunities he would never know in *México*.

Most of all, he deserves a father who loves him. Carlos.

When the red-haired woman looks back at her, Isabel pulls the CD player from her right sweater pocket and pretends to study the controls. But when she realizes that her pocket still sags with the weight of its contents, her lips wobble and tears spill from her eyes in spite of her brave intentions.

Michelle leans closer to the bronze panel, trying to figure out how the telephone works. In older elevators she's noticed hinged doors that presumably open to telephone handsets, but this car's control panel features a phone button, a built-in speaker and a tiny dot—the microphone?

Nothing happened when she pressed the phone button the first time, so she steps closer and presses it more firmly, ignoring the waves of disapproval that radiate from the redhead on the opposite wall. Michelle isn't thrilled about being stuck, either, but the hurricane is still hours away. The power will come back on. It always does.

The tension in her shoulders eases when the sound of a ringing telephone comes through the speaker. "You know—" she glances at the worried housekeeper behind her "—in the summer months we have power outages all the time. A thunderstorm rolls in, the lights go out, and the power kicks on a few minutes later. I'm sure we're going to be fine."

She crosses one arm over her chest, trying to appear relaxed, but the monotonous ringing is beginning to fray her nerves. Who is this telephone dialing, and why don't they answer?

She blows out a breath when the ringing finally ends with a click. A female voice chirps, "Majestic Elevator."

Michelle tosses the redhead a victorious smile. "Hi. We're stuck in one of your elevators in the Lark—"

"You have reached the answering service for Majestic Elevator Company. If you have reached this recording, all of our agents are busy helping other customers. Stay on the line and one of our staff members will be with you shortly."

The corner of Michelle's mouth twists. She'd like to

release a few of her momma's more colorful curses into that tiny speck of a microphone, but blue language isn't going to help, especially when one of her companions is crying and the other's wearing a look as hard as a stepmother's slap.

When a tinny strain of Muzak pours from the speaker, she grimaces and leans against the side of the car. "I think," she says, her voice rough, "we've been put on hold."

The redhead frowns and crosses her arms while the cleaning woman pulls a tissue from her pocket and blows her nose.

Michelle props one sneakered foot against the wall. "If they're this busy, people must be trapped in elevators all over town. You'd think they'd bring in extra staff on a day like this—"

"Hello?"

The unexpected voice snaps her to attention. "Yes? Operator?"

"That's me, honey. How can I help you?"

Michelle's words leapfrog over each other. "We're trapped in one of your elevators. Since most of the building is empty, there's no one around to help us get out—"

"Hold on a minute, let me get this down. You're in an elevator—where, exactly?"

"Um . . ." Michelle closes her eyes to think. "The eastern-most group. If you walk in the front entrance and go through the lobby, we'd be in the first bank of express elevators."

The woman chuckles. "Slow down, sugar. I need to know what city you're calling from."

This company services more than one city? Michelle braces both hands on the panel and tries to ignore the creeping uneasiness at the bottom of her belly. She'll be throwing up again in a minute, and she doesn't want to do that, not in front of these women.

"We're in Tampa," she says, speaking with slow precision. "The Lark Tower. The very tall building at the intersection of North Ashley Drive and Tampa Street."

All is silent but for the ghostly clatter of a distant keyboard, then: "The Lark Tower . . . at 420 North Tampa Street?"

Michelle sighs. "Yes."

The operator clicks her tongue. "Got it. I'll contact the local office so they can dispatch a technician."

"Wait a minute—you're not the elevator company?"

"I'm the answering service, honey. Majestic patched you over to me, most likely because it's a weekend."

· "Are you even in Tampa?"

The woman cock-a-doodles a three-noted laugh. "Sugar, I'm in Atlanta."

Michelle's relief vanishes, replaced by a rising irritation. "Thank you very much, but I'm afraid your plan is unacceptable. In case you haven't heard, Hurricane Felix is heading straight for us. Most of the city has evacuated. How are you going to get us out of this cage if there are no technicians in Tampa to dispatch?"

A moment of silence hums over the line, then the woman's voice goes flat. "I'm afraid I don't know how to advise you further, ma'am. Now, if there's nothing else I can do—"

"Don't you dare disconnect us!" The redhead snaps out of whatever fugue she's been in and steps toward the panel, her eyes blazing. "You will stay on the line until you get us some help."

Michelle shrinks back, stunned by the determination on the older woman's face. Where has Ms. Trench Coat been hiding *this* attitude?

"Ma'am," the operator says, an edge to her voice, "might I suggest that you ladies call 911?"

The redhead, who is not carrying a purse, slants a brow at Michelle; the unspoken query sends Michelle scrambling through her purse. "My cell phone has never worked in this elevator," she says, shifting until the emergency light shines into her nearly bottomless shoulder bag. "I'll try it, though."

She finds her phone, snaps it open and holds it up. Though the battery is fully charged, the signal bars flicker and then vanish as an error message appears: *No Service*.

She exhales, then looks at her companions. "I don't suppose either of you has a cell phone?"

The housekeeper shakes her head while the redhead slumps to the opposite wall.

So—their single cell phone is useless. And since the redhead's outburst did little to motivate the woman in Atlanta, maybe it's time to try another approach.

Time to turn on the charm.

"Miss—" trying to imagine the woman behind the

phone, Michelle focuses on the speaker in the panel "—would you mind telling me your name?"

The woman hesitates. "I'm only doing my job."

"I know, and you just might save our lives today. So, may I have your name? *Operator* sounds awfully impersonal."

"Ginger," the woman says, her tone heavy with suspicion. "Ginger McCloud."

"Good." Michelle forces a smile into her voice. "I'm Michelle. You see, Ginger, we have only one cell phone and it won't work in this elevator. So you're going to have to call someone for us."

"Sugar, that's not my job. I'm supposed to call the elevator-company dispatcher so they can send someone out. That's the policy."

"Then you'll have to make an exception to the policy. Please." Dismayed to hear a thread of hysteria in her voice, Michelle takes a deep, calming breath. "We're stuck and the hurricane is coming. This elevator doesn't have a phone, only a button, so you're the only person we can reach. Don't hand us off, please. We don't even know if anyone's still in the local office."

Somewhere in the distance, another phone rings. The operator's gum snaps over the line. "Just a minute, hon."

Michelle looks at the redhead, who rolls her eyes and mumbles something about incompetence. Michelle gives her a bland half smile and realizes that if the situation weren't so dire, this conversation might actually be funny.

Tomorrow she and Lauren will have to stop for a bite after their shopping expedition. Over cheese fries and soft drinks, she'll tell her best friend about Ms. Trench Coat and the sniffling maid and Ginger the kiss-my-grits operator. Lauren will be bug-eyed with disbelief; Michelle will swear every word is true, and they'll laugh until their sides ache. . . .

Unless tomorrow finds her still waiting in this elevator. Then she's not likely to be in a humorous mood.

She stands rooted to the spot, both hands flat against the wall, until Ginger returns. "Sorry. All right, I'll help if I can, but I'm not sure what you expect me to do."

"We need you," Michelle begins, "to call the elevator company in Tampa. I'm sure you can get the number from information. If they don't answer, call the Majestic office in Orlando or Sarasota: Call every elevator company in a three-hundred-mile radius if you have to, just get us some help."

The keyboard clatters again, then the woman sighs. "I'll do my best, hon. Y'all sit down and try to relax while I see what I can do. How many of you are in that cab?"

Michelle glances back at the cleaning woman, who promptly looks away. "There are three of us. Three women."

"Everybody all right? Any medical emergencies?"

Would it make a difference? Michelle is tempted to say that the redhead is about to blow an aneurysm, then decides against it. "We're fine, but we won't be if you take too long. We have no food, no water and no bath-rooms, if you know what I mean."

"I'll call the company in Tampa, then I'll call you back."

"No, no—hang on. I don't know if we can trust this phone. Don't disconnect us, okay? We'll wait."

Michelle hears the rustling of paper—a phone book?—then Ginger sighs. "This is going to take a while."

"That's fine." Michelle turns and nods at the others. "We've got nothing else to do."

"I'm going to put you on hold, then."

After an instant of silence, a thin stream of Muzak again flows into the car.

Isabel lowers her gaze to conceal the admiration that must be shining from her eyes. Rodrigo always said she was far too obvious about her feelings, but she has never been good at disguising her emotions. Today, however, she must hide all that is in her heart and mind.

If only she could be more like the brown-haired *gringa* at the front of the elevator. The way she spoke to the operator—so confident! Isabel would give a week's wages to be able to speak so.

She pulls a tissue from her left sweater pocket and swipes at her nose. Perhaps she can't help it. She has always been more like her soft-spoken mother than her boisterous father. Pedro Alvarado, who appeared taller than anyone else in the room even when seated, ruled as the undisputed king of their home and held the respect of his neighbors. *Mamá* honored him; Rodrigo obeyed him; his friends asked for his advice. When they went to the market, Isabel followed him, walking in the wake of admiring looks directed at Pedro Alvarado.

Though her father presided over their home with dignity, he had to set aside his authority when he went to work at the cotton mill. He did everything the boss asked him to do without argument. Even when he was told to repair the big drum used for smoothing the newly woven griege goods, he did not point out that he had never worked with that machine.

After the drum caught his hand and mangled his arm, Pedro Alvarado died without complaint. Fortunately for his family, the machine took only his arm, so Isabel's father was able to say goodbye before he died. As the foreman ran for a priest and weeping women crossed themselves, Pedro placed his head in his wife's lap and murmured his last words: *"Lo siento."*

Why was he sorry? Isabel could not imagine why her father needed to apologize. He had never done anything but work hard to raise his family. When other men in Monterrey began to bargain with the drug dealers, Pedro Alvarado refused. When a neighbor wanted to sew bags of liquid heroin into the bellies of six puppies and send them to the United States, Pedro quietly called the authorities.

Despite great temptation, he kept his focus on the cotton mill. "It is a poor man's job," he once told Isabel, "but it is honorable work."

Yet the only time Isabel saw her father's employers treat him with the respect due an honorable man was during *Navidad,* when tradition and the law demanded that company owners present each employee with the annual *aguinaldo,* or Christmas bonus. That stipend, equal to three months' regular salary, bought clothes for Rodrigo and Isabel and paid for repairs on the house. The *aguinaldo* allowed her parents to preserve their dignity each time they accepted paychecks that barely covered the family's living expenses.

Isabel had been fourteen when her father died, and in subsequent years she, her mother and brother continued to work in the Monterrey cotton factory. They remained silent when the bosses took advantage of the older people, short-changing them for hours worked, or forbidding them breaks when the sun grew too hot for anyone to stand. Isabel learned to quietly step away from the machines and help pick up women who had fainted in the heat.

Just once, Isabel mused while she watched one of the foremen strike an old woman who'd brought a stool so she could sit at the spinning machine, she would like to march up to one of the bosses and tell him what she thought of his cruelty. Yes, the work was legal, but the supervisors could be just as uncaring and wicked as the men who ran drugs.

But she needed her job, so she said nothing. She, *Mamá* and Rodrigo depended upon their weekly paychecks and the annual *aguinaldo.* And so Isabel learned to hold her tongue.

But this other woman, this tall *gringa,* has never learned to keep silent. Either she has never been frightened or she has overcome her fear. How does a woman develop such daring?

The answer comes to Isabel on a wave of memory. If one desires a thing badly, longing can concoct enough courage to override fear.

She knew such boldness . . . once.

"Go on." Maria's elbow scraped Isabel's rib. "You've been talking about him for weeks, so go ask him to dance."

"I might."

"What's keeping you?"

"I'm waiting. For the right moment."

To prove her point, Isabel turned away from the bar and propped both elbows on the counter, then looked out across the gathering of young people. No one seeing her in this indifferent pose would possibly know that the mere sight of Ernesto Carillo Fuentes sent blood coursing through all the canals of her body in a whooshing wave.

One of the best-looking young men in Monterrey, Ernesto stood across the plaza in snakeskin boots, a silk shirt and tight American jeans. A silver medallion featuring the face of Jesus Malverde, *México's* own Robin Hood, dangled from his neck while a diamond stud winked from his ear.

He was gorgeous . . . as were the girls he usually approached at this dance. But Ernesto was not dancing now. Laughter floated up from his throat as he dropped a fistful of pesos onto a waitress's serving tray and lifted a beer with his compadres. He looked relaxed and generous, like a man who might be persuaded to accept an invitation from a girl heavier and less beautiful than most.

"Go on," Maria insisted in Isabel's ear. "What have you got to lose?"

Isabel bit her lip. If she went over and Ernesto laughed at her, so what? She'd be no worse off than before. At least she would be able to say she had once spoken to Ernesto Carillo Fuentes.

Knowing that, she could die happy no matter what her family believed.

"Ernesto Fuentes is a drug dealer," her brother had shouted after learning of Isabel's secret love. "Where do you think he gets his money? From Colombians who pay Mexican men to run their drugs over the American border."

"He is not a drug dealer!" Isabel slammed her fork to the table. "He is a devout man—why, just this morning I saw him coming out of the Chapel de Jesus Malverde. They say Ernesto prays there every day."

"Jesus Malverde?" Her mother's hand flew to her throat. "He was not a good man. He was a *maldito,* a murderer and a thief."

Isabel flashed her mother a look of disdain. "He only took from rich people so he could give to the poor."

"No, Isabel. That chapel is an embarrassment to our city. It ought to shame anyone who truly loves God."

"What do you think Ernesto Fuentes does in that chapel?" Rodrigo glared at her from across the table. "He gives thanks for a successful run, that's what. When his drug mules get through, he goes to the chapel to celebrate with his men . . . and give thanks to Jesus Malverde."

"You're wrong! He's a decent man—you can see goodness in his face."

"Listen to your brother," her mother answered. "He knows about these things. He knows about trouble, and he stays away. And you should not trust a handsome face, Isabel. The devil lives behind a tempting smile."

Not always, Isabel wanted to shout. *Papá* had a good face!

Rodrigo reached for the ladle. "Do not worry about Isabel, *Mamá,*" he said, spooning gazpacho into his bowl. "Ernesto Fuentes would not look at a girl like her."

Isabel had wanted to clap her hands over her ears. Neither her mother nor her brother knew what they were talking about. If Ernesto were evil, he would not be so handsome or free with a smile. Evil did things to a man, marked him with scars and sneers, but in Ernesto's dark eyes and broad grin she saw only humor, wit and gallantry.

Tonight, for the first time in her life, she would summon a courage worthy of his. She would do what no one thought her capable of doing.

Girding herself with resolve, she popped a piece of chewing gum into her mouth, then pulled away from the bar. Her brother always said she took on a different personality when she chewed gum, and tonight she would need to be confident and coy, as different as she could possibly be.

She threaded her way through the dancing couples, then approached Ernesto and his friends. Cloaked in composure as fragile as spider silk, she hooked her thumbs through the belt loops of her low-cut jeans, tilted her head and asked the king of her heart if he wanted to dance.

His gaze skimmed over her, taking in the high-heeled sandals, the tight jeans, the sheer blouse and the medallion hanging above the shadows of her cleavage. Without warning, his eyes rose and locked on hers, focusing with predatory intensity. For an instant she feared her brother might be right.

Then Ernesto hit her with a smile that almost made her swallow her gum.

"*Sí, chica.* Let's dance."

10:00 A.M.

CHAPTER 9

Eddie Vaughn tosses another handful of popcorn into his mouth, then pitches a few kernels in Sadie's direction. The retriever snaps in midair, catching one of the puffy bites, then swivels to sniff for the snacks that got away.

A new crossword-puzzle book waits on the arm of the sofa, only inches from the bowl of popcorn in his lap. He had planned to let a crossword distract him from the tedious business of hurricane-watching, but he can't seem to tear himself from the Weather Channel. The newscasters keep alternating between scenes of devastation in the Yucatan and a hurricane map, over which Felix hovers like an unblinking white eye. A dotted line indicates the storm's predicted path, bisecting the state of Florida at Pinellas County and slanting toward Daytona before extending into the Atlantic.

During a commercial break, in which a smoky-voiced woman extols the virtues of a Jaguar, Eddie glances at his front window, where a sheet of plywood blocks the available light. No wonder the house feels like a bunker. Like burrowing animals, most of his neighbors have turned their homes into caves and dis-appeared. He won't see them again until Felix has moved on to harass the interior of the state.

If not for Sadie and the television, he'd feel like the last man on earth. The sensation is not unfamiliar; the last two years of his marriage were among the loneliest of his life.

The dog comes over and drops her chin on his upper arm. He scratches her ears. "We're doing okay, aren't we, Sades?"

Of course, he'd thought he and Heather were doing okay, too. His wife had become deeply involved in community theater, and no one was more surprised than Eddie when she came home and announced that she'd fallen in love with her director and wanted a life on the stage. Eddie tried to tell her that Thomas Bye, her director, was and would always be Tom Bystrowski, a meat-market manager at the Piggly Wiggly, but the girl was too starstruck to listen.

She left him; she divorced him; she married the meat-market man. As Eddie was packing the U-Haul for his move to Florida, he heard Heather was pregnant and Tom had been pushed out of community theater because a real director, one from the state of New York, had moved to Birmingham.

"Florida's good," he says, tossing another handful of popcorn to Sadie, "because there aren't any Piggly Wigglys around here."

When the hurricane coverage resumes, the camera has cut to a scene at Madeira Beach, not more than a ten-minute drive from Eddie's house. A reporter in a yellow rain slicker is staring into the camera and holding on to a hat with his free hand. "The wind has picked up here in the last hour," the reporter says, his image blurred by spatters on the camera lens. "We're seeing gusts of sixty miles an hour with sustained winds of about thirty. But look behind me Jim, can you get a shot of that? Some people simply refuse to take this storm seriously."

The camera operator obediently turns his lens toward the sea, where three wet-suited thrill-seekers are paddling in the usually placid surf. The Gulf is not calm today, and these young men are determined to get a good ride . . . perhaps at the cost of their lives.

Eddie shakes his head. The fools. He spent a summer lifeguarding at Panama City Beach, where twice foolhardy swimmers went out too far and nearly drowned him when he tried to bring them ashore. He never minded risking his life for people who cramped up or got caught in a rip current, but he's not sure he'd be willing to risk his neck for one of these hurricane cowboys.

Eddie scoops up a generous handful of popcorn as the camera cuts to the yellow-slickered reporter. "Felix is expected to make landfall at about seven o'clock tonight, so mandatory evacuation orders for beachfront residents have emptied the homes and motels along this shore. As for these surfers . . . well, I doubt they'll be out here much longer. The wind's getting wicked, and it's only going to get worse."

Sadie's whimper catches Eddie's attention—she is sitting in her prettiest pose, one paw uplifted, her eyes dark and beseeching. "You beggar." He grins and tosses another handful of popcorn in her direction. "Be sure to get it all, will you? Not sure we're going to have power for the vacuum."

From behind their desk, the grim-faced anchors at the Weather Channel announce that experts consider Florida's Tampa Bay to be the nation's second most dangerous location for a major hurricane. The most perilous spot, of course, is New Orleans, but no one needs to be reminded of that city's vulnerability.

"A hurricane's storm surge," the male anchor

explains, "can wreck buildings far from the beach and wash supporting sand from beneath structures and sea walls. It can engulf bridges, coastal roads and causeways, hampering rescue workers and those who evacuate at the last minute. That's why we're now telling Florida residents in the Tampa Bay region to stay put if they do not live in a flood zone." The camera zooms in on the reporter's eyes. "If you live along the beach and you haven't left the area, find a shelter inland and hunker down until the hurricane has passed. You'd better find that shelter now."

"The problem," the female anchor adds as the camera cuts to her, "is that the Gulf Coast is shallow—much more shallow, for instance, than the waters off Miami. The shallow waters allow for a higher surge and downtown Tampa is located at the point of maximum surge potential. Experts say that if a hurricane the size of 1992's Andrew were to hit Tampa, waves of twenty-five to thirty feet would smash into the city."

Eddie's house is not in a flood zone, but thousands of others are. How are those home owners coping with this news?

His gaze drifts toward the sliding glass door behind the kitchen table. Though the plywood blocks his view, the glass reflects a wavering image of the television screen. No sound seeps in from outside, leaving the air heavy with a peculiar muffled quality.

Instinctively, Eddie reaches for the dog, finds a silky ear and curls his palm around its warmth. Even with Sadie, the television and a crossword for company, he's not looking forward to the loneliness of the next twenty-four hours.

With the television droning in the background, he picks up the crossword-puzzle magazine and flips to a clean page. The puzzle is titled "Independence Day," and one across is a seven-letter word for *free*—

He flinches at the unexpected trilling of the telephone.

Michelle startles when in the middle of a dreadfully bland rendition of "Moon River," the Muzak stops and Ginger McCloud's voice blares over the speaker. "Hello? You ladies still on the line?"

She turns toward the elevator panel. "We're still here."

"It wasn't easy," Ginger says, "but I found a dispatcher in Pinellas County who put me through to one of her technicians. He answered the phone, but he says he's off the clock."

Michelle lifts her chin. "Can I speak to him?"

Her question is followed by a quiet so thick the only sound is the Hispanic woman's congested breathing. "Honey," the operator finally replies, "short of holding one phone up to the other, I'm afraid there's nothing I can do to manage that. We're a small answering service—we don't have a lot of high-tech equipment."

Michelle pushes herself up from the floor. "We're going to have to figure something out, then. I need to talk to that man."

For the past ten years she's made a career out of persuading people, and she's good at what she does. She's a professional, for goodness' sake. If she can convince corporate CEOs and CFOs to hand over thousands of dollars in the hope of gaining better positions, she ought to be able to persuade a mechanic to do his job.

But first she has to make sure this operator gives her the opportunity.

"Ginger? What's this technician's name?"

"Eddie Vaughn."

Michelle stares at the speaker and tries to focus. When she wants to charge a fee at the top of her sliding scale, she must assure her new client that he will secure a result commensurate with what he has invested. "More money expended," she promises, "results in more money returned."

So how in the world is she supposed to convince a blue-collar guy in Pinellas County that he can't afford to neglect three women across the bay? Money is not an issue, though the topic may soon enter the conversation. After all, every man has his price.

Dale Carnegie would recommend beginning the negotiation with the "can you do us a favor?" approach. What she's about to request, however, is a monumentally massive favor.

"Ask Mr. Vaughn—" She hesitates, irritated by the limitations of the situation. If she could see this guy, look him in the eye, things would be easier. "Ask him if he and his loved ones are safe right now."

She closes her eyes and strains to listen as Ginger repeats the question—presumably into another phone.

A moment later the operator responds, "He says he's fine and thanks for asking."

Michelle resists the impulse to groan. Why does the one available technician have to be a smart-aleck?

"That's good to know," she says, "but we're not fine. Since it's Mr. Vaughn's job to service these elevators, doesn't he think he ought to come over here and fulfill his responsibilities? If he hurries, he can get here, get us out and still make it home before the hurricane hits."

She bites her lip as Ginger parrots her words. After a pause, the operator's honeyed voice drips from the speaker again. "He says Tampa's not his territory, so you're not his responsibility. He also wants to know why you decided to go downtown when you knew the area had been evacuated. He says those streets have been closed off since daybreak."

Michelle rakes her hand through her hair. She wants to let this guy have it with both barrels, but this isn't the time to tell him what she thinks of such a cavalier attitude. He'd hang up, and then where would she be? Worse off than before, because Ms. Trench Coat looks as if she's itching to strangle someone, and Michelle is the closest target.

She addresses the panel again. "Listen, Ginger, this back-and-forth conversation isn't working. Can you please put the phones together? I need to speak to this man directly."

"I could try three-way calling, but I'd have to hang up—"

"No!" Michelle forces herself to take a calming breath. "Please. There has to be another way."

"Well—wait a minute. Maybe if I turn this other receiver upside down . . ."

Michelle catches the redhead's attention and frowns, but the woman maintains her locked expression. The housekeeper, however, has dried her tears and is leaning forward, her eyes bright with hope.

Michelle hears a clunking sound, a hum, then some sort of electronic yelp. Finally a baritone voice buzzes through the speaker: "Hello? Is this some kind of a joke?"

The voice is young and rumbling, not at all what she expected. In the static-filled background she can hear the comforting jingle of a State Farm commercial. *Just like a good neighbor . . .*

She can picture Eddie Vaughn with no trouble— thirty-something, soft belly beneath a flannel robe, fresh out of bed with his coffee mug in one hand and TV remote in the other. He's reclining in his easy chair, waiting for his wife to bring him breakfast. . . .

No wonder he doesn't want to leave the house.

"It's no joke. We're trapped in the Lark Tower." She raises her voice to be sure he can hear. "My name is Michelle Tilson, and I'm stuck in this elevator with two other ladies. You're Eddie Vaughn, right?"

She pauses, hoping he heard everything she said. She wants him to realize she's being civil, and she wants him to know her name. It's hard to turn someone down once you associate a need with a name . . . or a voice.

The television in the background goes silent. "That's right."

"Well, Mr. Vaughn, we really need your help. The elevator's stuck and I'm pretty sure the power's off. There's a backup generator to run the emergency systems, but I'm not sure how long the generators will last."

"Why are you ladies downtown? You had to know about the hurricane. It's been all over the news."

She blanches at the gentle sarcasm in his voice. "I can't speak for the others, but I came down early this morning and only meant to run upstairs for a minute. I'm pretty sure one of the ladies works the nightshift, and the other—" Her gaze moves to the intractable redhead, then she looks away. "I haven't had time to take a personal history from everyone, but we need your help. Please."

"Those roads are blocked off"

"It's not hard to drive around a barricade."

He snorts into the phone. "Are you sure there's no building engineer or security chief in the building?"

"I didn't see anyone. One guard was at his post this morning, but I don't think he knows we're stuck. If he did, he'd probably call *you*. So you see?" She smiles, hoping he'll hear warmth in her voice. "You're our only hope, Mr. Vaughn. Eddie."

White noise hisses over the line, followed by the swishing sounds of movement. "Where did you say you are?"

"The Lark Tower."

"If I make it over there, will I be able to get into the building?"

Michelle glances at her watch and remembers that Gus intended to close the lobby at ten. "The street entrance may be locked, but the parking garage is always open. Park on any level and you can't miss the elevators. We're in one of the express cars.

"All right. But before I agree to come, you all have to promise me something. Two things, actually."

Michelle grits her teeth. "What?"

"First, you have to sit calmly and wait for me to arrive. No messin' around in the car, okay? And when I get you out, you have to leave the building. Nobody hangs around to watch Felix roll in. I'm not going to risk my neck rescuing you twice."

Michelle immediately thinks of Parker, who has surely given up on her by now. He's probably on the road, racing home to be with his kids. If he's not, well, how's this elevator guy going to stop her from checking on him?

"Agreed," she says, without looking at the others.

"One more thing—you know a seven-letter word for *free?*"

Michelle blinks in exasperation. "What?"

"I was thinking *vacant,* but that's only six letters."

"Just hurry up, will you?"

For some odd reason, he whistles, then she hears a slamming door. "I'm already at my truck, lady. I'll be there as soon as I can get across the bay."

Michelle swallows hard. So—he's been getting

ready the entire time. "Thanks. Eddie."

After another series of murmurs and assorted clunks, Ginger's voice blasts over the speaker again. "That do it for you?"

"Yes. Unless you think it'd be useful to alert the Tampa police or our fire department."

The woman laughs. "I'll call 'em, but it sounds like you'd get better results if you rang up a superhero. Good luck, then."

"Wait—Ginger?"

"Yeah?"

"We might call you back."

For an instant Michelle's afraid the woman will say she can't be bothered, but the operator's response is surprisingly gentle. "Call if you need me, hon. I'll be here all day."

After Ginger disconnects, Michelle leans against the wall and looks out from the corner she's begun to consider her own. "I think," she says, sinking into a cross-legged position on the floor, "we might as well settle in and get comfortable. Any way you look at it, we're going to be here a while."

The housekeeper wipes her nose with a tissue, then, after a couple of awkward attempts at modest maneuvering, sinks to the floor and tucks her short dress around her thighs. The redhead remains standing for a long moment, then she slides down the wall until she's sitting across from Michelle.

Discomfited by the woman's hollow-eyed stare, Michelle pulls her cell phone from her purse and punches in 911. No response, no service. Nothing.

She drops the phone back into her bag and tries not to let her frustration show. She glances at the cleaning woman, who has stopped crying and seems calmer. The redhead sits with her legs crossed and her head lowered, one wrist balanced on each knee.

The housekeeper is the first to speak. "*Discúlpeme—*excuse me?"

Michelle looks toward the barely lit back of the car. The cleaning woman's mouth purses up into a rosette, then unpuckers enough to ask, "Help is coming, no?"

"That's what the man said."

"And we will all go together? We will go down and leave?"

Michelle shrugs. "Might as well."

"Thank you." When the housekeeper nods, Michelle realizes the woman is younger than she'd first thought. Her dark hair has come loose from her ponytail and floats around eyes that are large and smooth, their corners unlined.

No wonder she's upset. She's only a kid.

Michelle shifts her weight onto one hip and leans toward the cleaning woman. "I'm Michelle. And you are?"

The girl's shy smile temporarily banishes the shadows on her face. "Isabel."

Michelle plants an elbow on her knee, then rests her chin on her cupped hand. "Forgive me for being nosy, but have you worked here long?"

The housekeeper's eyes widen. "Long? No, no, not

long." Could the girl really be that shy? Michelle gives her a reassuring smile. "How old are you, Isabel?"

A deep flush rises from the girl's collar, marring her complexion with dusky blotches. *Diecinueve.*"

"That's what . . . nineteen?"

"*Sí.*"

Michelle nods in answer, then looks away. For some reason her questions seem to alarm the girl, so maybe Isabel would prefer to be left alone.

Michelle understands. At nineteen, she didn't trust anyone.

CHAPTER 10

"Shelly? When you're done sweeping up, we have some boxes in the back needin' to be unpacked." Mr. Morris, head of Maxim's custodial department, pulled a white envelope from his shirt pocket. "Before you start the unpacking, will you run this up to Ms. Calvino?"

Shelly leaned the broom against a shelf, then pushed at her sweaty bangs. The custodial job wasn't exactly a dream come true, but it provided enough to live on and had given her an excuse to leave home. Charleston, West Virginia, wasn't New York City, but it was a sight more cosmopolitan than Bald Knob.

She wiped her damp hand on her jeans, then accepted the envelope. "Ms. Calvino? She's . . . where?"

"Career Women, third floor. She's a tall lady, elegant lookin', blond hair. You can't miss her."

Shelly slipped the envelope into her back pocket as Morris walked away. She couldn't imagine what the head custodian would have to say to an elegant woman on one of the posh upper floors, but she'd only been working at Maxim's three weeks. A couple of the other girls had warned her that Morris was a single guy with fast hands, but he hadn't stepped out of bounds with her.

Apparently he liked more sophisticated women.

A wry smile twisted Shelly's mouth as she swept a heap of paper, dirt and assorted trash into an industrial-size dustpan. Maybe Morris had gone up to the third floor to change a lightbulb and liked Ms. Calvino's looks. Maybe the envelope contained a dinner invitation, or a suggestion that the lady break another bulb.

Shelly snorted, dumped the dirt into a garbage bin and paused, spying a battered copy of *How to Win Friends and Influence People* among the Styrofoam peanuts and discarded packing materials. That book would be right at home in her collection. She'd read about the Carnegie title in the bibliographies of other books, particularly those on finding success in the career marketplace.

With her thumb and index finger, she pulled the book from the trash, then grabbed the spine and shook the dust from its interior. A quick riffle of the pages convinced her she'd found a decent copy, so into her back pocket it went.

After returning the broom and dustpan to the supply closet, she checked her reflection in the mirror behind the door. A copy of *How to Increase Your Word Power* peeked from the front pocket of her overalls, giving her an odd, bumpy look. Frowning, she pulled the book from its place and slipped it into the back pocket with Ms. Calvino's envelope. She now had a pair of lumpy hips, but no one at Maxim's would look twice at a cleaning girl's backside.

The Maxim's handbook categorically stated that no on-duty employee was to appear on the sales floor in jeans, overalls or soiled clothing, but no one seemed to notice her as she walked through small appliances and made her way toward the escalator. Morris must have known no one would care about a skinny nineteen-year-old in braids, dungarees and a faded Mariah Carey T-shirt.

She took the escalator from the basement to the first-floor landing, where dozens of oversize Christmas presents had been piled into a pyramid. A cutesy version of "I'm Getting Nuttin' for Christmas" played on the intercom, a not-so-subtle reminder to the frantic mothers and fathers who were scouring the aisles for perfect gifts.

Shelly couldn't remember the last time she got a Christmas present from her mother. Her dad had always managed to bring her crayons or a new coloring book, but he died in a mining accident the year she turned ten. After that, people from the nearby Pentecostal church brought bags of groceries every Christmas Eve, but after setting the food on the porch they stood in a semicircle and sang carols loud enough to alert the entire park. Shelly appreciated the food—if not for those people, she'd never have known that people ate more than a chicken's wings or that fruit didn't have to come in a can—but the presentation so embarrassed her she vowed she'd celebrate her grown-up Christmases with TV dinners.

She bypassed Toyland on the second floor, then rode the escalator up to A Woman's World. The meandering rose-colored tiles led her past Better Sportswear and Lingerie, where she stepped off the tile pathway and wandered into the section reserved for Career Women. She didn't see any tall blondes, elegant or otherwise.

She stood in a gap between two racks of gaudy holiday sweaters and pulled the envelope from her back pocket. With every passing moment she risked attracting notice from one of the wandering supervisors, so maybe she should leave Morris's message where Ms. Calvino would be sure to find it.

She walked behind the counter, set the sealed envelope next to the cash register and backed away, feeling awkward and out of place. Not an inch of denim lay within a hundred yards of this register; apparently career women favored wools and linens and silk. She moved away from the desk, letting her fingers trail over the exquisite natural fabrics on the racks. No wonder things were more expensive up here. The clothing even felt different.

She was about to head for the escalator when a mannequin caught her eye. The faceless dummy wore a designer outfit—a halter top of light blue satin and a soft leather skirt in the same shade. Between her plastic fingers, she carried a matching jacket.

Shelly caressed the jacket sleeve and tried to imagine that softness caressing her arms. In an outfit like that, she'd look like a completely different girl. She'd feel like a million bucks.

Forgetting about the supervisors, she searched for the pieces on a nearby rack, pulled out the items in her size, and ducked into the hallway that led to the changing rooms. A glance beneath the doors assured her that Ms. Calvino had not sneaked to the dressing rooms for a cigarette. Morris's girlfriend was probably in the hall with the vending machines, munching on M&M's or downing a cup of coffee.

Shelly kicked off her sneakers, then unbuckled her overalls and pulled her T-shirt over her head. Ignoring the reflection of her tattered underwear in the long mirror, she slipped into the new clothing and breathed deeply as a transformation took place.

The skirt fit like a second skin. The satin halter top accented the boniness of her shoulders, but the jacket disguised that shortcoming. She spun in the full-length mirror, then tugged her braids to the back of her head. In this outfit, with her hair up and eyeliner around her eyes, she could pass for twenty-five, maybe twenty-six. Of course, there was no way she could afford this getup, not even if she saved for months and used her employee discount.

So switch the price tags.

The thought whipped into her brain so unexpectedly

that she glanced behind her to make sure she wasn't hearing the voice of an imp. Change the price tags? Easy enough to manage because Maxim's Department Store still did things the old-fashioned way; price tags were either pinned to garment sleeves or attached with ribbons and safety pins. She could gather these pieces in her arms, take the escalator downstairs to juniors' and replace these prices with tags from inexpensive cotton shirts and skirts. She could wait until after four, when the part-time help came in, to pay in the junior department. The harried housewife or young girl working there wouldn't recognize the outfit, or she'd be too tired, bored or distracted to care.

Shelly studied her image in the mirror. Was she crazy for even thinking about such a stunt? Could she and her bony shoulders pull off an outfit like this, or would people laugh as soon as she passed by? If she couldn't carry it off, she'd look like a little girl playing dress up. Everyone would know she was only Shelly Tills from Bald Knob, the girl who spent her days pushing a broom because she couldn't afford college and couldn't spend another day in her drunken mother's trailer—

So become someone else.

This time she recognized the voice in her head—the cultured tones belonged to the woman Shelly had always imagined but never dared emulate.

Pinocchio had Jiminy Cricket as his guide; she had Michelle Tilson—the polished, professional career woman she had always dreamed of becoming. Was Michelle only a dream . . . or a possibility?

Shelly bit her lip and stared into the mirror. From shoulder to hem she looked like a fashion model, but the illusion faded at her bare knees and vanished at her dingy socks. Her feet couldn't be helped, but she could work on what remained.

She unwound her braids, then pulled a wide barrette from the pocket of the overalls on the floor. After twisting her hair at the back of her head, she slid the barrette into the winding cord and clipped it into place. The look was more funky than chic, but it could work.

She pulled a container of lip gloss from another pocket and smoothed it over her mouth, then fished an almost-empty tube of mascara from the same pocket. Quick swipes of the left and right lower lashes left her eyes adequately smudged. She had no blush with her, but Momma used to pinch her cheeks just below the far corners of her eyes—there and there—and . . . done.

In the rectangular mirror Shelly saw Michelle L. Tilson, a sophisticated career woman who had never in her life received Christmas charity. Michelle knew how to win friends and influence people; she had a vocabulary so refined folks automatically assumed she'd attended all the best schools. Michelle didn't work in retail; she worked in an office. She didn't have a secretary; she had an administrative assistant and a staff.

Shelly caught her breath when she heard rustling from beyond the door. Someone moved in the hallway—another customer, or Ms. Calvino?

An unexpected knock sent a thrill of panic shooting through her. "Yeah? Yes?"

"How are you doing? Can I bring you anything?"

"No," Shelly managed to answer. Then, taking comfort from the locked door, in Michelle Tilson's voice she added, "Thank you, I'm fine."

"Ring the bell if you need me."

Shelly held her breath until the departing swish of the salesclerk's panty hose faded into silence. Ms. Calvino was probably returning to her post outside the entrance to the dressing rooms.

Exhaling in a slow and steady stream, Shelly pulled one arm free of the luscious jacket, then let it fall from her shoulders. She wriggled out of the skirt and unfastened the halter top. Her overalls still lay on the floor, so she put her T-shirt on, then stepped back into the familiar denim.

She sank to the edge of a bench and tied on her sneakers, then clasped her hands. What was the word she'd learned yesterday? *Audacity*—the willingness to tackle a dangerous or difficult undertaking.

If she were going to make something of herself, audacity would have to carry her through the next five minutes. The clock was already approaching four, so Ms. Calvino was probably busy at the register, getting ready to go home. Shelly could tuck the outfit under her arm and hurry past. By the time she made it down to juniors' and completed the switch, the downstairs register would be manned by a part-timer.

She replaced the designer garments on their hangers, then dropped one hand to the doorknob and bowed her head. What would happen if she were caught? She might be arrested. What would Momma say? The chorus of I-told-you-so would last as long as the mountains.

If the store manager didn't have her arrested, he'd certainly fire her. Without a job, how would she support herself? Her one-room Charleston apartment wasn't fancy, but it beat sleeping on the street. The macaroni and hot dogs she'd been eating weren't gourmet meals, but they were a lot more filling than empty dreams.

She closed her eyes as her thoughts drifted toward her mother, whose world these days revolved around a bottle. Her mother did nothing and produced nothing, yet somehow she managed to survive on Daddy's monthly benefit check. Shelly could always go home and live like Momma, but she wanted something better.

She wanted to be more than Eunice Tills's daughter. She wanted to be Michelle Tilson.

Michelle wouldn't sit in a trailer and watch the world go by; she'd take risks with her life. Michelle might not have money, but she had class, an excellent vocabulary, and knowledge derived from years of reading and people-watching. With those qualifications, enthusiasm and a designer outfit, she could get an office job that would take her a lot further than the custodial department at Maxim's.

Nothing in the quiet cubicle told her she was standing at a crossroad, but she knew it as certainly as she knew the sound of her mother's voice. The decision she made in the next five minutes could change the course of her entire life.

After a long hesitation, Shelly lifted her head and stepped out of the dressing room with three of the store's most expensive items tucked under her left arm. She strode straight toward the escalator, but her heart nearly stopped when Ms. Calvino called, "Did you find anything you liked?"

Shelly hesitated, but she didn't turn around. Instead, Michelle Tilson twiddled her fingers over her shoulder and said she'd try again another day.

Without a backward look, she rode the escalator down to the juniors' department, then ducked behind a tall display. A table had been covered with stacks of clearance items, mostly sleeveless tops and cotton skirts, so she took those tags and pinned them onto the designer pieces.

Nervousness gripped her as she approached the cash register. As she hoped, a part-time girl was working the floor, but talkative Ashley Stock wasn't the clerk Shelly would have chosen. She hesitated, then decided to plunge ahead with outrageous audacity.

"Hey, Shelly." Ashley greeted her with a smile. "You on your break?"

Shelly nodded. "Just thought I'd pickup a couple of things. I'm thinking about looking for a new job and need, you know, something to wear to the interview."

Ashley picked up the skirt. "Wow, this is nice. Haven't seen this before."

"It was—" Shelly pointed vaguely over her shoulder

"—in the clearance pile. I didn't see any others like it."

Ashley punched in the amount.

"Say," Shelly said, leaning on the counter, "have you seen the new guy in sporting goods? I hear he graduated from Florida State. Used to play football for them."

"Really?" Ashley picked up the satin top. "You like him or something?"

"Or something. He's cute."

Ashley slipped the jacket from its hanger. "You got a good deal on this, girl."

"I know." Shelly pulled her wallet from a pocket. "This'll probably clean me out, but I reckon it's worth it." She moved closer and lowered her voice to a conspiratorial whisper. "So . . . you want that guy to ask you out?"

Ashley's smile froze. "You know him?"

"No. But I could ask around, see who does. He's got to have friends somewhere, right?"

"Or maybe he's lonely and needs a new friend." Ashley punched the last number into the register, then frowned. "Uh-oh."

Shelly felt her stomach drop. "What?"

"Your employee discount. You want that, right?"

"Um . . . okay."

"So that's an extra twenty-five percent off." Ashley tapped another two keys, then totaled the sale. "There you go—an entire outfit for fifteen bucks. Can't beat that with a stick."

"Sure can't."

With the package under her arm and Ashley's "thank

you" ringing in her ears, Shelly took the escalator down to the basement where a stack of boxes waited to be unpacked. After finishing that task, she would find Morris and ask for the night shift. For the next few weeks, she'd need a couple free hours each day to interview for a more prestigious position.

An entire world waited outside West Virginia, and she would do anything necessary to explore it.

At nineteen, after experiencing the benefits of an exercise in audacity, Shelly Tills found that shedding her past was no more difficult than stepping out of a pair of overalls.

CHAPTER 11

Gina is leaning against the elevator wall, trying to take relaxing breaths and imagine herself on a spacious snowy mountaintop, when a piercing alarm shatters the silence. The strident *blaaat-blaaat-blaaat* jerks her back to reality and rockets her adrenaline level.

As her body tightens, she stares across the car at the brunette who identified herself as Michelle. A faint flicker of unease moves in the woman's brown eyes, then she glances at her watch. "Gus," she says, raising her voice above the din. "Remember?"

Gina leans forward, a hand cupped around her ear. "What?"

Michelle points at her watch. "It's a quarter after ten. I'm guessing Gus figured the fire alarm would be a good way to clear the office suites."

The maid is sniveling again, trembling as she dabs at her eyes and nose with a tissue. "Is a fire?" she manages to croak between sniffs.

The brunette shakes her head. "I don't think so."

A shiver passes down Gina's spine as the shattering sound continues. Will it ever stop? By the time the mechanic arrives, they'll be raving lunatics, driven out of their minds by this torturous racket.

And what if Michelle's wrong about Gus? A generator or something could have caught fire; flames could be shooting up from the lower floors at this instant. If so, they'll be toasted in minutes if they don't die from smoke inhalation first.

Gina covers her ears, trying to lessen the ear-splitting sound's impact by anticipating it, but each *blaaat* of the siren shatters her defenses. Over and over the alarm blares, scraping across her over-tightened nerves, without deviation. Now she understands why the army uses rock music to torment suspected terrorists. This repetitive racket is enough to give anyone the screaming meemies. . . .

She is about ten seconds from beating her head against the wall when the alarm stops. She tenses, bracing for another explosion of noise, but a balloon of quiet fills the car instead.

Finally, a moment of mercy.

Michelle breaks the silence with a subdued whisper. "I don't smell smoke, so Gus had to have pulled the alarm. There's no way he can do an office-to-office search to make sure everyone's out of the building."

The maid lifts a trembling hand. "They . . . will not come for us?"

Michelle gives her a twisted smile. "I wouldn't count on Gus. Did you see the way he walks? The man needs a hip replacement—there's no way he could climb stairs to help us."

Gina struggles to find her voice. "He might try—"

"I know Gus," Michelle interrupts. "He's got a good heart, but he's not the type to take chances. He probably hit that alarm, locked the front door and headed out, convinced that he'd done all he could be expected to do. But that's okay—Eddie Vaughn is playing the part of knight in shining armor, remember? He's on his way."

Gina closes her eyes. Yes, the elevator guy is on his way . . . across a windblown three-mile bridge that may be closing at any minute. In the meantime, she can't keep hoping for invisibility. Judging from what she heard through the telephone speaker, they're likely to be sitting in this elevator at least another hour.

She sighs and settles one shoulder against the wall, then gives Michelle a rueful smile. "I suppose I should introduce myself. I'm Gina . . . and I'm sorry for snapping at you a while back. With all that's going on today, I'm a little wound up. I hated to leave my kids at home, but I wanted to run up here and help my husband handle some last-minute things in his office." She shrugs. "I never imagined this scenario."

Michelle shakes her head. "Who could?"

Gina forces a smile, then lowers her gaze to the floor.

Sonny is a workaholic, but he can't work without power and he won't wait forever for the electricity to be restored. If he can't work, he'll go home. With that fire alarm blaring, he probably headed for the stairs and the parking garage, where he'll find his car and . . . see hers.

She blinks as the shock of realization hits. He'll see her car. He'll know she's come downtown to find him. He'll ask himself why she would leave the kids in this kind of weather, why she would come without calling first . . . and then he'll realize he's been found out.

What will he do next? The question has only two possible answers. He will either return to Gina and his family, or he will go protect the other woman.

Trapped in this cage, Gina is helpless to prevent either action.

She turns her face toward the door as frustration stirs memories of a dark time in their marriage. Sonny's mother died the year before Matthew was born, and Donald Rossman, Sonny's father, grieved quietly for two years. Sonny and Gina were delighted when he met and married June.

But when Donald entered a Kentucky hospital a few months later, they learned that June had convinced him to write a new will and change the beneficiaries on his life-insurance policies. "Of course I expect him to provide for June," Gina whispered to Sonny as they kept a vigil by Donald's hospital bed, "and I know your dad's a fair man. I'll appreciate anything he leaves us."

What she could never appreciate was his indifference to his only son.

Two days after Donald's funeral, they learned that he had left *everything* to June. As they prepared to return to Florida, Sonny put a few of his mother's handmade quilts and photograph albums into the back of the van, only to be stopped by June's attorney. With a policeman by his side, the lawyer demanded that every piece of property be returned to the house.

Gina wept all the way home. Donald had known they were struggling to establish a business and provide for two small children, yet he surrendered everything to a woman he'd known only a few months. "Lust," Gina told Sonny, her throat raw with grief. "It addled his brain."

Sonny no longer speaks of his father, but the pain still exists, simmering and hot, beneath his confident facade. One has only to mention Donald's name and the agony boils over, undercutting Sonny's assurance and self-esteem.

How can a man who has suffered under that hurt fail to see that he has been caught in the same trap? Sonny met a young woman and was overcome by lust; he is spending his children's inheritance on an outsider. Given time, he will mortgage their futures to satisfy his sensual cravings.

But his time has run out.

Gina lifts her gaze to the dark ceiling, where the lights refuse to burn. If her husband has done the smart thing and left the building, she'll catch up to him later. No one, especially not their father, will hurt her children like Donald hurt Sonny.

• • •

Gina stared numbly at the check in her hand: Pay to the order of Regina Meade Rossman the sum of fifty thousand and no dollars, dated September 4, 1985. A bittersweet bequest from her last surviving parent.

Her father had been in his grave three months before the lawyers settled his affairs. After taxes, expenses and selling his house and office building, fifty thousand dollars was all that remained of a once-sizeable estate built from her father's insurance business.

Her father had been more indebted than she realized, but that wouldn't alter her plan. Her suggestion would be slightly more modest, a minor adjustment to a proposal that could bring them independence, stability and, eventually, a steady income. Most important, her offer could help Sonny fulfill his dreams.

She had left work at noon, pleading a headache, and pulled into her parking space just as the mail carrier finished stuffing envelopes into the apartment's mail station. Thanking him with a smile, she pulled out her key and opened her box. Hard to believe, but the lawyer had kept his word and mailed the check on time.

She unlocked the apartment door and stepped inside, inhaling the scents of dust, mildew and the previous tenant's cigarettes. Daylight fringed the closed draperies and seeped onto the worn carpet, a nondescript shade designed to hide dirt. Gina tossed her purse onto a patched vinyl chair and moved into the kitchen, situated not more than ten feet from the front door.

She hated this apartment. She hated smelling it on

her clothes, coming home to it after a long day and making love to her new husband beneath its stained and cracked ceiling. Newlyweds deserved a fresh beginning, but on their salaries, she and Sonny had only been able to afford this pigsty.

Now she had fifty thousand dollars, enough for a down payment on a nice house in a good neighborhood . . . but Sonny had a dream. And while a house might bring her happiness, Sonny's dream would surely prove to be the worthier investment.

After starting dinner, she slid the check into an unmarked envelope, then slipped the envelope beneath a folded napkin. Humming to herself, she moved to the oven. Two chicken breasts bubbled in cranberry sauce; two baked potatoes hissed in foil jackets. She had a salad in the fridge and bakery rolls in a basket. Sonny would appreciate a good dinner—enough, she hoped, to listen to her proposal.

She stiffened at the sound of a key in the lock. He was home. Time to begin.

"Hmm, something smells good." Her handsome husband stepped into the rectangle that defined their small kitchen and dropped a peck on her cheek. He shrugged out of his jacket, then noticed the dishes on the table. "How long have you been home?"

She took his coat. "I told Mr. Thomas I had a headache."

"Do you?"

"Not anymore."

She draped his sports jacket over the back of an

empty chair, then sidled past him on her way to the oven. "I have something I want to discuss with you, though. An idea I've been contemplating."

He sank into his chair and loosened his tie. "Honey, I'm really tired. I'm not sure I'm up to talking about a bigger apartment even though I know how much you hate this place—"

"I could be happy here awhile. With no kids, we're really not that cramped."

His left eyebrow rose a fraction. "What do you have up your sleeve?"

"You want French dressing or Italian?"

"Blue cheese, if we have it."

She pulled a nearly empty bottle of his favorite dressing from the refrigerator, then drizzled it over the salad. She talked as she worked, her determination like a rock inside her as she carried the food to the table and explained her strategy: they would start an insurance company like her father's, but they would insure only low-risk clients. No smokers, no one more than twenty percent overweight, no one with a chronic illness. With a good actuary and careful planning, they could earn a profit within six months. Within a year, they could begin to issue more conventional policies.

Sonny's mouth twitched with amusement. "Honey, we can't open a business. We'd need seed money, an office, equipment. We could barely afford to pay the rent, let alone hire an actuary—"

She sat down, pulled the envelope from beneath her napkin and handed it to her husband.

"What's this?"

"A bequest."

He opened the envelope, then gave her a bright-eyed glance, full of memory, pain and awareness. "From your father?"

"Yes."

He didn't have to say anything, but in his eyes she saw the pain of *his* father's indifference, the sting of his stepmother's callousness. After a long moment, Sonny's gaze caught and held hers. "You really think we could pull it off?"

She raised her glass. "I do."

Sonny lifted his goblet and touched it to hers. "Then let's go into business together."

They rose from their seats and met in the middle, sealing their bargain with a kiss.

Caught up in a wave of sympathy, Michelle watches Gina unfold her bent legs and settle into a more comfortable position. Despite that bit of snappishness a few moments ago, the lovely redhead is obviously one of those women with a built-in sense of social grace. Michelle has always admired women who were born to success, but how they manage to remain impeccable and impressive in difficult situations has always been a mystery.

She'd be insane with worry if she'd left children at home with a hurricane approaching.

"Your kids," she asks. "How old are they?"

The redhead crosses her legs at the ankle. "Nineteen,

seventeen and fifteen. Old enough to take care of themselves, I know. But still, a mother worries."

"I don't blame you." Michelle glances at the panel of darkened elevator buttons. "This entire situation is frustrating."

"Yes," Isabel whispers. "I am frightened."

Michelle falls silent as the sound of the whistling wind penetrates the elevator shaft. Amazing, that they can hear it from this sheltered center of the building. When she signed her rental agreement two years ago, she learned that the Lark Tower met Florida's hurricane requirements and was capable of withstanding winds of up to one hundred miles per hour. At the time of its dedication in 1972, the Lark was a marvel of engineering, but Florida has beefed up its building codes in recent years and the Tower has never experienced the brute force of a category-four hurricane. Though the building wears its age with a certain grace, its glass exterior has weakened. Those wide, aging windows will be especially vulnerable to flying debris.

Michelle rode out the last hurricane, a category three that came ashore two hundred miles south, at her condo. Aside from a few fallen branches, Tampa home owners experienced only minor effects, yet buildings in Fort Lauderdale and Miami suffered severe structural damage and residents endured two weeks without power. If Felix proceeds as predicted, they're looking at a scenario that could be much worse—

She can't dwell on those possibilities. She won't.

"This is scary," she admits, looking at Isabel. "But I've been more frightened."

Gina's mouth curves in a smile. "When?"

Words spring to Michelle's lips: *This morning. When I realized I might be pregnant.*

She can't say that, though, not here. She needs to reserve that discussion for Parker, who will understand the tumult of emotions that gripped her as she held the pregnancy test kit.

But conversation in the elevator is a good thing. Talking will keep their minds occupied and help pass the time until help arrives.

Michelle folds her hands and smiles at the redhead against the opposite wall. "Have you ever felt really hopeless? Before today, I mean."

Gina almost laughs aloud. In the last few hours she's been overtaken by so many emotions it's hard to single one out from the pack.

But she knows hopelessness. Before the betrayal, before the anger, even before this frustration, she stood beneath the cold shadow of despair and felt its breath on her face.

She drops the reins on her thoughts and drifts back to a summer day at the beach. "One summer—it was 1990, I think—Sonny, my husband, and I had decided that I should take a week off and head to the beach with the kids. Sonny kept working, of course, but he'd drive over for dinner and we'd sit and watch the sun set over the gulf. Our daughter was a baby that year. Our son was three.

"One night I was lying on a beach blanket, propped up on my elbows, sort of in a daze. The day had been unbelievably hot and humid—one of those days when you feel like you're breathing through a wet wash-cloth. Sonny and Mattie were splashing at the pool while the baby and I watched the sun go down. After being alone all day with two kids, I was drained, almost too tired to think."

"Anyway, after the sun set, I turned around and saw Sonny coming toward me. I was about to ask what he'd done with Mattie, when suddenly I heard a woman screaming by the pool. That's when I knew— Sonny didn't have Mattie at all. The pool had him."

Even now, the memory has the power to shiver her scalp like the grip of a nightmare. "I ran toward the pool," she says, a tremor rippling her voice. "I don't remember it, but later people told me that I screamed with every step. By the time I got there, a man had dived in and pulled Mattie up, but he was as blue as ice. I handed Mandi to someone and tried to perform CPR on Mattie, but nothing I did seemed to help."

Gina glances at the others. The maid is not looking at her, but a quiver touches Michelle's chin. "Was he . . . okay?"

"The rescue squad came and took him away. They let me ride along, and I heard one of them radio ahead and say they were coming in with a DOA. Then the man who was working on Mattie yelled that he'd found a pulse. After that, I hung on to my son's hand and didn't let go until they pried me loose at the hospital."

Relief floods Michelle's features. "He was fine, then."

Gina shakes her head. "It was touch and go at the hospital. They didn't know how long he'd been underwater, so they didn't know if he'd suffered brain damage. And he'd inhaled water into his lungs, which made him susceptible to pneumonia, so they told me his chances weren't good. All that night I paced in that ICU corridor and begged God to let me keep my son."

From the edge of the emergency lamp's glow, the maid whispers, "Did He answer?"

"Who can say?" Gina can't stop herself from laughing. "That night I'd have prayed to Santa Claus if I thought it would work. Desperation does strange things to people—makes you want to make promises you know you can't possibly keep. Anyway, I promised God that I'd stop working and concentrate on my kids, do whatever it took to be the best mom in the world, if he'd heal my boy. The next morning, Mattie woke up and started talking like nothing had happened. But I've been unable to go near anything deeper than a bathtub ever since."

The Hispanic girl stares at her with chilling intentness for a long moment, then crosses her arms. "I believe in God. I pray to Him."

Gina pushes her hair back, the better to return the girl's stare. Of course the maid believes in God; she's Hispanic, which means she's Catholic. And probably as superstitious as a gypsy.

She smiles at the Mexican girl. " 'And almost everyone when age, disease or sorrows strike him . . . inclines to think there is a God, or something very like Him.' "

Across the car, the brunette chuckles. "That's funny. You make that up?"

"No. It's a verse from Arthur Hugh Clough."

"Oh." The brunette straightens, a frown puckering the skin between her eyes into fine wrinkles. "So . . . you didn't keep the promise you made that night?"

"I did—not because of some bargain with the Almighty, but because I realized how precious my kids were. By then it was an easy decision, because the business was doing well. Sonny didn't need me at the office and I was glad to be out of the picture. We decided our kids were the most important thing in our lives, so I was happy to make them my priority."

A tiny flicker widens Michelle's eyes. "Seems to me your kids would be better off watching you make something of yourself."

Gina smiles, simultaneously amused and annoyed by the brunette's naiveté "I didn't have anything to prove. I'd already graduated magna cum laude from Brown, married and helped my husband start a business. I wanted an opportunity to help make something of my children."

"Interesting perspective."

Gina tilts a brow. "Why do you say that?"

Michelle shrugs. "The women I knew growing up hardly ever left the house—especially my mother," she says, slipping out of her raincoat. "She'd get up, have a cigarette and drink gin for breakfast. A steady diet of soaps in the afternoon, crackers and soup for dinner if we were lucky, reruns and more booze at night: By the time I hit high school, my mother's rear had worn a hole into our sofa cushion."

Gina shifts her gaze to the elevator panel, sensing the younger woman's embarrassment. Michelle Tilson might be inexperienced in some areas, but apparently she had learned other lessons the hard way.

"You felt hopeless the night your son almost drowned," the brunette continues, folding her coat. "I lived with hopelessness for nineteen years. There weren't many jobs available in my little town, but I picked wild blueberries when I could and sold quilt squares cut from old dresses I bought at a church thrift shop. As soon as I had enough money to leave home, I packed a bag and hightailed it out of town. I swore I'd do anything to make it on my own, but I'd never live with hopelessness again."

Gina lets her head fall back to the wall. "Where was this place?"

"Bald Knob, West Virginia." Michelle snorts softly. "The kind of place you're always glad to say you're from."

Gina tilts her head, suddenly seeing Michelle Tilson in a new light. Perhaps this situation has a silver lining—this woman is someone who might become a friend. Once this sordid mess with Sonny is straightened out, she can see herself playing golf or having tea with Michelle Tilson, perhaps sharing a three-day weekend at the Saddlebrook resort. . . .

"I would never have guessed you were from the mountains. You seem quite . . . cosmopolitan."

"Oh. Well." Michelle's obvious resentment evaporates as she laughs. "I had TV, you see. Nothing else to do in the trailer at night. So I worked on my speech, forcing myself to talk and behave like the characters on *Home Improvement* and *The Cosby Show.*" Her mouth quirks with humor. "Claire Huxtable did more to mold me than my own mother."

Gina closes her eyes, grateful that neither of her daughters will ever be able to make such a statement. "I doubt that. Our mothers affect us more than we know."

"Maybe. But I feel like I've spent more time undoing my momma's influence than—well, never mind. I don't like to dwell on the past. That sort of thinking is unproductive."

In that reply, Gina catches the cadence of a southern accent. Michelle might have removed herself from the mountains, but she hasn't completely removed the mountains from her speech.

She is about to compliment Michelle on her accomplishments, but at that moment the overhead lights come on, an unseen engine hums and the elevator begins to rise.

CHAPTER 12

Michelle blinks in the sudden brightness, then glances at her watch. Ten-thirty. Could Parker still be in his office? The fire alarm would have rattled any ordinary human being, but Parker isn't ordinary when it comes to business. Plus, he said he'd wait for her.

She exhales a long sigh. "You see?" She hugs her raincoat to her chest and smiles at the housekeeper. "I told you the power would come back on."

She looks at the elevator panel, where the button for the twenty-fifth floor finally lights. Now they have moved out of the concrete shaft into an area with landings and doors she will never again take for granted.

Maybe her plan is still feasible. She can go to her office, grab Greg Owens's fake file and hurry to Parker's suite. From the sound of the wind she can tell the weather has worsened, but it won't be so bad she and Parker can't drive to her condo and talk about the future.

Twenty-six, twenty-seven. Only nine floors to go.

She pushes herself up. "This is good," she says, her eyes fixed on the elevator buttons. "We're almost home free, though we should definitely take the stairs down. I wonder if we can reach that repair guy and tell him not to come—"

Her breath catches in her throat as the lights dim and go out. The car shimmies to a halt, darkness closes in, and the bright square on the panel fades into blackness.

146

After a moment, the emergency light above the telephone speaker begins to glow again.

Michelle groans. Fresh misery extinguishes her hope as she slides back to the floor and lowers her head. To her left, Isabel presses her hand over her mouth as if she might otherwise cry out.

Across the car, Gina lifts her chin. "*Nil desperandum,*" she says, her voice filled with a surprising calm.

Michelle crinkles a brow. "I beg your pardon?"

"Horace. It means *never despair.*" Gina folds her arms across her lap. "You're the one who said we should expect the power to cut in and out."

"Yes, but I was hoping—"

"Better keep a tight rein on that hope," Gina says. "And don't forget about Murphy's law. If something can go wrong—"

"Why can't something go *right* for a change?" Michelle's misery vanishes, replaced by a rising rage. "And don't give me some two-thousand-year-old guy's opinion, because I don't care what Horace or Plato or Socrates had to say. They aren't in this elevator. They don't know what we're going through."

Gina stares back, her eyes bright with speculation, her smile sly with superiority. "They went through worse than this, I'm sure."

"I don't care. All I know is that I came down here for something important, but now I'm stuck and it's not only my day that might be ruined, but my entire career."

No longer caring what the other women think, Michelle slides her fingers between the elevator doors and pries them apart. They open as before, creating a space of about four inches, but this time that space reveals light and carpet and landings above and below a concrete divider.

"Hellooooo! Help!" she shouts, her lips inches away from the opening, then slips her arm through the gap. Her flapping hand is only a few inches above the carpet on the upper level, but it should be visible to anyone passing by. "Can you help us?"

She waits, listening, but apart from the caterwauling wind, both levels are heavy with after-hours quiet. Through the gap on the upper floor she sees a leather chair, a potted palm and a tasteful trash bin. She crouches to shout into the lower landing. "Hellooooo? Anyone there?"

"Save your voice," Gina says. A glaze comes down over her eyes as she props her elbow on a bent knee. "I'm sure all of us have important reasons for being here, but we're alone and we'll stay alone until after the storm passes. We have to wait. We have to be calm. And it might be helpful if we can focus on other things."

Michelle waits another moment, then pulls her arm in and watches the doors slide back together. She is on the verge of arguing out of sheer stubbornness when a small dose of common sense dribbles into her brain. As much as she hates to admit it, Gina is right about one thing: frustration is not a helpful emotion, and could be as crippling as panic.

She glances at Isabel, whose upper lip is adorned with pearls of perspiration. The sight reminds Michelle of a corresponding dampness under her own arms. No wonder—the air-conditioning isn't working and there's no outside ventilation. In an hour or two, maybe less, they'll be sweating like marathon runners.

She has to get a grip on her emotions. They all do. Michelle turns to face the others. "You're right. I'm sorry I lost it."

"Now we're even." The redhead rests her chin on her hand as a smile curves her lips. "Now—back to your story. Obviously, you learned something from your childhood misery. You came down from the mountain and made something of your life. How'd you manage college?"

"A scholarship," Michelle answers automatically. She glances toward the door, unhappy with the sudden change of subject. In another moment this woman will be asking questions about where, when and what Michelle studied. Though she has lied about those things a thousand times, it doesn't seem prudent to lie when her life is hanging by a cable.

No sense in tempting God . . . or whoever is controlling the universe today.

"I wish," she says, lifting her gaze toward the shadowy ceiling, "we knew what was happening outside. If we knew how the storm was progressing, maybe we could guess when they'll send rescue teams into the area."

Isabel lifts her head with a sudden snap. "Oh!"

Gina's eyes flick at the girl. "Don't be shy, speak up."

With a pained grimace, Isabel pulls something from her pocket, then pushes an object into the light: her pink CD player.

Michelle looks at the cleaning woman. How on earth is that supposed to help them?

Gina's mouth twists in bitter amusement. "Don't tell me—all this time, you've had a radio."

"I forgot." Isabel ducks as though she fears Gina will slap her. "I always listen to music while I vacuum. I never listen to *la radio*. But I have it."

When the redhead reaches for the player, Michelle blocks Gina's reach. "Why don't you listen," she says, nodding at Isabel. "See what you can tell us about the storm."

Gina withdraws her hand, annoyance struggling with humor on her face as she stares across the car. Michelle leans into the corner, not caring that she's nipped the older woman's pride. The redhead carries herself like a perfect lady, but a mile-wide bullying streak lies beneath that polished veneer. There's something about the way she avoids looking at Isabel unless she absolutely has to. . . .

Isabel slips the earbuds into her ears, then clicks the power button and twirls the dial. She listens, her brows lowering, then bites her lip and looks at Michelle.

"Well?" Michelle brings her hands together. "What's happening?"

Isabel switches the machine off. "Winds are one hundred forty-three miles per hour," she says, speaking slowly, "and it is raining hard. The radio man is worried about flooding."

"Flooding where?" Gina asks. "Along the Gulf?"

Isabel's gaze flicks at the older woman. "*Sí.* And the bridges and downtown Tampa."

"Rain." Gina lifts her gaze to the ceiling. "I thought that's what I was hearing."

She's been hearing rain? Michelle blinks, then closes her eyes to concentrate. At first she hears only the shriek of the wind, then her ears catch a susurrant whisper that seems to come from far away. So that's what the shushing sound is—the heavy rains serving as Felix's opening act.

"I'm surprised we can hear anything," Gina says, "dangling in the center of the building like this."

"But we're dangling in a shaft that opens to the roof," Michelle points out. "It's hollow, and you know how sound travels through open spaces, so maybe that explains it." She glances at Isabel, whose eyes are growing wider by the moment. "You made a good point a minute ago," she says, not wanting to panic the housekeeper. "We should talk about something to pass the time. Something positive."

"Like how you're *positive* that mechanic is going to get us out of here?" The curves of Gina's mouth go flat as she slips out of her trench coat. "I can't see how he's going to do that without help, and I don't know where he's going to get help when nearly everyone in the county has evacuated."

The cleaning woman leans forward, her eyes searching Michelle's. "The man you called . . . he is coming, *no?*"

"You heard him." Michelle drops her gaze before Gina's skeptical stare. "He said he was on his way."

With uncommon care, Gina folds her coat into a square, then props it between her back and the wall. "I wouldn't get my hopes up. The weather's worse than it was an hour ago, so he may not be able to cross the bridge. We may have to ride out the storm in this elevator—in fact, maybe we should count on it."

The housekeeper looks at Michelle, her dark eyes brimming with threatening tears. "My son needs me. Do you . . . do you have kids?"

"Not yet."

Isabel dashes wetness from her lower lashes. "My son, Rafael, is only eighteen months old. A baby."

The redhead snorts softly. "Enjoy him while you can. Babies grow up and turn into toddlers, and toddlers turn into teens. My kids are well behaved because I've never tolerated foolishness, but even my kids are occasionally challenging."

When the wind unexpectedly ceases for a moment, silence settles around them, an absence of sound that has an almost tangible density. Michelle inhales that silence, then finds herself about to choke on the strangely thickened air.

This won't do. If they stop talking, they'll begin to think of their loved ones, and when they think, they worry . . .

"Well," she says, her voice strangled, "we can't sit here and stare at the walls or we'll go crazy. We could . . . I don't know. Talk about our men?"

Gina arches her brows into triangles. "You like to play games at parties, don't you?"

"What's wrong with games?"

"Nothing, if you're fourteen."

Michelle meets the older woman's gaze. "I like ice breakers. They help people forget how miserable they are when they're forced into unfamiliar group situations. I could take a roomful of type-A personalities, assign them a social task, and have them interacting like old friends in ten minutes."

Gina snorts. "Interacting like competitors, you mean. My husband likes games, too, but he doesn't play for fun. He plays to win."

"What's the difference?"

The redhead draws a quick breath, then smiles slowly and turns to the cleaning woman. "You said you had a son. Want to tell us about him?"

Despite the stuffy warmth of the elevator, Michelle feels her cheeks flush with heat. Gina has purposely changed the subject in order to avoid an argument, and with that simple, graceful gesture, she has taken control of the conversation.

The woman is a master manipulator, but Michelle is no novice.

Obviously uncomfortable under Gina's directive, the housekeeper swipes at a hank of hair clinging to her damp forehead. "I don't know what to say."

"Come on." Michelle swings around to face Isabel. "You can take your time to think of something, but make it a happy story, okay? Maybe your happiest moment. After all—" her mouth twists in a confident smile "—we're not going anywhere until Eddie arrives."

Isabel swipes at her nose with a tattered tissue and wonders what she can say. A happy story? These *gringas* barely talk to her, then they ask for *una historia feliz?* Is she supposed to clean their building *and* entertain them?

Still . . . maybe it wouldn't be bad to remember a time before the trouble started. Before Ernesto.

She thrusts the tissue back into her pocket and breathes deeply, forcing herself to move past a cloud of raw memories. She had a happy childhood, but these women would not appreciate the simplicity of life in Monterrey or understand how food in the belly equaled happiness in the heart. They might not value the care her mother took slicing homegrown peppers or grilling tortillas on the griddle. Yet while they might not be familiar with hand-prepared foods or poverty, they might understand love.

She dabs again at her wet nose and searches for the right words. Hard as it is to remember happiness, it's even harder to translate the feeling into English.

She looks at the younger woman. "I grew up in Monterrey, where almost everyone worked in the cotton mills," she says. "My *mamá, papá, y hermano*—my brother—worked there, too, so I started at the mill when I was fourteen. I was too young, but my mother said nothing when I told the boss I was older. We needed the money, but I also wanted to be with my family. Everything was good until my *papá* caught his arm in one of the machines. He died."

The brunette holds one hand up and places the other across it. "Time out," she says, her eyes crinkling at the corners. "We want to hear about good things, not industrial accidents."

Isabel draws a breath between her teeth. She had been about to add that those first few weeks were a happy time, but how can she talk about the mill without mentioning *Papá's* accident?

She looks away and searches for another story. "My marriage day," she finally says. "When Carlos married me, I was happy. But the happiest day was when Rafael was born an American citizen."

The woman called Michelle turns to face Isabel and leans against one of the bronze doors. "Tell us about Carlos," she says, hugging her knees. "Did you date for a long time? Is he handsome? Does your baby look more like you or your husband?"

Isabel blinks, then gives the woman a bland smile, remembering that she and this *gringa* are from two different worlds. She met Carlos only three minutes before he saved her life; he married her three weeks later. And the baby, who had been in her belly when she met her husband, looks nothing like the man he calls *Papá*.

Her gaze shifts to the pattern on the tile floor. "I owe Carlos everything."

"Where'd you meet him?"

"A town in North Carolina . . . where I got off the bus."

When the red-haired woman lifts a brow, Isabel knows they want the entire story. But how can she speak of Ernesto? Already these *gringas* think her poor and stupid. If they knew about Ernesto, they would also think her wicked. And if they knew what happened in the office on the thirty-sixth floor . . .

They must never, ever know that.

Still they keep watching and waiting, so what can she tell them?

"I love my Carlos." She gives each of the women a brief, distracted glance and tries to smile. "When I got off the bus I had no money, so he took care of me and bought me a ticket to Florida. He found me a place to stay and three weeks later he took me to the church where a priest married us. He is a good father, and he keeps me safe. What more could any woman want?"

"What, indeed?" the red-haired *gringa* says, and even across the gulf that separates them, Isabel recognizes the tang of bitterness in the woman's voice.

꒷꒦

CHAPTER 13

"Baby, if you love me, you will."

Isabel stared at Ernesto through a haze of nausea. How could he be so insensitive? He knew about her pregnancy, he knew she was *enferma.* So how could he insist that she go to New York?

"Ernesto." His name, once so lovely on her tongue, tasted like bile. "Ernesto, please, I am sick."

"It'll pass, baby. Soon you will be feeling good."

He reached out, cupped her chin in his broad hand and looked into her eyes. "Doesn't being my woman make you feel good?"

Yesterday she would have said yes.

Six months ago, during their first dance, she'd given Ernesto her heart. Two days ago, in her bathroom at home, she'd discovered that he had given her a baby. This morning she'd broken the news; he'd smiled and told her to go home and rest. When she'd come looking for him this afternoon, he'd barely glanced at her before asking her to go to New York.

If he'd meant to take her on a vacation, she'd have been thrilled beyond words. She'd have forsaken her family and lied to her *madre* for a chance to see New York on Ernesto's arm.

But he didn't want her to go as a *turista.* He wasn't

planning *una vacaciones* or a sightseeing trip; he wanted her to deliver drugs to his New York contacts.

He wanted her to hide cocaine in her belly.

"No, Ernesto," she begged, searching for some sign of yielding in his eyes. "It would not be good for the baby."

His hand rose to stroke her hair. "Nothing will hurt the *bebé.* You will be safer than most of my girls. If you are stopped, you will not be arrested because the Americans will not X-ray a pregnant woman. No X-ray, no proof."

She shook her head like a dog stunned by a swift and unexpected blow. "What if they don't believe I am pregnant?"

"They will make you pee in a cup, then they will see for themselves. You will be safe, *chiquita.* No one will bother you."

Sick with the knowledge that he could use her in such a way, she placed one hand on her stomach. "Ernesto, I don't want—ohh!"

His hand twisted in her hair until the pressure ripped at her scalp. She cried out, then closed her eyes and gasped as he leaned closer to exhale a beery breath in her face. "This isn't about what you want; *chica.* This is about what you will do for me. Other girls have done it, and look at them—they have happy babies, no? So you will do it."

"I am not like those other girls. I am too afraid—"

"I will ask Jesus Malverde to give you courage. He will be with you and bring you back to make me happy."

"But—"

"If you do not do this . . . perhaps you will never see your brother alive again. I know Rodrigo, I know where he goes after work. I think my son would like to know his uncle some day, but that will be your decision."

He released his grip on her hair, but as he walked away, a clump of long strands fell from his fist to the floor.

Isabel pushed herself to a sitting position and couldn't help noticing the billboard outside the apartment window. Stop, the government-sponsored sign read, Love Can Cost You Dearly.

The picture beneath the words featured a young woman being led away in handcuffs while in the background her silk-shirted, blue-jeaned, drug-dealing boyfriend smiled and smoked a cigarette.

As rain streaks the cab windows, Eddie Vaughn clicks his tongue and studies the wavering pavement. "Yesterday," he tells Sadie, "the white lines on this highway told me where to drive. I know those lines haven't moved, Sades, but I'm not seein' them. If you spot one, give a shout, will you?"

The dog shifts her weight on the seat and sits a littl straighter, knowing she's been asked to do somethin

Eddie chuckles and returns his gaze to the wet ro Sometimes he'd give his last dollar to know how m of his conversation the dog comprehended. He used to mock him, saying he put too much st what Sadie understood, but sometimes he is sure the dog grasps far more than his ex-wife.

"Whoa, girl." He extends his arm to shield the retriever as he applies the brake. The instinctive action is unnecessary, for Sadie's harness is attached to the seat belt, a precaution he insists on taking whenever his best friend travels with him.

Ahead, on what looks more like a pond than a road, yellow beacons flash a warning. Swirling red and blue lights signal the presence of an emergency vehicle, so maybe a cop will be able to tell him what's going on.

The only other car on the road, a Ford Explorer, pulls a U-turn before it reaches the yellow lights. Eddie presses forward, driving as fast as he dares until he reaches the roadblock.

The Pinellas County deputy draped in an orange poncho is a woman. Water streams from the brim of her plastic-covered hat as she bends toward the window to shout an unintelligible order.

Unintelligible: fourteen letters, difficult to understand. You could fill half a column with that one.

Eddie presses the window button and flinches as cold ʾin invades the sanctity of the warm cab.

ʾVe've gotta keep people off the bridge," the deputy her voice hoarse. "We've got storm surge ʾn soon."

rs through the gathering gloom and studies ʾad. The three-mile Howard Frankland ʾıla of Pinellas County with Tampa. ʾe rides about twelve feet above the bay, all but "the hump," a towering, sloping span designed to permit the passage of tall ships.

"Listen—" Eddie tries to speak in a normal voice, but the deputy shakes her head and cups her hand around her ear.

"It's like this," he yells, leaning out the window. "I'm an elevator-repair technician. We've got some women stuck in a downtown skyscraper and I've got to help 'em out."

The woman stares at him for a moment, then his words fall into place. "You've got people in downtown Tampa? But those roads were blocked off last night."

Eddie grips the steering wheel. "I guess they found a way around the barricades."

The deputy rolls her eyes, then points toward the bridge. "If you go over, you won't be able to come back for a good while. This bridge is going to be underwater in a couple of hours. The Skyway's already closed and the Causeway will be swamped any minute."

Eddie squints at the long gray bridge, barely visible in the pouring rain. "I guess I'd better find a rock to crawl under, then."

Though the look in her eye makes it clear the deputy is questioning his sanity, she leans in again. "You got gas? There's no gas within a hundred miles of here."

"I filled up yesterday. And I have a spare gas can in the back."

"Well . . . all right, I'll let you through. But you be careful, you hear? Winds are awful strong on the hump."

"I'll take my time."

"Don't take too long."

He rolls the window up as the deputy grabs on to her hat and ducks into the wind. A moment later she swings one of the barricades aside, leaving just enough room for his truck to squeeze onto the approach to the bridge.

He hasn't driven forty yards when the sky opens and releases a deluge. He turns the wipers to their top speed, but he can hardly see past the wall of water streaming over the windshield. Beside him, Sadie whimpers and lies flat, her plumed tail drooping off the bench seat.

"Don't fret, girl." Eddie keeps his gaze on the road, knowing one false move could land him up against the guardrail or in the bay. "We're gonna be fine. Just two miles of straight road, then the hump, then we're in Tampa. We're practically there."

When Sadie whimpers again, Eddie reaches into his pocket and pulls out a liver-flavored dog biscuit, which the retriever accepts with delicate pleasure.

Eddie feels his mouth curl into a one-sided smile. As long as the dog is willing to eat, things can't be all that bad.

Eddie rolled over and felt his arm drop into emptiness. He opened one eye, momentarily confused. This wasn't his bed, not his apartment. He was stretched out on a narrow sofa in a stranger's living room.

He closed his eyes and deliberately let his mind run backward. Yesterday . . . Pete Riddleman had thrown a party to welcome the new lifesaving crew to Panama

City Beach. After the orientation meeting, they'd all gone over to Pete's place, where Mr. Riddleman had stashed plenty of beers in iced tubs. At eighteen, neither Eddie nor the other newcomers were old enough to drink in Florida, but Pete's father had winked and said as long as they stayed at the house and didn't drive drunk, everything would be a-okay.

Eddie rolled onto his back and forced himself to focus on the ceiling. Across the room, a couple of guys snored into air that smelled of cigarettes and sour beer. Riggs and Murtaugh argued on the television as a *Lethal Weapon* DVD repeated its play cycle.

Eddie lifted his head, felt an invisible two-by-four slam the empty space between his eyes, then let his throbbing skull drop back to the sofa pillow.

A hangover. His first.

He lifted his hand and gingerly massaged the bridge of his nose. How did people cure this misery? His friends could sleep it off, but Eddie had pulled the first shift; the condominium bosses expected him to be in his chair by nine o'clock.

What time was it?

Careful not to lift his head, he raised his left arm and moved his wristwatch into his field of vision. Eight-thirty. Still time to make the chair . . . if he could coax his body into an upright position.

He let his arm drop, then groaned when the limb struck his stomach. His newly awakened belly roiled with nausea, and the thought of coffee only increased the turbulence.

He pressed his lips together, closed his eyes and reminded himself that the john was only a few yards away. Through the living room, if his memory could be trusted, and to the left. There he'd find a toilet. Shower. Sink. Maybe an Alka-Seltzer or an aspirin in the medicine cabinet. He wouldn't be choosy.

He breathed hard through his nose, marshaling his strength, then pulled himself upright. Bodies lay scattered over the floor—young men sacked out on pillows, on blankets, one guy sprawled on his back in a bean-bag chair. Eddie rose and ignored all of them, bulleting his way to the sanctuary of the bathroom.

He barely made it to the toilet before his stomach revolted at the sudden change in position. He retched for what felt like an hour, then rose in a stooped posture and moved to the sink. He rinsed his mouth and splashed his face with cold water. He clung to the edge of the vanity and peered into the mirror.

Bleary-eyed Eddie Vaughn would lose his first post-graduation job if he didn't get down to the beach on the double.

He splashed his face again, scrubbed his skin dry with a towel and staggered back through the living room. None of the other guys stirred as he moved to the kitchen, where Mr. Riddleman had piled his collection of car keys in a brandy snifter. Eddie fished out his key chain, winced at the jangling sound it made, then waved a silent farewell to Pete, who was sleeping on a chaise longue by the pool.

In his car, he tapped out the rhythms of Wilson Phillips's "Hold On" as he wove in and out of the beach traffic. Nine o'clock on a Friday morning, but every driver on the highway was out for a relaxed Sunday drive.

Except Eddie.

At ten minutes past the hour, he zipped into a parking spot, dropped two quarters into the meter and grabbed his gear from the back of his Jeep. He sprinted past the bed of tall sea grass, his sneakered feet pounding the wooden boardwalk, then came to an abrupt halt.

A knot of people had assembled near the empty lifeguard station. A dark-haired woman in a black bathing suit crouched at the center of the circle, a pale boy face-up on the sand beside her. A man knelt across from the wailing woman and desperately tried to blow life back into the boy's lungs.

A grim-looking onlooker propped his hands on his hips as the woman sobbed, then his gaze brushed Eddie's. His hot look seared Eddie with scorn and reproach.

An investigation later established that the boy had gone into the water at 8:50 a.m. and had been caught in the riptide only a moment later. Because the child had begun to swim before a lifeguard had been expected on duty, a civil court ruled that the condominium wasn't liable and Eddie could not be faulted for the boy's drowning.

The legal decision did nothing to assuage Eddie's guilt. If he had not partied the night before, he probably would have reported to his stand early . . . and the boy would still be alive.

After successfully completing twelve months of lifeguarding without further mishap, Eddie moved back home to Birmingham. He set aside his plans for college and checked out vocational schools instead. He thought about firefighting and briefly considered police work, then he fell in love with elevators.

Through careful maintenance and the occasional rescue, in the elevator business you could save a life every day.

Despite her intention to remain calm, by eleven-thirty Michelle is as frustrated as a race car driver stuck in commuter traffic. In order to stop thinking about Parker, she's forced herself to focus on the problem with Greg Owens, but she can't do anything until she reads the man's application. Once she sees how the columnist has presented himself, she should be able to find him a legitimate job offer within a week or two.

The thought of sidestepping the reporter's assault brings a smile to her face, but she can't deny the irony. Greg Owens, champion for the cause of integrity and ethics, has resorted to deception in the hope of exposing an employment scam. To remain free of his sticky little web, Michelle will counter with complete honesty. If not for the danger of further fallout, she might even be tempted to expose Marshall Owens's false application.

But what kind of jobs might he have applied for? He

might have claimed to be a teacher or a writer. Depending on his background, he might have claimed to be a coach or in retail. She could ask the school principal who e-mailed her this morning for possible leads at local schools, and Lauren might know someone at the mall. If they meet at Lord & Taylor tomorrow—when they meet—Michelle could stop by the store office and ask for a sample application.

She pulls her purse from the corner and rummages through its depths for her notepad and a pen. She wants to jot down these ideas before she forgets them; she wants to feel as if she's doing something useful while she sits here staring at the walls.

She finds her notepad, drops it onto her lap and thrusts her hand back into her purse. After grabbing a handful of objects at the bottom of her bag, she brings them into the light: a wrapped cough drop, a highlighter, a paper clip, a gum wrapper and two pens, neither of which work when she drags them across a sheet of paper.

From the other wall, Gina watches with a look of patient amusement. "You might check—" she points toward the purse "—to see if you have anything edible in there. By the time the storm passes, we might be hungry."

Michelle gives her a wintry smile. "We won't be here when the storm passes. Eddie's coming."

"He may be," Gina counters, "but unless he's bringing help, I don't think he's going to get us out. Even a piece of hard candy might boost our energy."

Tired of arguing, Michelle dumps the contents of her purse on the floor. The other women lean forward as she takes inventory: "Two tea bags—one Earl Gray, one chamomile."

"Nice," Gina says. "If only we had teacups and hot water."

"A USB flash drive," Michelle continues, "a couple of wadded tissues, one AAA membership card, one tube of raspberry antibacterial hand lotion, six pieces of sugarless gum and my passport." She looks up, anticipating the question in Gina's eyes. "I'm not going overseas, but I do travel occasionally and I hate showing my driver's license at the airport. The passport has a much better picture."

Gina tucks a strand of hair behind her ear. "I would do the same thing."

"One pair of prescription sunglasses, a bottle of Motrin, a travel-size mouthwash, a handful of receipts, my cell phone, my wallet, my pocket calendar. My notepad, highlighter and two pens, both of which are apparently out of ink."

Isabel sighs and leans back against the far wall while Gina folds her arms. "Nothing edible? You must not have been a Girl Scout."

"Look," Michelle says, her voice coagulating with sarcasm, "at least I brought a purse. Where's yours?"

A secretive smile softens Gina's mouth, but she doesn't answer.

NOON

CHAPTER 14

Michelle sits in silence, her eyes fastened to the sweeping second hand on her watch. Time is a funny thing. As a kid, an hour seemed woven of eternity; as a businesswoman, sixty minutes flies like a bullet.

Yet in the elevator, time hangs over them like a noxious cloud. How long has it been since she talked to Eddie Vaughn—two hours? On a good day the drive from central Pinellas County to downtown Tampa might take forty-five minutes; today is not a good day. But surely the weather hasn't deteriorated so much that he won't be able to make it.

She sighs, looks at her watch again, then claps her hand over the face. She'll drive herself crazy if she fixates on the clock. Eddie Vaughn is on his way; she will believe that. He'll arrive any minute now and he'll save their lives.

One hero on a white horse, courtesy of 1-800-SAV-A-GAL.

The other women have grown quiet. Isabel fell silent after her abbreviated attempt at storytelling, and Gina closed her eyes soon after Michelle emptied her purse. The redhead wears the placid face of a woman at rest, but Michelle knows better. Gina didn't lower her eyelids so she could sleep; she lowered them because she was weary of her companions.

Michelle closes her own eyes, veiling her thoughts of Parker. How she wanted to see him this morning! He has to be gone by now, and he's probably worried. Will he look for her, maybe drive to her condo? Or will he simply go home and trust her to take care of herself?

"One thing I admire about you," he told her once, "is your independence. You don't sit around waiting on me. I can't tell you what a relief that is."

The compliment warmed her even as it stung. If he wanted to protect her, shouldn't he want her to be a little less independent? She's always been proud of her self-sufficiency, but it would be so nice to know that someone wanted to take care of her so she could lay her burdens down. . . .

"You're thinking of someone."

The remark snaps Michelle back to the present. Gina is watching, and her green eyes have narrowed with speculation. "You have a transparent face."

Mercifully, the dim light in the car hides the full extent of Michelle's embarrassment. "You must have caught me in an unguarded moment."

"Are you thinking about him?"

"Who?"

"Earlier I believe you said we ought to talk about our men. We heard about Isabel's Carlos, but I'm curious about the man who brought that enigmatic smile to your face."

Michelle smiles. "Maybe I should sit facing the wall."

"Easier to tell me about your man. I don't see a wedding ring . . . so he's a boyfriend?"

"For the moment." Michelle bites her lower lip, then glances at Isabel, whose face has lit with interest. "He's older, a widower, successful in his business. An amazing guy, really. We've been together about a year, and I think—well, I hope—we may be ready to get serious. We were supposed to meet this morning to discuss the future, but—" She shrugs. "I guess that'll have to wait."

The redhead smiles, but the distant look in her eyes tells Michelle that her brain has focused on something entirely different.

Michelle leans forward. "What are you thinking about?" The redhead arches a brow. "Don't you hear it? The wind has picked up."

Michelle strains to listen. The whistle of the wind has been constant for the past hour, but beyond that sound she hears new noises—thumps and bumps and splintering scrapes.

She gasps in a shiver of panic. "What is that?"

"Some of the windows must have blown out," Gina says, her voice flat and matter-of-fact. "This building is almost thirty-five years old—it can't handle much stress." Despite her calm, her face has gone pale, and a drop of perspiration trickles from her hairline. "I'm afraid your mechanic isn't coming."

"He is." Michelle clenches her jaw to kill the sob in her throat. "He's been delayed, that's all."

"Did you ever think," Gina continues, "what a tragedy it would be to learn how to live on the day you die? I've been sitting here reviewing my life, wondering what I ought to have done differently so I wouldn't be here at this moment—"

"We're not going to die today," Michelle says. With an effort, she pushes herself off the floor and turns toward the elevator panel. "I'm going to call Ginger. She'll get Eddie on the phone and you'll see that he's close. He's probably trying to find a way through those blasted barricades."

She speaks with more bravado than she feels, and her hand trembles when she presses the telephone button. She waits, her ear above the speaker, and when nothing happens she presses the button again.

Silence.

"It's a bad connection," she insists, jabbing the button a third time. "Any minute now the phone will kick in. . . ."

But it doesn't. She is waiting for nothing.

She's done it before.

To recognize the twelfth-grade daughters
of Boone County, West Virginia,
who have achieved exemplary academic standards,
the Daughters of the American Revolution,
Oak Hill Chapter,
invite you to a tea to honor recipients
of the Star Student Award.
The Holiday Inn in Oak Hill
The seventh of June, 1991, four o'clock p.m.
Young ladies may bring an escort.

The engraved invitation stood on Shelly's dresser, propped next to a precious bottle of Halston cologne. The invite arrived weeks ago, and every time Shelly looked at it she felt like a trash-picker who'd found the bottom half of a winning lottery ticket.

The honor was nice, but she'd never been to a tea and didn't stand a chance of finding an escort. Even if some eligible Prince Charming crept out from a mountain holler, she couldn't afford a decent dress.

Where was *her* fairy godmother?

Still, the card was a pretty thing, shiny silver and white, and she might not ever see anything as nice until she picked out her own wedding invitation . . . provided she found a way out of Bald Knob and a man who wanted to marry her.

She'd kept the card purely for decoration, but yesterday afternoon Brian Hawthorne, class president and star linebacker, asked her if it was true.

"Is what true?"

"You won the Star Student award. Mrs. Purvis said only two girls from our school even came close, you and Jennifer Milton."

At first Shelly thought he was crazy, especially since nobody else at school seemed to know a thing about the tea and the ceremony. She looked into his eyes, searching for signs of desperation or mischief, and saw nothing but round blue orbs flecked with green and gold.

"Yeah, they're having some kind of fancy tea to give out the awards." She shifted her books from her hip to her arms. "But I'm not goin'."

"Why not?"

She shrugged. "What do I know about tea? Besides, all the other girls will have an escort. I didn't want to drag some guy all the way over to Oak Hill just so he can be bored and sip from a fancy cup."

Brian laughed. "Well, I figure you ought to go, so if you need somebody to take you, I'm up for it. Besides—my mom's a member of the DAR. She won't let us be bored."

She searched his eyes again and saw only twin reflections of her own timid image.

"Okay," she finally said. "I'll go. Not because I like you or anything, but because I reckon a girl ought to go to a fancy tea at least once in her life."

Brian's grin had practically jumped through his lips. "Great!"

The thought of that smile warmed her as she spritzed Halston on her neck and wrists. The question of what to wear had pressed heavy on her mind, but a quick search through the cedar chest produced a sleeveless white dress with a V neck. Though her mother had married in that gown, Shelly didn't think Momma would mind if she wore it to the tea. Years of loneliness and several hundred bottles of booze had obliterated any happy memories lingering in its folds.

Shelly sniffed at the garment before laying it out on the bed. The fabric smelled of mothballs, but she didn't have enough time for a trip to the dry cleaner's. The steam iron had removed the creases and probably set a sprinkling of orange spatters near the hem, but good enough would have to do. Nothing mattered but getting to the awards ceremony.

Brian had promised to pick her up at three-thirty. Shelly showered at two, then took extra time applying her makeup and curling her long hair. When she was satisfied with her face and hairstyle, she slipped the dress over her head and breathed deeply to fill out the bodice. Her mother had always been bosomy, but Shelly refused to stuff her bra the way some girls did. If she couldn't pass muster with what Mother Nature had given her, tough.

She pulled on her best gold bracelet, the pearl necklace she'd inherited from her grandmother and a sterling silver ring that had cost her the proceeds from twenty quarts of wild blueberries.

After glancing ruefully in her closet, she wished again for a fairy godmother—a pair of glass slippers would have been highly appreciated. A collection of dirty sneakers littered the floor, sprinkled with old socks, two pairs of stuffed-animal slippers and one pair of sandals. The white sandals matched her dress, but the left shoe's ankle strap had lost its buckle.

Shelly pulled the broken shoe onto her lap. She could cut off the useless strap, but she wouldn't be able to walk with a shoe that wouldn't stay on her foot. She had no choice, then, but to try to repair it.

After searching every drawer in the trailer and the shed, she came up with three options: duct tape, adhesive bandages or staples. The staples bit into the top of her foot and then gave way. The bandage strips lacked staying power (no surprise, since this bargain brand barely stuck to a cut finger). The duct tape wouldn't be the most attractive solution, but it was certainly the strongest.

With an eye on the clock, Shelly slid the tongue of the strap into the broken buckle, then encased both pieces in gray duct tape. When she was sure the repair would hold, she put on the other shoe. Standing, no one could see the tops of her feet. Sitting would be a problem, but if she kept her right leg crossed over the left and her skirt pulled down, maybe no one would notice.

At three-fifteen she was ready to go.

She paced in the living room, the skirt of the white gown swishing against her legs as she walked from the TV wall to the kitchen. Her mother lay on the couch, a cigarette between her fingers, her free arm thrown over her head, her eyes glued to a rerun of *M*A*S*H*. At every commercial break, she lifted her head, gave Shelly a bleary look and said, "Face it, girl, you ain't the type to drink tea."

By the time the four o'clock soap opera faded from the screen, Shelly realized Brian wasn't coming. She sat in her dead father's recliner and watched the shadows lengthen across the room. Had Brian met his buddies at the diner and told them what he'd done? Were they hee-hawing about her even now?

The thought lacerated her.

She wouldn't let them laugh. They might think her a misfit, they might not invite her to their parties, but she had every right to accept an award she'd earned. She would go to that tea in her mother's yellowed wedding dress and her own duct-taped sandals. She would show up, sweaty and defiant and late, and she would revel in secondhand glory.

Because one day she would leave Bald Knob. She would exchange her hopelessness for success. She'd forget about this trailer and these people. When she broke a shoe, she'd throw it out, and she'd never, ever wear anything with even a teeny, tiny stain on it.

And if by chance one of her classmates found her in the great, wide world, she'd look at him in consternation, furrow a brow and say, "Bald Knob? You still living in that flea-bitten town?"

She tucked her battered purse under her arm and headed toward the door. "Bye."

"You going somewheres?" Her mother rose up on an elbow and cast a wide-eyed look over the sofa pillow. "In my weddin' dress?"

"See you later, Momma."

Gripping the last shreds of her courage, Shelly Tills stalked out the door, marched down the creaky porch steps and grabbed the handlebars of her bicycle.

Twenty miles lay between her and Oak Hill, with ten of those miles spread over a strength-sapping incline.

But she'd find the energy to pedal up Mount Everest if doing so meant she could confront Brian Hawthorne and his friends and shame them into silence.

Gina leans forward and stretches the ache from her shoulders, then lets her hands fall back into her lap. If only she'd remembered to grab a magazine from the nightstand before she got in the car . . .

She grimaces at the absurdity of the thought. If she's not careful, she'll drive herself crazy with if-onlys. What's done is done; the present and future are all that matter. She must endure this interval of confinement, then she'll be free to do whatever she must to protect her children.

Her plan has been postponed, that's all, though the storm has added a new wrinkle to the situation. Despite Michelle's blind faith in that mechanic, it's going to take a dedicated rescue team to get them out of here. The governor will have learned from others' mistakes after Katrina, so he'll implement rescue efforts as soon as the storm has passed. Professional people will scour these buildings; the rescue may merit media attention. Sonny, who has to know where she is, will be on the scene, eager and solicitous about her welfare.

When they are finally escorted from this building, photographers will snap their cameras and reporters will listen for sound bites to play on the six o'clock news.

Sonny will take her home, where the kids will welcome her with open arms. She'll soak for an hour in her whirlpool tub, then she'll slip into her robe, take the pistol from her coat pocket and shoot her worthless husband between the eyes.

She'll be suitably distraught when the police arrive. With the children by her side, she'll point to the door that leads from her bedroom to the pool. "There," she'll say. "An intruder. He came in and murdered my husband."

When the police wonder about a motive, Gina will gently suggest that the publicity attracted the attention of a wild-eyed lunatic, possibly someone who lost a relative in the hurricane. Crazed with grief, he came to the house because he thought Sonny didn't deserve to have his wife safely returned to him. . . .

She lowers her head and rubs her temple. Okay, so there are a few problems with the scenario—fingerprints and gunpowder residue, all kinds of details to consider. But she'll figure something out. She has hours to think and plan.

She glances at the others. The maid, who seems more nanny than daredevil, is coiled into the shadows at the back; Michelle is watching the elevator buttons as if she expects them to spring to life at any moment. The woman is unrealistic to the core, but optimism might be part of her nature. She reminds Gina of her college roommate, Trina, who attacked everything from her studies to her love life with the confidence of a girl who knows the power of her charms.

If she weren't so damnably frustrating, she might be good company.

Gina props her shoulder against the wall and lowers her head. Despite her distress, her thoughts keep drifting toward Sonny. Why is that? Force of habit? Like phantom pains from a limb no longer attached to a body, she may always think of Sonny as if he's only in the next room.

But even bad habits can be eradicated. One thing's for sure—Sonny has never loved her the way this

Carlos fellow loves the Mexican girl. Gina still can't believe Isabel's story—how can a man meet a woman, feel sorry for her and commit to her, just like that? He had to have another reason, some angle to play, but Gina can see nothing in the girl's face or figure that would suitably reward a man for taking an unremarkable girl into his life.

She finds herself recalling a moment clipped out of time, perfectly preserved by the alchemy of memory: Sonny at the kitchen table in navy slacks and a white shirt, the sleeves rolled up to his elbows. A sharpened pencil rests on his ear.

Her younger self sits across from him, a secondhand typewriter beneath her fingertips, a nine-month-pregnant belly balanced on her lap. She is barefoot because the day is a scorcher, while a portable fan on the floor tries its best to move the heavy air.

Sonny is poring over actuarial tables, preparing to send out quotes for a stack of prospective customers.

"Sonny—" she frowns at a scribbled note on a page "—I can't read this."

"Hmm?"

"Your letter to John McKee." She picks up the steno pad and turns it to face him. "See this?" She taps the spot with a fingertip. "What is that supposed to be?"

She holds the notepad aloft while she finishes proofing an already-typed page; when she looks up, she finds Sonny staring at her. "What?"

He says nothing, but leans his head on his fist and smiles. "Sonny, don't tease. What are you doing?"

"Looking at you," he says. "At my beautiful, intelligent, wonderful wife."

And at his words her heart jolts, her pulse pounds and her first honest-to-goodness labor contraction steals her breath. "Oooooh." She drops the steno pad and pushes away from the table. One hand flies to the small of her back. "Oh, Sonny!"

"Baby, are you—is it—"

"Time," she snaps between clenched teeth. "I think it's time."

While Sonny races for the suitcase, the car keys and the list of family phone numbers, Gina stands and watches in alarm as her water breaks and floods the kitchen floor. Matthew comes into the world two hours later, emerging from between her legs to land in Sonny's capable hands.

And Sonny . . . weeps. He lifts the wet baby and kisses it, then he brings Matthew to Gina and kisses her forehead, her nose, her cheeks, all the while thanking her for giving him a son.

She lifts her head and blinks the images of the past away. Sonny had been no less grateful and moved at the birth of his daughters, and with each child Gina felt that no two people could be more closely bonded than she and her husband.

In those days, she never dreamed her marriage could die. But over the years she has gradually transferred her passion for Sonny to her children, who have thrived in its light and love.

Sonny never even noticed . . . or did he?

CHAPTER 15

Isabel curls into the corner and wraps her arms more tightly around her legs. Though the car is warm and perspiration has dampened her forehead, an uncontrollable current moves through her body, shivering the coward that lives within her skin.

These *gringas* are trying to act brave, but still they talk of dying. What do they know of death? The one with red hair says she has been reviewing her life, but her hand is weighted with a diamond big enough to choke an iguana. What will she review, all the presents she has received? The comfort she has known?

The other woman, the younger one, speaks too loudly and too quickly. She is trying to fool herself into thinking they will be rescued at any moment, just as Isabel once thought the *policia* would protect her family.

She used to dream of such crazy things. She dreamed of dancing with a handsome man and being called beautiful. She dreamed of having babies and going to church with her husband and laughing with the other village women as she worked to care for her own family.

Yes, she has a family now, but she is too afraid to go to church, too terrified to hope for happiness and too ashamed of her fear to pray for courage. Carlos pretends not to care that Rafael is not his son, just as he pretends she is beautiful. He is a good man, sometimes a foolish man, and he will be dead if Isabel does anything to attract the wrong kind of attention.

If she makes a single mistake, her family will be killed.

Ernesto promised he would find her if she ran away. The authorities in America can be bribed, he warned her, and they watch everyone, all the time. *So if you run from me,* chica, *I will find you. I will pay many American dollars to find where you are, and I will come in the dark and cut you while you sleep.*

Carlos does not understand why she wants to work the night shift.

Why she can only sleep in the day.

Isabel pressed her head into her mother's lap and sobbed. As tears rolled over her cheeks, hot spurts of loss and shame, she confessed everything, even Ernesto's threats. "I am only glad," she finished, "that *Papá* is not alive to see the way I have disgraced him."

"Shh, Isabel." *Mamá* stroked the tears from Isabel's face, her fingers cool against her daughter's flushed skin. "*Silencio, chica.*"

After a while *Mamá* pulled Isabel into her arms, dried her tears and told her not to worry. "Your *papá* was not afraid of the drug dealers," she said, her own tears barely dammed. "We will not be afraid, either. We will go to the authorities and tell them what Ernesto has asked you to do."

And then, to demonstrate her courage, *Mamá* went to the *teléfono* and called the police. A sergeant took her name and said he would see her *mañana*.

Across the room, Isabel listened as tears flowed down her face. But she was no longer weeping; her tears were a simple overflow of feeling for her parents, both of whom had courage enough to stand up for what was right.

She remained by her mother's side for the rest of the night, keeping an eye on the clock as they folded laundry and listened to the radio. She dreaded Rodrigo's approach because she would have to tell him what she'd done. He would listen. And then he would tell her she'd been a fool to approach Ernesto Fuentes.

Rodrigo had not come home by the time her mother put out the lamp. "You know your brother," *Mamá* said, a tight smile on her lips. "Young men stay out too late."

That night Isabel lay in a rectangle of moonlight that slanted through the window and drifted over her bed. Music came through the window, the soothing sound of her neighbor's guitar, but though her thoughts were thick with fatigue, she would not let herself sleep until Rodrigo came through the door.

Shortly after one, she heard footsteps in the court-yard. She threw back her blanket and padded to the front door, then peeked out the window. No one moved in the moonlight, but a pale shape lay on the cobble-stone path.

A smile tipped the corner of her mouth. Had Rodrigo come home drunk? If so, she would not be the only one suffering from shame in the morning.

Drawing her nightshirt closer around her neck, she opened the door a crack. When no one jumped out from behind the courtyard wall, she opened the door wider and peered into the night.

What she saw made her blood run cold. Rodrigo lay motionless on the path, tinged with blue and clad only in his underwear. His bare legs had been crossed at the ankle and fastened to the ground with a spike; his arms had been extended and firmly fixed through each wrist. Blood trickled from a stab wound not in his side, but at his heart.

Above his head, where Pontius Pilate had posted *This is the King of the Jews,* another tyrant had staked a different note: *Esta Puedo Ser Su Madre.*

This could be your mother.

Isabel ran forward and clutched the note to her breast, then rocked back on her bent legs and shattered the silence with her screams.

Michelle shifts her weight and tries to find a more comfortable position. One of her hip bones keeps grinding against the tile floor and she can't deny that her bladder feels fuller than it did the last time she checked her watch. What are they going to do if they're trapped for several more hours?

Gina aims a perfectly painted fingernail in Michelle's direction. "It's going to get worse, you know."

"What do you mean?"

"The discomfort, the stress, the need for a bathroom." Gina's gaze drops to her empty hands. "We're going to be a mess by the time we get out of here."

"Oh, I don't know." Michelle glances at the walls, which gleam like chocolate in the emergency light. "We might be tired and a little hungry, but I don't think I'll be in desperate need of a bathroom for a while. I can hold out until Eddie gets here."

The redhead's mouth twists in bitter amusement. "You really think he's coming?"

"I do."

"Then I hate to break the bad news. That man is probably tucked away somewhere safe and he's written us off. Face it, dear heart, no one is coming for us until after the storm has passed. Sunday night, maybe Monday morning, they'll send out rescue teams. If we're lucky, we'll be out of here Monday. If we're not lucky . . ." She lowers her head to her bent knees and clasps her hands around her ankles, then turns her face toward the closed doors.

Michelle waits, but Gina doesn't finish her thought. Hopelessness is seeping through the car like poisonous gas. Soon they'll all be affected unless—

"Maybe," she says, looking at Isabel, "if we keep our minds off the hurricane and try not to think about running water, we'll be okay."

Gina's shoulders contract in a shudder. "The last thing in the world I want to think about is water." When she turns her head toward the center of the car, Michelle is glad to see that the woman hasn't completely surrendered to despair.

"Hey," she says, nudging Gina's foot with her sneaker. "Why don't you tell us more about your family?"

The corner of the redhead's mouth dips in an odd smile. "So now we're going to play Show and Tell?"

"We're just going to tell. I've already dumped my purse, so unless you two are hiding something, neither of you has anything to show."

Gina props her chin on her hand. "Okay. My husband is named Sonny, and for twenty-one years, I've been a faithful wife."

"And you have three teenagers?"

"One handsome son and two beautiful daughters."

Michelle smiles, feeling for the first time that she and this aloof woman might have something in common. "My boyfriend," she says, "has three children. But he has two boys and a girl."

Gina pulls her bent knees to her chest, but her eyes remain distant and abstracted. "Children are precious," she says, her eyes drowsy and abstracted. "In fact, I think the happiest day of my life was when my son was born. I thought I would never love anyone as much as Sonny, but then my son came along. Suddenly my life began to revolve around that boy . . . and I've been centered on my children ever since.

She lifts her head and looks directly at Michelle. "They say women fall in love with their babies because of some temporary hormonal surge, but don't believe them. I adore my kids. Always have, always will."

Michelle drops her hand to her belly and feels the

burgeoning warmth beneath her palm. How will a baby change her life? Years ago she believed the occupation of motherhood was only slightly more estimable than fast-food service, but she's beginning to see things from a different perspective.

"My kids aren't perfect," Gina continues, propping her cheek on her knees. "But I'd do anything to protect them—anything at all."

Her last words are edged with a sharpness that cuts through the soft spell cast by her tone. Michelle stares into the woman's stony features as a ripple of alarm undulates down her spine. Do most mothers feel that protective? Hers didn't.

She leans back and tries to picture herself in the stands of a soccer game, her fist clenched in the face of some bully's mother.

Yeah, she could do that. She's worked hard to cultivate a sophisticated facade, but underneath she is still as rough and tough as Bald Knob granite.

Suddenly aware that her skirt was far shorter than anyone else's, Michelle tugged on her hem, then followed Howard Jones into the cubicle in front of his office. "This will be your space," he said, gesturing to the desk, chair and padded walls as if he were granting access to a royal box at the opera. "You'll be close enough to hear if I raise my voice even a little bit."

She nodded and refused to look at him, knowing that the gleam in his eye had nothing to do with her meager word-processing skills. Six months as a Kelly girl had taught her a lot about men and their secretaries—a girl could get into trouble in a hurry if she didn't establish strict boundaries right away. A too-quick smile, a too-friendly expression, an offer of a ride to lunch . . . any of these innocent things could lead to trouble if a boss were inclined to step out on his wife.

She'd worked as a temp for the Jones Personnel Agency last week; Howard had been so impressed with something about her that he'd offered her a permanent position. Because she liked gathering experience from many different companies, Michelle wouldn't have accepted the offer except for two things: Howard's wife worked in the office to his right, and Olympia Densen-Jones insisted on paying the office help $8.50 an hour, double the minimum wage.

After living for months on baked beans, tuna fish and hot dogs, Michelle was looking forward to fresh fruit and an occasional meal out.

Olympia breezed out of her office and gave Michelle a quick smile. "I'm glad you're here. Howard—" she cut a glance to her husband "—aren't you supposed to have a nine o'clock meeting with Tom Oliphant?"

Howard flushed. "Um, yeah. I was on my way."

"Bye, then." Olympia tilted a polished cheek toward him. "See you when you get back."

Michelle looked away and suppressed a smile. Howard Jones's name might be listed first on the business cards, but anyone who spent five minutes in this office would learn who really called the shots.

"Well, then." Olympia pressed her hands together as

her husband left. "Howard was so impressed with you last week. He said you have a real aptitude for the business."

Michelle shrugged away the compliment. "I'm not so fast on the computer."

"You can learn the computer. What we need are folks with people skills, and something tells me you have plenty of those." Her eyes rested on Michelle's face and lit with speculation. "We're in the business of matching people with jobs, and we're good at it. If you're as creative and bright as I think you are, you'll be a natural."

Michelle stiffened, uncomfortable with such free-flowing praise. "I'll try to do the best I can for you."

"Don't try—just do." Olympia swiveled on her leather pumps and placed her hand on the top of a tall metal filing cabinet. "What we do is teach our clients how to market themselves—not everyone looks as polished as you did when you came through our door. We're in the business of creating what I call pleasing people packages. We take what clients have to offer, dress it up a bit, and offer them to a prospective employer. Once our clients have been through our polishing sessions, they almost always get the job."

Michelle folded one arm across her chest. Maybe this job would pay off in ways she hadn't expected. "You dress people up?" she asked, hoping she didn't sound like a hick. "In new clothes?"

Amusement flickered in Olympia's eyes. "Sometimes. But mostly we dress up their résumés. For instance—" she opened the top drawer of the filing cabinet and pulled out a folder "—take Bill Baker, a former mail clerk for one of the mining companies. By the time he left for his first job interview, he thought of himself as a former director responsible for fielding, targeting and expediting crucial corporate communications. And here's Sally Courtland. She came to us as a secretary and left here an administrative assistant. Same job, same responsibilities. But a little judicious résumé enhancement can lead to higher pay and a much better job."

Michelle blinked. "So—I'm an administrative assistant now?"

"You bet. And you work for a placement professional."

"But isn't that . . . a little misleading?"

Olympia slid the folders back into the file, then closed the drawer. "I read your application," she said, leaning against the cabinet. She folded her arms and looked at Michelle as something sparked in her brown eyes. "And how is Bald Knob these days?"

Michelle swallowed hard. "Fine, I guess. I haven't been back in a while."

"It's a nice place," Olympia said, her tone steady and smooth. "But not for women like us. Not for people who want to make their mark on the world."

"You know Bald Knob?"

Olympia tugged on her gold earring and stepped into Michelle's cubicle. "I know it," she said in a softer voice, allowing the tips of her manicured nails to click over the keyboard. "And I won't go back there. Neither should you . . . unless you really want to."

"I don't."

"I didn't suppose you did. So you can't think like folks in a small town. You have to adapt." She smiled, then gripped the back of the rolling chair with both hands. "Everyone in this business expects a certain level of exaggeration. The employers paint their positions in optimistic colors and our clients dress to impress. In the corporate mating ritual, playing the game is half the fun."

Michelle leaned against the door frame, unable to understand her new employer's motivation. "I appreciate this job, I really do, but—"

"What?"

"I don't understand why you're doing this. I mean, I'm not the most talented girl you've had working in this office."

Olympia smiled and looked toward the front, where a half dozen other women sat with telephones pressed to their ears. "Maybe not," she said, the corner of her mouth rising in a wry smile, "but you remind me of myself at your age. Someone helped me out, and I think it's time I returned the favor." She hesitated for a moment, doubtless reliving some memory, then she patted the back of the chair. "Come on, Michelle, take a seat. I have a stack of new clients I want you to call. Bring 'em in, check 'em out, write up a plan of action. For the first few weeks, I'll be looking over your shoulder, guiding you every step of the way."

Michelle stepped forward and sank into the chair, then rolled closer to the desk. She looked up as her new boss moved toward the doorway.

"Olympia?"

"Yes?"

"You wouldn't happen to be my fairy godmother, would you?"

She'd thought Olympia would laugh, but instead a knowing look entered the woman's eyes. "You're going to make it, Michelle Tilson."

Eddie glances to his right, where every few seconds a wave crashes into the seawall and launches a plume of spray. Tampa Bay, which usually ranges in color from a sunlit green to deep blue, is now the same murky shade as the sky. He can't help feeling as though the world has liquefied into a colorless gray morass. . . .

Morass: six letters, something that overwhelms or impedes. Too bad that word doesn't figure in his current puzzle-in-progress.

The rain-shrouded Howard Frankland Bridge looms in his rearview mirror; downtown Tampa lies ahead. To his right and left, at the edges of the four-lane highway, light poles stretch toward the sky like skeletal arms, their halogen bulbs pushing vainly against the encroaching gloom.

Beside him, Sadie rests on the seat in a down position, her tail drooping toward the floor. "Look at this, girl," he says, spying another white stripe on the highway. "We've managed to stay in the lane."

His voice crackles with hoarseness; he's had to shout to make himself heard above the thrumming rain. He knows it's foolish to keep announcing progress reports to a dog, but the sound of his voice seems to comfort Sadie.

Her presence certainly comforts him.

He takes care to keep his vehicle to the right of the white line and eases forward, moving toward downtown Tampa and exit forty-four. What was that hymn his grandfather used to sing? "Peace Like a River." The old man said that troubles were crashing storm waves that could knock any man off his feet, but faith was an anchor, as comforting as a warm puppy—

Well, maybe that last part came from Charles Schulz.

A light fog rises from the pavement like steam, raised by the force of raindrops striking the warm asphalt. Water streams like sheets over the windows while an occasional rogue drop sneaks through the rubber seals and drips onto his left shoulder.

All this dreadful weather, and Felix is still seven hours away.

On the radio, a country artist is singing the story of six men caught in a coal mine: *Two miners are obsessin', two men are regressin', and two confess to messin' with each other's wives. . . .*

Eddie can't help but wonder what's happening with the women in the elevator. The woman he spoke to, Michelle, seemed like the confident type, but even confident people can crack under pressure.

If he had his druthers, he'd want to work with calm

men instead of panicked females. Growing up in a house with six sisters has taught him that chickens are easier to corral than agitated women.

He glances at the dog, then reaches out to rub her ears. "You could set a good example for them, couldn't you, Sades?" The dog snores in response.

Michelle is about to ask if Gina's kids have inherited her red hair when she hears the distinct sound of breaking glass. For no reason she can name, the sound raises the hair at the back of her neck.

"That can't be good," Gina whispers, her gaze darting toward the door. "Do you think that's the wind . . . or looters?"

Michelle swallows hard. She hasn't even considered the possibility of looters, but she's beginning to believe anything could happen today. The streets are blocked off, but she found a way in and so did Gina. Like most urban centers, Tampa has a sizable homeless population, and some of those people are averse to government shelters. Anyone could walk into the parking garage and find the stairwell.

"Do you think—" she pauses to run her tongue over her dry lips "—do you think we'll be safe even if we get out? Gus said he was going to leave after he evacuated the building."

"Looters want only one thing—loot." Gina's eyes gleam with contempt. "They shouldn't bother us. I'd hate to think, though, what might happen to anyone who tried to stop them."

Michelle lowers her head onto her hand as a company of new terrors takes up residence in her imagination. What if they escape the elevator only to be accosted by crazed looters? What if they're attacked, raped? She could be traumatized . . . and lose the baby.

"We need to obey your elevator man and stay calm," Gina says. "We're safe in here and we'll stay safe until the storm passes and the authorities commence rescue operations. We might be a little hungry and dirty when this is over, but we'll survive."

Michelle smiles at the floor. Gina has shifted to a calm, no-nonsense tone, probably the voice she uses to reassure her children. Though she can't know they'll make it out of this cage, the assurance in her voice settles Michelle's nervous stomach and persuades Isabel to relax against the back wall.

"Staying in here is a nice plan B," Michelle says, smiling at Gina, "but I'm sticking with plan A and hoping Eddie gets here soon. I'd rather leave sooner than later, wouldn't you?"

Gina crosses her arms and exhales heavily. "I'm not holding my breath."

At exit forty-four, Eddie eases the truck off the ramp and heads south, toward downtown. He can see Tampa's skyscrapers from the elevated highway, though their rooflines are buried in low-hanging clouds.

In one of those buildings, three women are waiting for him.

He's not surprised to see flashing red and blue lights at the bottom of the exit ramp. A police cruiser sits crossways in the middle of the intersecting road, blocking access to the southbound lanes.

Again, he crawls to a stop and prepares to roll down the window. For a long moment he sits, waiting for the cop to realize he's not going to head back onto the interstate, then the cruiser's door opens into the rain.

The beefy cop lumbers forward, reluctance evident in every line of his posture. When Eddie rolls down the window, he finds himself looking at narrow eyes, a square jaw and a jutting chin.

"You can't go downtown, son." The cop points to the entrance ramp on the opposite side of the intersection. "So you might as well get back on 275 and head home."

Eddie pulls a business card from the ashtray and hands it over. "Three women have got themselves trapped in the Lark Tower," he says. "If I don't get them out now, they'll be spending a few days in that elevator. That could be rough."

The cop holds the card up in the rain, then lifts his gaze. "You suicidal or crazy?"

Eddie grins. "So—you gonna move the cruiser?"

The cop shakes his head, then lifts his hand and lets the wind snatch the wet card. He thumps the roof of the pickup. "Bet you were grateful for a nice, heavy truck when you came over the hump."

"Happy to have every one of these six thousand pounds."

"Sure I can't talk you outta this?"

"I'm sure."

The cop wipes water from his cheek with the back of his hand, then nods. "Sure hope you find a safe place to ride it out, 'cause I'm afraid the nearest shelters are all full. The surge is comin' in as we speak."

Eddie rolls up the window as the cop walks back to his vehicle; a moment later the pickup is moving onto North Tampa Street and approaching the Lark Tower.

This part of downtown is older and slightly shabby, nothing like the upmarket tourist areas by the convention center. The traffic lights are out, so he drives cautiously past deserted parking lots and one-way streets. Oak trees dot the sidewalk, still secure in their concrete planters, but their canopies are twisting in the wind.

He glances at his watch and frowns. He got the emergency call around ten; it's now nearly one. He's spent the last three hours driving fifteen miles, and though the storm is still building, disaster doesn't operate on a predictable schedule. One of those women could have found a way to pry open the doors; all of them could have plunged to their deaths by now—

The entrance to the Tower's parking garage appears at his right, an empty white square. He jerks hard on the wheel, momentarily upsetting the dog's balance, and pulls into a whitewashed corridor. Now that rain is no longer hammering the roof, dense silence settles over the cab.

Eddie follows a curving driveway, then brakes when he comes to a gate. At his left, a machine advises him to press a button for a ticket. On a whim he presses the button; no ticket emerges. Of course not, the power's off.

For an instant he considers barreling through the black-and-white mechanical arm (in the face of impending destruction, who would care?), but reason assures him that the women have done what he asked and waited calmly. He steps out of the truck, pulls the arm into an upright position, then hops back in his seat and pulls forward.

The second floor, a sign assures him, is for visitors; all spaces on the higher levels are reserved for tenants. But the storm surge is coming and Hurricane Frances, which bypassed Tampa in 2004, caused the Hillsborough River to rise fifteen feet at downtown's Platt Street.

If he has to drive the women out of here, the higher he parks, the less distance they'll have to cover.

Eddie turns the steering wheel and drives upward as quickly as he dares. The experience is like navigating in a cave—with no windows; the darkness is penetrated only by small lamps above the exit signs at the center of the structure.

When his headlights flash across a six painted onto a wall, Eddie discovers that he has reached the uppermost parking level. He pulls alongside the glassed-in lobby that houses two banks of elevators, then cuts the engine.

Is he too late? He's not familiar with these elevators, and sometimes people modify them in dangerous ways. Just last month three people got stuck in an elevator in Minneapolis; instead of waiting for help, they pried open a modified door and jumped to the floor below. The third man, however, didn't land safely, but fell backward down the shaft.

Have these women kept their promise? Or have they panicked in the face of the coming storm?

Eddie gets out, whistles for Sadie and pulls his toolbox from the space behind the front seat. As the dog belly-crawls across the bench, he turns on his flashlight and examines the surrounding structure. The building has been around a while, for the long pipes of a retrofitted sprinkler system hang between unlit fluorescent light fixtures overhead. Electrical conduit snakes along the walls and air-conditioning units have been squeezed into irregular corners.

The sound of his breathing is loud in his ears as the beam of his flashlight bounces over empty parking spaces and silent AC units. A chilly black stillness surrounds him while the wings of a vague premonition brush his spirit. A ghost building.

When Sadie's nails click on the concrete, he locks the truck and moves toward the elevator lobby. His flashlight reveals two entrances—one for the six express elevators and one for the elevators that service the first twenty-five floors.

Where are the women? He closes his eyes and tries to recall what the woman said, but all he can remember is the word *express.*

"I guess—" he looks at Sadie "—we should start climbing stairs."

1:00 P.M.

~✲✲~

CHAPTER 16

Michelle is wondering if there are enough calories in sugarless gum to sustain life when a voice rises from the yawning space beneath them. "Hellooooo! Can anybody hear me?"

Her anxieties dissolve in a wave of relief. She grins at the others as she rises to her knees and crawls to the door. "I think the cavalry has just arrived."

Gina swipes a hank of sweat-drenched hair from her forehead. "You're kidding."

Michelle parts the doors as far as she can, then bends to yell into the dark gap between the threshold and the lower landing. "We're up here! Are you Eddie Vaughn?"

Laughter, masculine and vibrant, rises from the tunnel below "Good grief, ladies, couldn't you get stuck on a lower floor?"

Michelle sits back, not certain how to respond. How can the man joke at a time like this?

"Ignore the wisecrack," Gina advises. "Just tell him to get up here."

Michelle leans toward the door and tries to peer downward, but she can see nothing but darkness and concrete. "Where are you?"

"I'm waving a flashlight. Can you see it?"

"No."

"That's okay." His voice seems to come from a mile away. "Which car are you in? Right, left or center?"

Michelle stops to think. She'd been so busy talking to Gus she scarcely noticed which car she entered—

"Center," Gina supplies, so Michelle shouts out the answer. "Okay. Do you know what floor you're near?"

Michelle turns toward the others. "Where did we stop? Wasn't it twenty-seven?"

Gina nods. "I think so."

"I think we're near the twenty-seventh floor," Michelle yells. She waits, but hears no response. "Did you get that?"

"Oh, yeah." Even through the disguising echo, she hears resignation in the technician's voice. "I'll be up shortly—that's a lot of stairs."

She holds her breath until she's certain he's moved away, then she grins at Gina and Isabel. "You want to know my happiest moment? I think this may be it."

Gina exhales and braces herself against the elevator wall. What do you know—Elevator Man has come to the rescue. She didn't think the mechanic would make it across the bridge, but here he is, cracking jokes and behaving as if this kind of thing happens all the time.

If the man knows his stuff and brought the right tools, maybe they *will* walk out of here today.

"Listen." A note of alarm in Michelle's voice arrests Gina's attention. "Did you hear that?"

Gina strains to listen, but all she hears is the hooting

wind. Isabel catches her eye and shakes her head.

Gina tilts a brow at the brunette. "What did you hear?"

"I could have sworn I heard a dog barking. And I'm—well, I don't like dogs."

Gina resists the urge to roll her eyes. "Relax. The wind can play tricks on you, especially when you're nervous." She leans against the wall, aware that they still have a long wait ahead of them. "You never told us about your happiest moment."

"Yes, I did. It's now."

"No fair—we'll all be thrilled to get out of here. So give us a story or we'll tell Mr. Vaughn you've decided to stay overnight."

"Tyrant," Michelle says, but there's no malice in her tone. She moves away from the door and settles back in her corner. "Since I haven't been married or had a baby—" her eyes take on a guarded look "—I suppose my happiest moment would be the day I hung out my own shingle. I'd been running a personnel agency in West Virginia, but when circumstances changed, I realized West Virginia wasn't big enough to accommodate all the things I wanted to do. So I moved here, registered my company as a Florida corporation and established Tilson Corporate Careers."

She shrugs modestly and lowers her gaze, and in that moment Gina catches a glimpse of the girl Michelle had been before life chiseled the last traces of awkwardness, uncertainty and inexperience from her features.

"I've been calling my own shots ever since that day," Michelle says, flattening her palm. Her expression hardens as she eyes her nails with a critical look. "And it's felt good. Maybe that's why being stuck in this elevator is so unbelievably frustrating—I'm used to being in control."

Gina nods. "I can tell."

Michelle looks up, searches Gina's eyes, and smiles. "So are you. I'd bet my last dollar on it."

Gina uncrosses her legs, which have begun to tingle from a lack of circulation. What the brunette doesn't realize is that today Gina has taken back control of her life. Nothing has worked out the way she planned, but it will.

The day is not yet over.

Shelly groaned and breathed in the scent of pine needles. She had been climbing the old pine tree with Job Smith, but his momma rang the dinner bell so he had to go home. Shelly had been about to leave, too, but on a branch only a few feet away she spied the biggest, fullest pinecone she'd ever seen. Mrs. Rich, their third-grade teacher, had promised they could make bird feeders out of pinecones, peanut butter and seed, but you couldn't make a decent feeder without a big, puffy cone.

She clung to the papery tree bark and turned so she could sit on the branch. With one hand around the main trunk, she eased her bottom over the branch, reaching for the cone with her right hand. Her arm wasn't long enough.

She bit her lip and looked around. A spray of new needles jutted from the limb she sat on, so she broke it off at the branch, getting her hand sticky with sap in the process. Holding the fragrant spray like a feather duster, she leaned sideways and flicked at the cone. There! It moved.

She leaned again, her muscles stretching, and swatted at the pinecone. She heard a swish as the needles brushed its surface, then the cone fell . . . and so did Shelly.

She rolled onto her back and winced as color ran out of the world and pain shot up her right arm. The limb she'd been sitting on loomed high above, its shape wavering in her vision.

"Help!" Her lips formed the word, but her lungs didn't have enough air to push sound out of her throat.

She gulped, forcing down the sudden lurch of her stomach. What if nobody came looking for her? What if this was one of those nights where Momma didn't cook and Daddy didn't come home? She could be layin' out here all night, freezin' and waitin' for a bobcat or bear to come along and gobble her up.

Her face twisted, her eyelids clamped tight to trap the sudden flood of tears, but they streamed from the corners of her eyes and ran into her hair. She didn't dare make noise, lest she alert some wild thing of her presence.

She didn't know how long she lay there, but before the sun went down she heard the voice of her daddy. "Shelly Louise!" The call, vibrant and strong, came from the direction of the trailer park. "Shelly Louise, where are you?"

"Daddy!" She sat up, sobbing with gladness, as her arm began to throb again. And even though she was afraid her father would yell at her for wandering off so close to suppertime, she called again, "Here, Daddy!"

But when he saw her and came running, his eyes held nothing but tenderness. "Ouch, baby," he said, looking at her arm. "You hang on, and I'll get you fixed right up."

He unbuttoned his shirt, then wrapped the warm flannel around her arm, binding it close to her chest. Then he lifted her into his arms and carried her out of the woods, toward lit windows that glowed like welcoming eyes.

There, nestled between her daddy's strong arm and his heart, Shelly realized what love was. Love came when you needed help; love was big enough and strong enough to make the hurt go away.

When her daddy died two years later, she wondered if she'd ever find love again.

Eddie pauses on the landing at the fourteenth floor and leans hard on the railing. Sadie turns her head into the beam of the flashlight and looks at him.

"I know," he says, answering her unspoken question. "I know they're waiting. But I'm not as young as I used to be and this is a *lot* of stairs."

Content with his answer, Sadie sits at his side, then lifts her head to parse the darkness.

Mindful of the battery, Eddie switches the flashlight off. The stairwell, a windowless rectangular tunnel cut through the center of the building, is as dark as pitch. Even though he's surrounded by tons of concrete, insulation and filler materials, the insistent sough of the wind reaches into this space.

The hurricane is on its way, moving closer every hour, making better time than some of the hapless tourists trapped on the interstates. The machine rooms that control, operate and suspend the Lark Tower's elevators are located on the roof—probably the most vulnerable area of this aging structure.

Hapless: seven letters, unlucky, unfortunate. Often confused with *feckless,* eight letters, unwilling or unable to be useful. . . .

For about the twentieth time, he wishes he knew the building better. If the Lark Tower were part of his territory, he'd have access to the utility rooms and a couple of ladders. If he knew the security chief, he could ask about backup generators and maybe get some help.

If wishes were horses . . . he'd be running a rodeo.

He takes a deep breath, holds it a moment, and switches the flashlight back on. "Come on, Sadie. Only fourteen flights to go."

He places his foot on the next step and forces his flagging feet to maintain a steady rhythm. Right, left, right, left.

Heather would say he was nuts, of course, but she'd never understood his desire to do his job. She'd talked him out of training to be an emergency medical technician, even accused him of wanting to be an EMT only because he wanted to play the hero. She'd definitely be on his case if she could see him now. But she can't see him because she's miles away and married to another man. A figment of Eddie's past.

Right, left, turn, turn, right, left, right.

Truth is, he'd like nothing better than to do his job in peace, without fanfare of any kind. Yeah, it's nice when folks notice and appreciate his hard work, but by the time he reaches the typical trapped elevator, the people are either so angry or so panicked that they don't spare much thought for the guy checking out the controls on the roof—

It's okay that they don't appreciate his efforts. Like his ex-wife and his sisters, they don't understand.

Because they've never experienced the agony of too little, too late.

He glances upward, unable to see anything in the darkness above. He doesn't want to go to the roof today, but he shouldn't have to. The important thing is freeing the women, not restoring elevator operation. By the time Felix blows over Tampa, he's pretty sure the Lark Tower's elevators are going to be among the city's least pressing problems.

Right, left, turn, turn, fifteenth floor, right, left.

Belinda, his closest sister, has her own opinions about why he enjoys helping others. The last time they were together, she ran her finger down his cheek and made tsking noises as she shook her head.

"What's wrong?"

"Poor baby," she said, her voice gentle. "Still risking your neck to save the world?"

"It's my job, Bel."

"It's more than that. I think you risk your neck because—well, you know."

He caught her hand. "Apparently, I don't."

She curled her fingers around his. "Because, little brother, these days you're afraid to risk your heart."

Eddie shakes his head as the memory dissipates. Belinda is wrong, of course; he'd give his heart gladly if he could find a woman worth his time. But right now the last thing he wants is a high-maintenance relationship.

Right now, the thing he wants most in the world is to prove himself un-feckless.

Eddie Vaughn's arrival has quickened Michelle's pulse; now she struggles to be patient. She taps her fingers on her knees, visualizing the moment of their release like a butterfly fluttering just beyond her fingertips . . .

Her fingers stop moving as an unfamiliar sound reaches her ear. The air around them has been vibrating with myriad woofs and thuds and creaks, but this sound is different. It's alive. It's—"

"A dog." Gina lifts her head from the wall. "You were right, I heard the dog. It's somewhere nearby."

Michelle's childhood phobia lifts its head and snarls. Despite the terror of the last few hours, the thought of facing a dog makes her hands go slick with sweat. "Why would a dog be in the building?"

Isabel presses her hand to her chest and squeals as something thumps against the top of the car.

Gina looks up at the ceiling. "That was either debris falling down the shaft, or—"

"It's Eddie." Michelle speaks in a rush of confidence. The technician promised to come and he kept his word; now this amazing man will get them out of this cage. She doesn't know how he'll do it, and she doesn't care.

But why is he on the elevator roof?

Like the others, she stares at the plastic panels overhead as the elevator quivers. Even through the moaning winds, she hears the chink of metal against metal, a heavy clank, the exhalation of a deep breath.

She feels like shouting when a rush of fresh air invades the car.

"Everybody all right in there?" The clear, vibrant sound of Eddie's voice pebbles her skin while a circular light dances over the plastic panels overhead.

"We're fine," Michelle calls, an unexpected catch in her voice. "And thank you for coming. We weren't sure you'd follow through."

"Lady, I think you could talk Mahatma Gandhi into joining the NRA."

Though Michelle searches the ceiling, she can't see the hero who's come to rescue them. But she'd bet her last dollar he has a nice face.

Gina grips the side railing as if she's afraid Eddie's weight will overload the car. "Do you really think you can manage this by yourself?"

Their unseen rescuer laughs. "I'm not alone. I brought my dog."

"That's no comfort at all." Gina tightens her hold on the rail. "And why are you on the roof?"

"Because the car-top exit is in the rear right corner of the ceiling." Eddie's voice is crisp now, and direct. "I need one of you ladies to slide the light panel away. Can you help me with that?"

"I'll try." Michelle stretches up on her tiptoes, but she can't reach the sheets of Plexiglas. "I'm not tall enough." She crosses her arms and frowns, then looks at Gina. "Did you ever build a pyramid in gym class?"

One corner of the redhead's mouth dips in a frown. "I was never the athletic type."

"You don't have to be athletic. You only have to keep still a few minutes. If you and Isabel will get on your hands and knees, I can step onto your backs and reach that panel."

The cleaning woman's forehead knits with puzzlement, but Gina understands—and apparently doesn't like the idea. "You think I'm going to kneel on this dusty floor?"

"You were sitting on it."

"Yes, but—"

"Come on, it'll only take a minute."

The housekeeper hesitates, then crouches on the floor. "Move a little closer to the wall," Michelle instructs her. "And, Gina? I really need you to help. My weight is too much for Isabel to handle alone."

The redhead mutters under her breath, but she moves

211

to the corner and bends, taking her place beside the girl.

"Closer, please." Michelle bites back her irritation. "You have to be shoulder to shoulder."

Gina sighs heavily, but moves closer to the cleaning woman. She's still not close enough, though, so when Isabel looks up, Michelle gives her a move-over gesture.

Eddie's voice floats down from overhead. "How's it going in there?"

"Fine," Michelle calls. "We'll have that panel out of the way in a jiffy."

Isabel sidles toward Gina until the two women's shoulders are touching. Michelle chews on her lip, then pulls off her sneakers. "I'll be quick, I promise."

"What if you break my back?" Gina says, looking over her shoulder. "My bones aren't as strong as they used to be."

"I don't think I can hurt you if I place my weight at the base of your spine. Try not to worry about it."

"Easy for you to say. You're not down here on the floor." Michelle blows her bangs from her forehead. "You want to trade places? Just say the word."

Gina hesitates, then lowers her head. "Just do it already."

Michelle places one hand flat against the wall, then studies Isabel's back. She can't remember the last time she's even thought about building a pyramid.

"Hurry up," Gina calls, exasperation in her voice. "This dust is going to make me sneeze."

Michelle catches her breath, then steps onto Isabel's

back, quickly balancing her weight by placing her other foot on Gina. Isabel grunts and the redhead breathes hard through her nose, but Michelle tries not to think about them as she looks up and reaches for the overhead panel. Almost instantly she is overcome by dizziness, so she returns one hand to the supporting wall and tries to keep her eyes straight ahead while she tugs at the plastic sheet.

"How is this thing attached, Eddie?" she calls, her frustration rising when the panel resists her probing fingertips. "It won't slide, so how am I supposed to—"

"Push up first, then over," Eddie answers. "You don't have to take it down, just push it up a bit so I can grab the edge."

She reaches for the panel again, feels it above her fingertips, then shoves it upward. The space brightens, and when she lifts her head she finds herself staring into the stubbled face of a man wearing a striped cotton work shirt. Below the words *Majestic Elevators* and the emblem of a crown, a name is embroidered on the pocket: *Eddie.*

"Hey there." Eddie grins down at her, his blue eyes shining in a narrow face. "You ladies called for a cab?"

"Thank heaven you came," Michelle says, unwilling to look away. She will name her children after this man; she may mention him in her will. "I was beginning to think we were the only people left in the county."

"Are you done up there?" Gina's strained voice rises from beneath Michelle's feet.

"Sorry." Her cheeks burning, Michelle steps back to the floor, careful not to jolt the elevator.

Gina stands and brushes dust from her hands. "Thank you for coming," she says, her tone polite as she glances at the man on the roof. "I'm sure it's rough out there on the streets."

"Elevator jockeys live for danger," Eddie says, grinning. "And I didn't have anything else to do."

Gina crosses her arms. "Still, we appreciate you coming. No one else around here seems interested in doing his job. You'd think that the security guard or the building manager would stick around to make sure everyone had been properly evacuated."

Michelle listens in disbelief as she reties her sneakers. How can Gina complain to a man who has risked his own safety coming to rescue them?

Either Vaughn doesn't notice Gina's attitude, or he doesn't mind her grousing. "Okay, ladies, it's like this," he says, glancing up. "Due to what looks like a power outage, you've stopped between the twenty-seventh and twenty-eighth floors. Unless you want to take your chances and hope the power comes back on, you can let me get you out of here. But because I don't have a ladder, this extraction might be a little tricky."

Gina looks down and mutters under her breath. "I knew it. The man isn't equipped to do the job."

Michelle glances toward the elevator panel, where only the dim emergency light burns. "Do you think the power might come back on?"

The brightness of Eddie's smile diminishes a degree. "Who knows? It could cut in and out all day, or it may stay out three weeks. But I don't think you want to wait that long."

"But—" Michelle points toward the roof "—if we're up there and the power comes on, we could be knocked off. You might be some kind of elevator cowboy, but I'm not about to ride one of these things."

Eddie laughs. "Don't worry, even with power, the car won't move if the door or the ceiling exit is open."

Michelle nods slowly. "Okay."

"Wait." Gina steps forward again, her arms folded as tight as a gate. "What will happen if we stay put? Let's suppose the power comes back on and the hatch is closed."

"Well—" Eddie rubs his chin "—that all depends. If the car has lost touch with its controllers, it will probably return to the lobby. But since I didn't program these cars, I'm not sure what they'll do."

Gina shoots Michelle a sharp look, then retreats to her corner.

"My plan," Eddie continues, ignoring the redhead, "is to bring you up through this exit. From here we can step down to the landing and from there we can take the stairs. The stairs are situated in the interior of the building, so we'll be sheltered from the impact of the wind. The stairwell, in fact, is probably the safest place to ride out the hurricane."

Michelle cuts a quick glance at Isabel, who has retreated to the back wall and is hugging herself. She doesn't look at all thrilled about climbing into the darkness of the elevator shaft.

Gina brings one hand to her hip. "Why can't you open the elevator doors and let us step out? That would be so much safer."

Eddie shifts his gaze to her face in an oddly keen look. "That's not the best option in this situation."

"Please, Mr. Vaughn, don't patronize me. If you want to play George of the Jungle, that's your affair, but I think I'd prefer to simply jump down onto the landing."

Eddie looks away, showing his teeth in an expression that is not a smile. "The situation is not as simple as you think. Right now I'm sitting about eighteen inches above the twenty-eighth floor. You, ma'am, are standing about four feet above the twenty-seventh. You may think it'd be easy to jump onto that lower landing, but you're not realizing that most people tilt backward after jumping from above. Ordinarily, I'd have a ladder in place to block the open shaft, but I'm fresh out of ladders and you're fresh out of luck. Because I'd hate to see you fall into the hoistway you're so desperate to escape, I'm recommending an exit through the roof I don't mean to seem disrespectful, ladies, but I doubt any of you want to go to the bottom all that quickly."

"I get it," Michelle says, a flood of gooseflesh rippling up each arm. "Say no more."

"Believe me—" Eddie meets her gaze "—this rooftop hatch is the safest way out. And I'm here to lend a hand."

Michelle looks at Isabel, whose eyes have gone darker and rounder. "Do you understand?"

The girl nods without speaking.

Michelle tips her head back. "So—without a ladder, how are we supposed to get up to you?"

Eddie leans into the car and points to the silver rail on the back wall. "You can help each other up like you did before, with the pyramid. If necessary, use that railing to support your weight as I pull you out."

"Wait a minute." Gina steps under the opening and glares up at the technician. "I understand how two of us could lift someone up and out. I can even see how Isabel here could lift me up—I'm not that heavy. But I don't see how the last woman can get out without a ladder. Your arms aren't that long, Mr. Vaughn."

One of Eddie's hands locks around a thick nylon strap across his chest. "See this? It's my safety harness. I can take it off and pass it down to the last woman. It's hooked to a lanyard, which is attached to a brace. I can pull the last woman up."

Gina's face remains locked in neutral for a moment, then she arches a brow. "I suggest you send the harness down now," she says, iron in her voice. "After all, you're used to elevators. We're not."

Michelle feels a sudden wave of pity for the man. If he'd known he was braving rising winds and crashing waves to rescue a shrew, he might have refused to leave home.

Eddie blinks, then focuses his gaze on Michelle. "You want the harness, too?"

She cuts a look to Gina, whose gaze remains resolute. "Um . . . well, I'd probably feel more secure with it on."

"I would like the harness." Isabel's soft comment slips into the silence. "The lady is right. I would be scared and I might fall. But if I can wear the straps, I will be brave enough." The cleaning woman steps up and peers at the rectangular opening in the ceiling. "For Rafael," she whispers, "I will go first."

Without another word, Eddie unsnaps the clasp at his chest and wriggles out of the contraption. "Don't ever let it be said that we don't aim to please."

A moment later, a tangle of blue nylon drops into the elevator car. Isabel stoops to pick it up, then frowns at the jumbled mess.

"Step into it," Eddie calls. "Circular straps around the legs, one strap across the lower back, buckle across the chest. Adjust to fit."

Gina steps aside and chews on a fingernail as Michelle helps Isabel into the contraption, then holds up the remaining loose end.

"That piece," Eddie says, dropping a line through the opening, "hooks to this lanyard, which is attached to the crosshead. Anything connected to that piece isn't going anywhere the elevator's not going."

"Whatever you say," Michelle says, reaching for the line. She snaps the carabiner at the end of the lead to the D-ring of the harness, then gives Isabel a reassuring smile. "Snug as a bug in a rug."

"*¿Qué?*"

218

"Never mind." Michelle steps back, then turns to Gina. "Going to help me boost her up?"

Gina shrugs. "Might as well."

"Okay." Michelle links her hands and bends her knees, bracing herself for the young woman's weight. "Do you remember doing this when you were a kid? You step into my hands—"

Isabel snorts softly. "I know how to do this." She places one crepe-soled shoe into Michelle's locked fingers.

"That's good," Eddie calls. "Now put your other foot in the other lady's hands."

After Gina laces her fingers together, Isabel brings her right foot up. Slowly, as the trembling housekeeper clings to their shoulders, Michelle and Gina straighten their knees and lift Isabel toward the technician's outstretched hand . . .

A tumult of breaking glass and growling wind shatters Michelle's concentration. From somewhere close the dog barks while a roar echoes through the shaft, trembling the car. Isabel recoils from the hatch and Eddie pulls his hand from the opening. "Hang on, will ya? I think a window shattered. I've got the doors propped open, so it'll take me a minute to check things out. . . ."

Michelle hears the solid thumps of his departing steps, then something jolts the car. Isabel topples forward, falling away from the other women, and the dangling lanyard slaps Michelle's cheek. She looks up, hoping Eddie can provide an explanation, but the shaft is now alive with creaks and flaps and the yawning stretch of metal. Eddie, she realizes, has stepped away and she hasn't felt his returning tread on the roof, but suddenly there he is, his face appearing and vanishing in the open exit, accompanied by a flash of green that rustles as it passes by . . .

Was that a *potted palm?*

The technician's hoarse cry blends with a canine howl and Isabel's terrified shriek. Through the roaring din, Michelle breathes one name: "Eddie?"

Her rescuer does not answer.

She shrinks back as raindrops fall into the car, flung by a teasing wind that howls in the elevator shaft. Cold sweat prickles beneath her arms and her heart pounds like a trip-hammer as glass pebbles and sheets of paper rain through the open hatch.

After a fierce assault, the wind retreats and the debris stops falling. But though her eyes keep returning to the rooftop opening, Michelle sees no sign of Eddie Vaughn.

She covers her face with her hands, exhales slowly and peers through her fingers at the others. Like a panicked fish on a hook, Isabel struggles to free herself from the safety harness, then curls into a knot at the back wall.

In her corner, Gina's face has gone idiotic with shock. "Is he—did he—"

Michelle closes her eyes and watches the scene replay itself on the back of her retinas—the invasion of a wind so strong it slammed the elevator against the wall of the shaft and hurled debris at the man who had come to save them.

She covers her mouth as a fresh wave of nausea strikes.

CHAPTER 17

Gina feels her own gorge rise as the sound of the brunette's agonized retching fills the car. She looks away, hiding the look of revulsion that has to be on her face, but the combination of Michelle's vomiting and the maid's weeping is straining her nerves. She will scream in a minute; she will open her mouth and release the frustration that has been building since this morning. . . .

No. She can't lose control, not here, not now. Unlike her mother, who used to become apoplectic if the dog peed on the carpet, Gina has never been prone to hysteria. Life is filled with unfortunate events and a confident woman learns to accept the bad with the good. What you cannot change, you accept; what you cannot accept, you change.

Which is why she's going to make an adjustment in her marriage as soon as she is released from this elevator. *If* she is released from this elevator.

Reminded of the nasty event that has brought them to this low point, she lifts her head and peers at the ceiling. What, exactly, happened to the repairman? From the horrified look that twisted Michelle's face, Gina surmises that the brunette saw him fall down the shaft. In any case, he's gone. The opening in the ceiling now reveals nothing but a thin stream of gray light.

She strains to listen for signs of life outside the car, but she can't hear anything but the howl of the wind and the occasional patter of falling debris. No cries or moans. Even the dog has gone silent.

The technician probably died on impact. She's read about people who survived falls from incredible heights, but Eddie Vaughn didn't look like the type to beat the odds. More scarecrow than Schwarzenegger, he is more likely to be sprawled at the bottom of the shaft than hanging from a loose chain or climbing his way up an elevator cable.

Too bad. He'd been foolish to come out here alone and unprepared, but he had been chivalrous enough to give up his safety harness—a fact she'll have to mention to the reporters after their release. He probably thought he could rescue them with no trouble, but the easiest person to deceive is oneself. . . .

She draws her knees closer to her chest, suddenly aware of a trembling that has risen from her core. Why is she shivering? The stale air in this car is anything but cool, yet still her heart rattles in its cage of ribs.

She considers the question, then a sudden thought almost makes her laugh aloud—had she been secretly hoping the mechanic could get them out? If so, her subconscious must be more childlike than she realized.

All morning common sense has informed her that they are going to spend at least a couple of days in this car. They'll have to talk about practical sanitary arrangements soon, but those matters can wait until after the other two have finished with their emotional tantrums. Until they accept reality, she will focus on those outside this awful elevator.

Her children are safe at home, thank goodness, and Sonny is probably wrapped in his mistress's arms. Justice would be served if the hurricane flattened the woman's building or blew it out to sea, but today fate seems to be stacking the odds against the wronged wife, not the adulterer.

When she glances at her watch, her nervous concern shifts to an urgent and more immediate fear. By now, the kids are awake and moving around. Have they realized she's missing? Have they made calls to locate her? They know nothing of the private investigator's report hidden under her mattress, so they might assume she's gone to be with Sonny. The poor dears have to be worried.

She can't stop fretting about them. Have they heard that it's wise to stay inside and seek the safety of interior rooms when the hurricane moves ashore? Does Mattie know that the emergency radio is in the laundry-room cabinet? The house is new; the windows guaranteed, but what if the garage door buckles? Because one component failure can lead to another, one little worm of wind can snake its way in and rip off a roof. . . .

She's done all she can to protect her darlings, but often the greatest danger occurs after a storm has passed. Matthew could go outside and step on a downed power line; Mandi or Samantha could drink contaminated water or eat spoiled food from the freezer.

Gina chews on her thumbnail as a dozen questions rise to needle her brain. Why did she leave the house this morning? Sonny is a cretin and deserves to die, but when people hear that she's missing, they'll whisper that any woman who would leave her children in harm's way has to be the world's most irresponsible mother.

It isn't true, and yet . . . though this admission would sound absolutely outlandish if she spoke it aloud, until the elevator stalled she had enjoyed every moment of her morning. For the first time in years, she has taken charge of her predictable life and made bold plans without Sonny. She has even—

She glances toward the other women, then turns her face toward the wall, unwilling that they should glimpse her thoughts in her eyes. She can't admit this to anyone, but neither can she deny it.

Even this disaster has exhilarating moments.

A man has died on her account. How often does that happen? And though she feels awful about Mr. Vaughn and admires his willingness to help, he suffered the results of his own foolhardy actions. If he wanted to remain safe, he shouldn't have surrendered his harness to the Mexican girl.

Just as Sonny shouldn't have stolen from his children. But he did. And so, like Eddie Vaughn, he will reap the results of his own foolishness.

She lifts her head and checks on the other women. The maid has fallen silent except for an irregular sniffle; Michelle has finished retching and is wiping water from her eyes. She does not lift her head at the touch of Gina's gaze; the woman is probably embarrassed. Who can blame her?

Gina rests her head against the wall and retreats into her own private thoughts. Moving slowly, so as not to attract attention, she lowers one arm to the fabric square that is her folded trench coat. Her fingers tiptoe through the folds until she finds the opening to the bulkiest pocket, then her hand slips between the layers and curls around the cool metal of the gun.

The trembling at her center slows and stops. She inhales a deep breath, lifting her chin as the future sharpens into focus.

She will get out of here. She will handle the publicity, make sure her children are safe. And then she will deal with Sonny—she will find a way to take him completely, permanently, out of their lives.

"I think," Michelle says, her voice jagged and jittery, "this is the most frightened I've ever been in my life." Her gaze catches and holds Gina's. "Are we ever going to get out of here?"

"We certainly are." Gina smiles to reinforce the note of confidence in her voice. "It's only a matter of time."

For the first time in weeks, Gina thought she could feel a tinge of autumn in the evening breeze. She stood with Samantha at the foot of the bleachers as other parents and students filed by. The crowd, engorged with joy at the Gaither High Cowboys' win over the Sickles Gryphons, chattered and laughed as they emptied the stands and moved into the night.

Gina leaned against the chain-link fence around the football field. Matthew had played his heart out, bringing a smile even to Coach Higgins's sour features. He'd scored two touchdowns, running the ball over thirty yards each time. The fans had gone wild each time, pounding each other and stomping on the benches until Gina thought she and Samantha were likely to bounce out of their seats.

She slipped her fingers through the links and stared at the gold goalposts. Sonny should have been here.

He'd read about the game in the paper tomorrow morning, of course. He'd sit across from Mattie at the breakfast counter and try to pry a few words out of their son, but he might as well try to start a conversation with the dog. On a Saturday morning, after a hard game and a late victory party, Mattie wouldn't feel like talking.

To her left, the band members filed out of their reserved section, moving to a steady cadence provided by the percussion section. One high-stepping sax player strutted by, swinging his horn, and Gina pretended not to notice the wink he gave Samantha. She looked adorable in her Cowgirl outfit, even though the hem on those shorts had caused a major war an hour before they'd left the house. Sammy insisted that all the girls wore short shorts to football games; Gina countered that no daughter of hers was going out in a costume consisting of an exposed fanny and fringe.

Finally, they compromised. Sammy sewed a row of fringe at the bottom of her white shorts, lowering the apparent hem by at least two inches. The fringe matched that on the bolero vest she wore over her light-blue shirt, so the entire effect was enchanting.

Score one for Mom.

Samantha stepped closer to Gina's side and jerked her chin toward the stands. "Here comes Mandi."

Gina turned in time to see her older daughter pick her way down the stairs, remaining in step and swinging her flute down-left-right-up as if her future depended on it. Mr. Gleason was tough on the band kids, requiring them to remain in a disciplined formation almost from the time they arrived until the time they exited through the main gate. He allowed them to mix, mingle, and go for soft drinks during the third quarter, but otherwise he made them toe a tight line . . . and the kids loved him for it.

Gina made a mental note to ask the band director for his secret.

Samantha nudged Gina's ribs. "Do you think she'll say hi to us?"

"Wouldn't count on it." Gina tipped her head back and stared at the cloud of insects swarming around the bright stadium lights. "But you can try."

Samantha giggled and moved to Gina's other side, where she'd have more direct access to her sister. Gina watched, half-interested, as the flute players came down the steps, turned a sharp right corner, and marched toward the open area where Gina and several other parents waited.

"Hey, Mandi!" Samantha raised her voice to be heard above the noise. "Mandi! Over here!"

Samantha waved as if she hadn't seen her sister in years, and Gina suppressed a smile when Mandi's pleasant expression vanished beneath a get-me-out-of-here look.

"Mandi! It's me, your sister!"

Mandi stopped staring at the head of the student in front of her long enough to send Samantha a drop-dead glare.

"That's enough," Gina said, dropping her hand to Sammy's shoulder. "You wouldn't want her to tease you like that."

"I wouldn't care."

"When you're fourteen, you'll care."

"Gina!"

She turned in time to see Gladys and Herb McGee striding toward her.

"You must be awfully proud of that boy!" Herb's big hand swallowed Gina's as he pumped her arm. "What is he, a junior?"

"That's right."

"He's got big things ahead of him, you mark my words. Scholarship, maybe? To FSU? He's quite a football player, Gina. I know Sonny must be about to bust his buttons."

"He is." Gina smiled at Gladys when Herb finally released her hand. "Did you all enjoy the game?"

"Say . . . where is Sonny?" Herb rose on tiptoe to scan the milling crowd. "Probably down at the sidelines bragging to the other fathers."

She smiled again, her face aching with the effort. "Sonny had to work tonight."

Herb gaped in exaggerated amazement. "Why—that's awful. You tell him he's working too hard. No man ought to miss a game with the crosstown rivals."

Gina nodded. "I'll tell him."

Gladys linked her arm through her husband's and pulled Herb away. He was still exclaiming over Sonny's workload when she caught Gina's eye. "We'll see you next weekend."

Samantha tugged on her sleeve. "Mom? Can I go get a Coke?"

Gina squinted toward the snack bar. "Aren't they closing?"

"Please, Mom? There's people there, see? I just want a Coke."

Gina sighed, then glanced at her watch. Nine-fifty, so the players shouldn't be too much longer. She didn't know what kind of speech the coach delivered in the locker room after a winning game, but so far he'd taken half an hour to deliver it.

She pulled a dollar bill from her purse and gave it to Samantha. "All right, but hurry back. I want to catch Mattie before he heads out with his friends."

Sammy took the money and sprinted away, leaving Gina alone. She glanced toward the closest exit, clogged now with uniformed band members whose formation dissolved the moment they passed through the gate. One of the boys, sweaty in his uniform pants, T-shirt and suspenders, had doffed his jacket to chase a girl who'd filched his cowboy hat.

Gina scanned the area around the snack bar, then spotted Samantha moving through the crowd of band boosters who were cleaning up. A twinge of guilt made Gina wince; as new band parents, she and Sonny ought to spend a Friday night behind the counter.

She clenched her fist. What work could possibly be so important? Sonny should have been here.

She turned toward the gate and spied Mandi talking to her friends. She'd wait by the parking lot, pretending to be independent and parentless, until Gina and Sammy left the field. Then Mandi would wave to her friends and walk to the car in her mother's wake.

Gina laughed softly. A few years ago she could remember feeling the same way—wanting desperately to be independent, being embarrassed to have to depend upon Mom for a ride, for money, for anything.

She folded her arms and stepped up to one of the fence's supporting poles, then leaned against it. The door to the visitors' locker room had opened; several of the Sickles players came out, wet-haired, fresh-faced and carrying green-and-gray gym bags that seemed to drag their shoulders into a posture of discouragement. As silent as a defeated army, they moved out in single file, led by their coaches, who headed toward a chartered bus.

Poor kids. Gina had seen Mattie wear the same look

after a major loss, and nothing she could say or do seemed to cheer him up. Fortunately, his depression vanished with the start of a new week.

She straightened as the door to the home locker room opened and the players began to exit. She looked for her son's copper-colored hair, but she couldn't find him in the crowd. A group of players grinned, hooted and slapped hands as they cavorted in the grass, then the skinny kid who served as team manager cut through them, dragging a mesh bag bulging with footballs.

Surely they were ready to go. Gina straightened and took a few steps forward. For some silly, macho reason the boys weren't supposed to mingle with the crowd after a game, but if she walked to the open area behind the goalposts, Mattie could meander over and hear her quiet congratulations before he headed toward his car and the victory party.

She had nearly reached the area behind the end zone when she spotted her son with Chuck Hoff, the tow-headed kid who'd been Mattie's best friend since middle school. They were laughing together as Matthew quietly accepted mock punches and congratulations from his teammates.

She unfolded her arms and lengthened her stride, anxious to catch Matthew and Chuck before they got away. Sonny should be doing this.

She hadn't walked more than ten steps when an oddly primitive warning sounded in her brain. The Gaither players, still jiving and celebrating, were taking their time about leaving. The remaining Sickles players, who practically vibrated with resentment, had to file past the Gaither boys. . . .

Might as well combine gasoline and flame.

She swerved to dodge a pair of entwined middle-school sweethearts and hurried toward the football players. Where had all the coaches gone?

She stepped into a hole and pitched forward in the grass. Ordinarily she would have been embarrassed, but no one seemed to notice. If only Mattie would look and come help her!

She pulled herself up, then winced when she tried to put weight on her ankle. She'd probably sprained it, but it couldn't be helped. All that mattered was getting those boys off the field and on their way.

A warning spasm of alarm erupted within her when she looked up and saw one of the Sickles players walk past Mattie and deliberately bump him. Mattie turned, his arm lifted, his smile flattening into a thin line. He said something, the other player replied, and before Gina could act, remnants of the two opposing teams squared off under the lights.

Adrenaline fired her blood as tension crackled between the players. Obviously, they'd picked on Matthew because he'd scored against them. Her son wasn't the type to fight, but, like his father, he wouldn't back down.

She hobbled into a blizzard of insults. The leading Sickles player stood with his hands loose at his sides, his gym bag on the grass at his feet. He'd clamped his jaw and was breathing hard though his nose.

Did kids hide weapons in their wet towels?

She faced her son who, like his friends, was still hyped up on testosterone. "Matthew," she said, using her sternest voice. "You need to get in your car and go."

Her sixteen-year-old warrior cast a glance of well-mannered disdain in her direction, then faced his opponent. A muscle quivered at his jaw.

"That your mommy?" the other player sneered. "Want her to take the heat for you?"

"I've got a handle on things," Mattie said, his face set in the ears-back look dogs give each other before springing forward.

Gina stepped into the narrow space between the two players and lifted her arms. Both young men towered over her, but she had to maintain this fragile peace. "If you fight," she said, her words strangled by the panic welling in her throat, "you'll have to fight around me."

A couple of the Sickles players murmured in the background while Matthew's arm flexed. She breathed in the scent of male ferocity and sweat, knowing he would hate her for this; he would blame her for destroying his reputation and threatening his manhood.

He'd say she made him look like a wuss.

One of the Gaither players launched a stream of curses against the Sickles team; a Sickles player responded in kind. Gina kept her arms up and lifted her chin, her heart hammering her rib cage as the threatening players edged closer—

"What's going on here?" One of the referees, still in

233

his black-and-white shirt, shouldered his way through the crowd. He blinked at Gina, then turned immediately to the boys. "You guys break it up and move along. Sickles, your bus is about to pull out. Unless you want to walk the five miles back to your school, you'd better hit the road now."

Gina exhaled in a steady stream as the muttering players retreated, one or two pausing to flash a crude but eloquent bit of sign language in her direction. Mattie moved away, too, safe in the company of his friends.

She waited until the last player had stepped onto the asphalt parking lot, then she looked at the ref.

"Do me a favor?"

"Sure, lady."

"Let me borrow your shoulder?"

Under bright lights and a cloud of flying insects, Gina covered her face and rested her forehead on the man who had come to her rescue. The bewildered referee patted her shoulder until she straightened and palmed tears from her cheeks.

You okay, ma'am?"

"Yes, thank you. I have to find my daughters and take them home."

The ref's tongue worked at the inside of his cheek for a moment, then he grinned. "That was a pretty gutsy thing you did."

"Oh. Not really." She ran her fingers along her lower lashes to wipe away any smeared mascara. "Any mother would have done the same thing."

"You sure you're okay?"

"Yeah. Thanks."

Then, to prove her point, she folded her arms, lifted her chin, and set off in search of Mandi and Samantha. Sonny should have been there.

2:00 P.M.

CHAPTER 18

Michelle swallows hard and wipes her mouth with the back of her hand. The sour taste of vomit lingers at the back of her throat while a thin sheen of sweat covers her chest and forehead. The other women have retreated to their corners, probably because they find her offensive. They must be repulsed by her; she wouldn't blame them if they were. At this moment she despises herself.

What has happened to her? She's Michelle Tilson, always confident and always in control. When life doesn't flow her way, she takes the helm and charts a new course, doing whatever it takes to cruise through troubled waters. She adapts and perseveres and survives, but in the last hour all her efforts have resulted in ruin.

Eddie's death is all her fault. If she hadn't bullied the answering-service operator, he would still be safe at home. But instead he crossed the bridge and headed into a storm to save a group of women who demanded his safety harness and watched helplessly as he tumbled down an elevator shaft.

She lifts her head as a new sound reaches her ear. From someplace above them, Eddie's dog is whimpering. Despite her fear of all things canine, the sound lances her heart.

"Listen," she whispers, her voice breaking. "What are we going to do about that?"

Gina gapes at her as if she's suddenly begun to speak Chinese. "What do you mean, what are we going to do? We can't do anything to help ourselves. Why should we care about a stupid dog?"

Michelle claps her hands over her ears as the animal breaks into a heartrending howl. "I don't think I can stand that noise. It knows, it knows what happened!"

"Then it knows we didn't have anything to do with that man's accident," Gina snaps. "The elevator company should have sent a team with ladders and the proper tools. Instead they sent Ichabod Crane and his hapless hound—"

"At least he came. No one else would take the chance."

"But they should have! We're in desperate need here! When the hurricane blows ashore we're going to be caught like sardines. I don't know a lot about elevators, but I know we're hanging from cables that are attached to the top of the building. If the roof of this building goes, so might we. One quick ride south, and it'll all be over."

A low, tortured sob breaks from Isabel, who is still wrapped in a tight knot, her arms around her knees.

Her shoulders shake as she weeps.

For a long moment Michelle is too paralyzed to respond to either woman. They are helpless; they are miserable; they all feel terrible about Eddie Vaughn. They're going to have to answer for him; maybe they're going to have to answer for everything they've ever done.

Her grandmother believed in Judgment Day. In an awe-inspiring, angry God who only smiled when he wore the face of Jesus.

Gina glares at Isabel. "You are getting on my last nerve, so stop crying."

Michelle lifts her chin. "You don't have to yell at her. She feels bad about Eddie—we all do."

"We need to get over the mechanic," Gina answers. "We have to come up with some kind of strategy if we're going to get through this ordeal. We need to make a plan."

Michelle blinks at the older woman, unable to believe what she's hearing. Though Gina is certainly no warm fuzzy, she can't be as unfeeling as her words imply. This snappishness has to be some kind of post-traumatic stress reaction.

"Shh." Michelle crawls toward the distraught cleaning woman, then rests a tentative arm on the woman's shoulder. "We're going to get through this. We just have to have a little faith."

Gina whips her head around. "Faith? In whom?"

Michelle searches for an answer. "Gus knew we were going upstairs. The answering-service operator knows about us. And . . . well, my grandmother always said God sees everything. He knows we're here."

Gina snorts, then props one elbow on a bent knee. "Oh, yeah, the Almighty got a lot of people out of New Orleans when Katrina struck. And all those people he plucked up from the tsunami—how could I forget about them? He sends out heavenly rescue squads all the time, doesn't he?"

Despite Gina's sarcasm, Isabel's sobs slow and subside. After a few moments, she pulls a tissue from her pocket and blows her nose. "Thank you," she mouths silently.

Michelle responds with a nod, then lifts her arm and slides a little closer to her corner. What is to become of them? Despite her attempt at comforting Isabel, she can't help feeling that Eddie was their only hope. The distressed dog can't help them and the elevator hasn't moved in—

She groans as a new realization strikes. Eddie said the elevator won't run if the ceiling hatch is open. So if the power happens to come back on, they won't move to the next floor. They'll be stuck here, exposed to whatever happens to fly down the shaft, for however long it takes for the hurricane to pass and rescue operations to begin.

Like the Katrina victims who sweltered and died in their attics, they could be trapped for days. They might die from dehydration in this car. She might never see Parker again, never have an opportunity to tell him she wanted to marry him.

Never be able to share her secret.

Michelle draws a deep breath and looks at the red-head, who has leaned back against the wall, her face resettling into calm lines. Perhaps it was good for them to let off a little steam. Perhaps it'd even be good for them to confess a few things.

"I wasn't going to tell anyone—" she lowers her gaze to her hands "—but if we don't make it out of here, I'd like someone to know. If we aren't rescued, three people won't die in this car. There'll be four victims. This morning I discovered I'm pregnant."

Gina's placid expression softens as a smile crinkles the corners of her eyes. "Congratulations. Is this good news?"

Michelle barks out a laugh. "I wasn't sure at first, but the more I thought about it, the more excited I became. I was on my way to tell my—"

"A file." Gina lifts her head like a cat scenting the breeze. "You said you came here to pick up a file."

"That's right." Michelle nods. "My office is on the thirty-sixth floor. But my boyfriend works on that floor, too, so I was going to tell him after I picked up that client file. He knew I was coming and he promised to wait. We were going to leave the building together. I was hoping we could ride out the hurricane at his place while we celebrated my news."

Gina's eyes narrow slightly. "Are you sure your man isn't married?"

The remark is designed to sting, and it succeeds. Michelle's lower lip trembles as she returns Gina's stare.

"I told you, he's a widower. And even though he has three kids, I hope he'll be excited about another baby." She blinks as a sudden flood of tears stings her eyes. "If we don't get out of here, he'll never even know."

Gina tucks her hair behind her ear. "Does your mystery man work for the attorney general's office? I know some of those guys from—"

Isabel interrupts by breaking into loud sobs. Michelle turns, alarmed, as the housekeeper again covers her woebegone face with her hands. "What's wrong now?"

"They will arrest me!" the girl says, her words muffled. "I didn't mean to get into trouble, but they will see my cart, they will blame everything on me. The attorney general is a powerful man, and he will know everything—"

"Relax." Gina catches Michelle's eye and winks. "Dan Foster's a pretty big wig, but he's not as powerful as he thinks he is."

"She's right," Michelle adds. "They can't blame you for getting caught in the elevator. And it's not your fault we bullied our way in here."

"No, no." Isabel shakes her head and wipes the tip of her red nose with the tissue that is now little more than clumped paper. "The general will put me on trial and my *fotografía* will be in the paper. People will talk, the news will spread. He is looking for me now. When he finds me, I am dead."

Michelle glances at Gina, an unspoken question in her eyes, but the redhead only shrugs.

Michelle pats the cleaning woman's knee. "I'm sure you are mistaken. Why would the attorney general want to kill you?"

Isabel wipes her eyes with the back of her hand, then presses her trembling lips into a thin line. She stares at Michelle for a long moment, as if judging her ability to keep a secret.

"We're not going to turn you in, if that's what you're thinking," Gina says, her voice flat. "Whatever you've done is of no interest to me."

The housekeeper peers out at them through tear-clotted lashes. "Two years ago, in *México,*" she says, her voice wavering, "*mi novio*—my boyfriend—was Ernesto Carillo Fuentes, one of the most important men in Monterrey. I became—how do you say it? *Embarazada,* like you. A baby."

Michelle supplies the word: "Pregnant."

Isabel nods through her tears. "*Sí.* I thought Ernesto would be happy, and he was, but not for why I thought. He wanted me to carry *cocaína* in my belly. He said it would be easy because the American guards will not X-ray a pregnant woman."

Gina, who is examining Isabel's face with considerable absorption, gasps aloud. "You carried cocaine in your belly?"

"I've heard about this," Michelle says. She lowers her gaze and looks into Isabel's eyes. "You didn't do it, did you?"

As Isabel buries her face in her hands and goes quietly to pieces, Michelle lifts a brow and considers the cleaning woman from a new perspective. She's always believed that success requires two things—hard work and a willingness to bend the rules when necessary. Judging from the way Isabel's carrying on, she's done more than bend the rules.

So which rules, exactly, has she broken?

"Will you please bring your seat backs and tray tables to their upright and locked positions?"

As the flight attendant repeated her instructions in Spanish, Isabel leaned forward and looked across the aisle. Juana, another of Ernesto's girls (though not, like Isabel, carrying his child), buckled her seat belt as casually as if she smuggled fifty thumb-size pellets of cocaine across the border every day.

Isabel shivered as a sudden chill climbed the ladder of her vertebrae. Before she'd boarded the plane, Ernesto had warned her that the drugs in her belly were worth a great deal of money—enough that the men who waited in New York would kill her if she tried to escape. She would have to go with them, do exactly what they said, and cooperate until she passed every ounce of cocaine. To think about keeping even one of the pellets would invite disaster. When all the tightly compacted capsules had been counted and cleaned, the New York contacts would give her a good dinner and send her away with five hundred American dollars, a package for Ernesto and a return plane ticket.

"If all goes well," Ernesto said, nuzzling her cheek, "you will be back with me before the weekend. But if you run—" he pulled away so she could see the threat in his eyes "—they will track you down and slit your throat. If you lose the package they give you, I will gut your mother . . . and then I will come after you." A devilish smile spread across his thin lips. "No one crosses me and lives to tell about it, *chiquita*. No one."

Isabel felt a fresh scream rise in her throat and choked it off. How could someone who looked so appealing be so evil? *Mamá* had been right—deceit is a lie that wears a smile.

The flight attendant at the front of the plane picked up a microphone. "We are now making our descent into New York's JFK Airport. When you exit, be sure to have your customs card filled out and ready to hand to the officials."

Isabel grimaced, then pulled her I-94 card from the seat pocket. How was she supposed to know the address where they'd be staying? What had the others written?

She looked at Juana and exhaled when the older girl held the card at an angle so Isabel could see what she'd printed: 625 East Sixty-eighth Street, New York.

Isabel filled out the form, then caught Juana's eye to smile her thanks. The older girl laughed. "*Es el apartamento de Lucy y Ricky Ricardo,*" she whispered, pointing to the address. "*En el programa de television.*"

A dart of panic pierced Isabel's heart, but Juana only giggled and raised the back of her seat. Isabel did the same, then held the arrival card between her damp palms until the roaring plane jolted to the runway.

Ernesto had sent six girls on this flight—along with Isabel, Juana, Berta, Paloma, Rosa and Susana were traveling with bellies and intestines packed with cocaine capsules. Berta, Isabel noticed as she stood to pull her small suitcase from the overhead bin, did not look at all well. Pearls of perspiration dotted her forehead and upper lip, but perhaps she was nervous.

Isabel didn't want to consider the other possibility. If even one pellet burst inside a girl's body, she would die. She might survive if she could make it to a hospital, but none of the men waiting for them in New York City would consider approaching a hospital if one of them became ill.

Isabel fell into line behind Juana as they exited the aircraft, but she knew she was supposed to step away from the others as soon as they entered the gate area. Ernesto always sent several mules at once in order to deflect suspicion. If one girl got caught, he reasoned, the authorities would be so busy interrogating her that the others could slip through.

With her suitcase in hand, Isabel followed Juana up the Jetway, then stepped to the right in the airport gate. She moved to an empty seat and unzipped her bag, pretending to look for her passport while the other girls mingled with the tourists, businessmen and grandparents on their way to visit family in the United States.

When the last passenger had exited the Jetway, Isabel pulled a stick of gum from her bag, then zipped the case and walked toward the bustling hall where the others had disappeared. Though she had been perspiring all day, she felt suddenly slick with the clammy sweat of fear. So many people, and all of them in a hurry! How would she be able to tell the good people from the bad?

Ernesto's New York contacts would be watching from the customs exit. Though she had never seen them, a vivid picture rose in her mind—they would be a darkly handsome, narrow-eyed group standing with their arms crossed and their jaws tight while they silently counted heads. When they realized one of their sheep was missing, they would question the waiting girls. Juana and the others would be so intimidated, in a matter of minutes the men would have Isabel's name and description. They would send someone into the airport, and they would search for her. They might even tell the customs officials to watch for Isabel Juanita Alvarado.

They would not be happy.

Though Isabel was so nervous her teeth clicked like castanets, she had decided not to join the other girls. Ernesto's contacts would be furious, they would post a guard and watch the airport for days, but endless hours at the cotton mill had taught Isabel patience. She would wait them out, she would pray for her *mamá,* and she would keep her baby safe.

Ernesto would not believe she had run. He had killed Rodrigo to frighten her into submission; he had been sure she would obey his commands and come shivering back to him.

But before she'd left for the apartment where she would have to swallow the cocaine capsules, she had placed a briefcase under her mother's bed. *Do not call the police,* she'd written, *but leave Monterrey at once. Do not look for me. Take this money—it is enough for travel, but not so much Ernesto will come after you—and go to a city where no one knows us.*

I am sorry for all the trouble I have caused.

Te quiero, Mamá. Vaya con Dios.

Mamá and Rodrigo had been right about Ernesto; she had been wrong. She had already lost her brother, but she would not lose her mother.

If doing penance for her sin meant never seeing her mother again, she would sacrifice that love as an act of contrition. She would leave Monterrey and never return to *México*.

A brave woman would stand up to the drug dealers; she would find someone who could be trusted, and she would tell him everything about the girls who were carrying cocaine into *los Estados Unidos*.

She was not a brave woman. She did not deserve a new life in America, but her baby deserved more than a father like Ernesto.

3:00 P.M.

CHAPTER 19

Unable to resist a wave of curiosity, Gina watches as Michelle leans toward Isabel, her face set in lines of concentration. "So . . . what did you do?"

Isabel wipes her tears, then takes a deep, shuddering breath. "I swallowed the drugs and came to New York, but instead of meeting Ernesto's men, I hid *en el baño.*"

Gina looks at Michelle. "What did she say?"

"The restroom, I think," Michelle answers, her eyes soft with sympathy. She turns back to the maid. "Didn't they think to check the restrooms?"

The girl's dark lashes shutter her eyes. "Too many people around for the men to come in. They sent one of the girls in to look for me, but I gave her money to say she did not see me. At night, when the cleaners came in, I would move to a gate and pretend to wait for a plane, but in the mornings I would get something to eat and go back to the restroom. When I thought it would be safe to leave, I covered my head with a sweater I found on a bench. I wanted to be sure Ernesto's friends would not know me."

"What, um, happened to the cocaine?" Michelle asks.

Isabel swallows hard as a flush mottles her neck. "Down the toilet."

Gina barks a laugh. "I'm surprised her thugs weren't hanging out at the sewage treatment plants."

"They weren't her thugs." Michelle tosses the comment over her shoulder, then focuses again on the maid. "How long did you stay at the airport?"

"*Cinco días.* Five days."

"After that, you came to Florida?"

When Isabel grimaces, Gina wonders if the girl is struggling to remember . . . or wishing she could forget. "When I was ready to leave, I had only two thousand pesos. Some of it was Ernesto's money, but most of it was mine."

Gina stretches her legs into the empty space at the center of the car. "You should have been fine, then."

Michelle scowls. "That's not even two hundred dollars. You can't get a decent hotel room for that in the city."

"I had one hundred eighty-eight dollars," Isabel says. "I changed the money behind the security gates. When I thought the men might have stopped watching for me, I went through customs and took a cab to the *estación*—" She looks at Michelle, her face twisting. "You know the name? A big *estación*?"

"Grand Central?"

"No, Greyhound *de autobús.* I gave the man all the money I had, and he said it would be enough to get me to Charlotte. So I bought a ticket and got on the bus, but when I sat down and looked out the window, I saw—" A shudder shakes her.

"What?" Michelle asks. "What'd you see?"

"Ernesto." Isabel's voice thickens. "He had come from *México,* and he had someone watching for me at customs. That man couldn't catch me before I got on the bus, but he called Ernesto so they could follow. Ernesto talked to the man at the bus station and knew when I would arrive to Charlotte. He knew everything."

The wind continues to moan in the shaft above them, but now Gina scarcely notices. Staring at Isabel, she realizes the Mexican girl would have been about seventeen when she landed in New York—the same age as Mandi. How would her daughter handle that situation? Mandi isn't involved in any kind of drug abuse, thank goodness, but despite all the precautions a parent might take, one never knows who a teenager will encounter at a party or a friend's house. . . .

Her daughter, she admits with great reluctance, might be just as susceptible to the charms of a handsome young man. But she'd never submit to emotional blackmail; if she found herself in a situation like the one Isabel faced, she'd come home, pour her troubles into Gina's lap and wait for her mother to make the world right again.

And Gina would. No matter where they lived, she'd grab a rifle and go hunting for drug lords before she would let her daughter serve as human camouflage for some snakeskin-booted lowlife.

She would also arrange a quiet abortion for her daughter. She would do anything to erase the situation from Mandi's memories, to pretend none of it ever happened.

And yet . . . all of it happened to Isabel. The girl has lost everything, been driven from her country and borne her tormentor's child. Mandi would crumple under such pressure, maybe even consider suicide.

Gina has to admit the Mexican girl has courage.

"Ernesto stood outside the bus and stared at me," Isabel says, her body rigid, her fists clenched. "He couldn't get on, but I knew he would follow."

"You could have slipped off the bus at any stop," Gina says, folding her arms. "You could have left that miscreant behind."

"I didn't know what to do." Isabel's soft voice is tinged with terror. "I felt trapped, so I sat in the seat and cried. That's when Carlos saw me. He sat beside me and by the time we reached Raleigh, I had told him everything."

When Isabel lifts her head, the clear light of devotion shines from her dark eyes. "In Raleigh, Carlos got off the bus, walked into the office, and called *la policía*. Ernesto and three of his men had been following in a car, waiting for me to come off the bus, but they drove away when *la policía* came. While they were gone, Carlos bought me another ticket and walked me to another bus. We came to Tampa and got married before Rafael was born."

"Do you ever worry?" Michelle asks. "About Ernesto finding you?"

The maid's answering smile is frayed around the edges. "Every day."

Gina clears her throat. "Sounds to me like you

might be here illegally. Did you get a green card?"

Michelle turns and gives her a black look. "Cut the girl some slack. She was running for her life."

"I don't have anything against her personally, but it's a legitimate question," Gina insists. "Our borders are being overrun with these people—they're taking jobs from Americans—"

"I work the graveyard shift, emptying trash cans, dusting shelves and washing windows," Isabel interrupts. "Nobody else wants this job. And Carlos is an American citizen. We did not marry for a green card—we married because Carlos loves me. I don't know why, but he does."

Gina nods, less interested in the woman's employment situation than in the loving look that lights her eyes whenever she whispers her husband's name. Did Sonny ever love her like that? Would he have married her if she had been penniless, on the run and pregnant with another man's child?

Not likely. Gina has given up everything for him, yet the biggest sacrifice Sonny's ever made for her was forfeiting his golf game on the Saturday she gave birth to Samantha.

Shifting to sit on her bent legs, Gina moves closer, tightening the circle of conversation. "Your situation was rough, but you escaped that danger and now you're happy with your husband. I can see how much you love him, and I'm happy for you. Now . . . imagine how you'd feel if you discovered that your beloved Carlos has been having an affair."

Her secret hangs in the air—revealed, spoken, pent up no longer. The maid acknowledges Gina's confession with a grim nod, and the look in Michelle's eyes shifts from irritation to sympathy.

Gina lowers her gaze as the shell of her bravado cracks under the pressure of their eyes. "After twenty-one years of faithful marriage, what do I have? A cheating spouse who steals from me and my children. A man who has opened offshore bank accounts because he hopes to hide most of his assets before he visits a divorce lawyer. A man who wouldn't know poetry from a platitude. Some reward, huh?"

Lines of concentration deepen in Michelle's forehead as she groans. "That is truly awful. I'm so sorry."

Gina smiles a silent touché. "I don't want pity—I deserve a medal. Let me tell you, being married to Sonny is no picnic. I helped him start his business on our kitchen table, did I tell you that? I worked my rear off helping him make a name for himself. He's a bigwig, powerful and well-known in Tampa. We're invited to all the right parties, we live in a good neighborhood and drive nice cars, but all I ever cared about was our kids. Well, yesterday a private investigator delivered proof—my husband's been spending a fortune on some sweet tart of the month instead of investing for our children's future. When he didn't come home last night, I decided to do something about his philandering."

Gina looks up to find Michelle studying her with a slightly perplexed expression, as if she's considering a question she lacks the courage to ask. The girl really needs to develop some courage. If they're going to be trapped together in this steel cage, they may as well be honest with each other . . . well, almost. As much as she'd love to tell the world what she intends to do to Sonny, that plan won't succeed if anyone knows her true intention.

Avoiding Michelle's eyes, she straightens her spine and presses it against the unyielding wall. "This morning, after I found the passbook for the offshore account, I decided to ask for a divorce. I was coming to the office to break the news when—" She gives Isabel a crooked smile. "Well, you know what happened."

The maid shakes her head. "I am sorry for you."

"Don't be. I think Zsa Zsa Gabor had it right—husbands are like fires. They go out when left unattended." Gina pulls her raincoat to her chest until the comforting weight of the pistol rests on her breastbone. "I've had it with Sonny. The marriage is over. As soon as we're rescued, I'm going to give him the news and call the best divorce lawyer in town."

Michelle leans toward her, concern in her eyes. "Are you sure about this? I know you're upset, but twenty-one years is a lot to throw away. You have to think of your children."

"I am thinking of my children." Too drained to explain further, Gina closes her eyes. "After you've invested the best years of your life building a man's family and career, maybe you'll understand. I still have feelings for Sonny, but what I'm feeling isn't love."

"Maybe," Michelle says, "you'll feel love again tomorrow."

Gina ignores the comment. "Passion is passion, I suppose. The man has always been able to drive me crazy."

Maybe she should amend that—men have always driven her insane. Sonny, Matthew and even Sonny's father have, on occasion, tied her heart into knots. The greatest loves of her life have also brought her the most pain.

Beginning with her dad.

Gina threw down her hairbrush and frowned at her reflection in the bathroom mirror. Her hair was impossible—the wrong color, the wrong texture, the wrong length. She'd asked the stylist to give her a look like Farrah Fawcett's, but the girl hadn't cut the bangs right. They'd looked okay when Gina had left the salon, but now the stubborn fringe wouldn't cooperate.

She opened the bathroom door. "Mommmmm!"

Her mother's face appeared at the end of the hallway. "What?"

"That girl at your salon didn't know what she was doing! My bangs won't feather like they're supposed to."

Mom came forward, wiping her hands on her apron. "Your hair looked lovely when we left. Maybe you're not holding the brush right."

"I'm holding it just like the girl did."

"Honey, you can't expect to get the same results as Joanie. After all, she's a trained stylist and you're seventeen—"

"I know what I'm doing, Mom, and nothing's working." Gina retreated before her mother's patient smile, then sank to the edge of the bathtub. "Bruce is coming over in an hour and I'm not ready."

"You want me to try and fix it?"

Gina didn't think a woman who'd worn the same style for the last twenty years would be able to help, but she didn't complain when her mother picked up the brush. She caught a section of hair at Gina's forehead, wrapped it around the boar bristles, and turned on the blow dryer. Ever so lightly, she waved the appliance over the circular brush.

Gina drew a breath between her teeth. Why was her mother always so gentle? You had to be tough to wear Farrah hair; you had to pull it and curl it and bend it and fluff it. At this rate, she was never going to be ready in time.

"Never mind," she said, taking the dryer from her mother's hand. "That's not right—it's going to look ridiculous."

"It'll look fine."

"You don't know a thing about it, Mom—you wouldn't understand." Gina snapped off the dryer, then looked in the mirror and blew out a breath, lifting the limp hair over her brows. "We don't have what I need, so I might as well call Bruce and tell him not to come. I won't let him see me looking like this."

Her father would have told her to stop being so melo-dramatic, but her mother placed a delicate hand on Gina's shoulder. "What do you need?"

Gina whirled to face her. "I saw this commercial for a new shampoo called UltraMax. It's supposed to prime your hair for blow drying and make it more manageable."

A corner of her mother's mouth rose in a half smile. "You really think shampoo is going to make a difference?"

"Haven't you heard their commercial? 'It'll go the way you want it to, lift the way you want it to, drift the way you want it to . . .'"

Mom caught Gina's hand and squeezed. "I get the idea."

"Please, Mom, will you run up to the grocery and get me a bottle? If you leave now, I'll have time to wash and dry my hair before Bruce gets here."

Her mother sighed and checked the clock in the hall. "I promised to watch *Donny and Marie* with your dad—"

"That show doesn't start until eight and you should be back long before then. Please, Mom?"

Her mother sighed heavily, then nodded. "All right. But you'd better hope your dad needs something, or he'll accuse me of spoiling you again."

After her mother left the bathroom, Gina moved to the hallway and listened as her father complained about the late hour, the rainy weather and Gina's self-ishness. Especially Gina's selfishness.

Her mother's voice rose above her dad's growl.

"She's a seventeen-year-old girl—the world is supposed to revolve around her."

"She has a car—why doesn't she go herself?"

"She won't be with us much longer, and I don't mind going. So stop fussing and hand me my purse."

Five minutes later, Gina heard the starting roar of her mother's car. She pulled aside one corner of her bedroom curtain and smiled as her mother's Chrysler backed out of the driveway, its windshield wipers beating in tandem.

Her smile vanished an hour later when a local sheriff knocked to inform them that Georgina Elizabeth Meade had been killed after skidding on the rain-slicked road. The Chrysler hit a telephone pole, which snapped at the base and fell on the car, crushing the roof and Georgina's skull. "Looks to me," the cop said, his voice strained, "like she never saw it coming."

Gina collapsed into her boyfriend's arms, burdened by guilt as much as grief, while her father followed the sheriff outside and stood bareheaded in the rain.

Dad rarely spoke to her after the accident. During the following months, she came home from school, heated a casserole or TV dinner and ate in front of the television. She did her homework in her room and accepted a weekend job. Though they lived in the same house and shared the same last name, tragedy and blame built a wall between her and her father, a barrier reinforced by every indifferent day.

Her dad admitted as much on a night when she came home late and found him sitting on the floor in the den, drunkenly sobbing over a photograph album. "You," he said, glaring at her through red-rimmed eyes. "You have the stone-cold gall to walk around here looking like her and talking like her when you aren't worthy to kiss her feet! You selfish, stupid girl! Sent her out in the rain because you were too lazy and spoiled to lift a hand for yourself."

"Daddy, please!" Gina knelt at her father's side, her gaze clouding as she inched trembling hands toward his slipper-clad feet. "I'm so sorry! I didn't want her to get hurt. It was an accident!"

"Never," he said, remarkably lucid for one who smelled so strongly of alcohol, "never speak to me. I'll do what Georgie wanted and send you to college. I'll even pay for your wedding, but I will never talk to you again. If not for you, I wouldn't have lost her. The only reason I haven't turned you out on the street is because Georgie would want me—" emotion choked his voice "—to keep you."

A hot tear rolled down Gina's cheek. "Don't you think I'd change places with her if I could? I'd die, Daddy, if that would bring her back to you. I'd do anything, if you would forgive me—"

Without another word, Dad clutched the photograph album to his chest, stood and stalked out of the room, leaving Gina alone on the gold shag carpeting that had been her mother's pride and joy.

Michelle pushes a fringe of damp hair from her brow and sneaks a glance at the redhead, who has fallen into an introspective silence. No wonder the woman was in a dark mood when they entered the elevator. Though Michelle has had no personal experience with divorce, Lauren's parents split a few years back, and she has confided that their breakup left her questioning everything she had previously believed about marriage and family.

Michelle crosses her legs to relieve the pressure on her hip bones. Even her parents, as messed up as they were, never considered divorce. Her father must have been the most patient person on earth. On the other hand, he didn't always come home at night. Momma said he was working late, but even Shelly Tills knew that miners didn't work more than an eight-hour shift. If Daddy wasn't sitting in his recliner after dark, he either couldn't come home . . . or he didn't want to.

Still, she couldn't believe her father had ever taken up with another woman. When her mother managed to stay away from the bottle, he was gentle and affectionate, a good husband. Sometimes he'd ask Momma to come out on the front porch to watch the stars come up over the ridge, but as soon as it got dark she'd complain of being cold and want a drink to "chase off the chill."

After a while, Daddy stopped asking Momma to come outside with him. But Michelle was certain he'd never taken up with another woman.

Without looking directly at Gina, she manages a shaky smile. "I'd be careful if I were you. I've heard that people who think divorce will cure their ills soon find out that the remedy is worse than the disease."

Gina releases a hollow laugh. "Trust me, that won't be true in my case. I want Sonny out of my life as soon as possible."

Michelle rests her head on her folded arms. "I can't imagine ever feeling that way about my boyfriend. If Parker cheated on me I'd be upset, but he'd still be the man I love and the father of my child. I'd try to talk things out before I ever thought about leaving him."

"Excuse me?"

Michelle lifts her head. "I said I'd try to talk things—"

"Did you say *Parker?*"

"Oh—yes, I did." Michelle smiles when surprise fills the older woman's face. "That's right, you might know him. Parker Rossman."

"P-Parker Rossman—" the syllables tangle on Gina's tongue "—is the widower. The father of your baby."

Michelle recoils from the redhead's gaze, which has fixed her in a green-eyed vise. "That's what I said."

"Parker Rossman—" Gina fumbles with the folded coat in her arms "—has a family who calls him Sonny. And he's not a widower, he's married."

Michelle shakes her head. "You have to be mistaken."

"I'm not. You see, Parker Rossman is my husband."

Michelle stares at the woman in bewilderment while some still-functioning part of her brain registers that Gina has pulled something from her coat—and the unwavering object in her hand is a gun.

CHAPTER 20

"Hello?"

Michelle looked up to see a man at the door, a bouquet in his arms. She moved to her purse, assuming he worked for a florist, then halted. Even in downtown Tampa, delivery persons did not wear suits and silk ties.

"Parker Rossman," the stranger said, extending his right hand as he stepped into the office. "Your neighbor from down the hall."

"Michelle Tilson." She shook his hand, then tilted a brow at the flowers. "Did someone die?"

"Not unless you decide to kill me for impertinence. Instead, I hope you'll accept these as a welcome to the building." Parker placed the bouquet of daisies and wildflowers in her arms, then stepped back and slipped his hands into his pockets. "Gus told me an attractive young woman was moving into the empty suite between my office and the AG's domain. I figured I ought to stop by and help you find your way around the thirty-sixth floor."

She smiled. "Have I met this Gus?"

"The security guard downstairs—older guy, kinda portly. He's nice—you'll like him. Always genial, never pushy. He doesn't even mind when my kids bug him for separate visitors' passes so they can race each other in the elevators."

Michelle made a mental note as she placed the flowers on an empty desk. Attractive, nice, generous, and a parent. Three out of four wasn't bad.

She leaned against the desk and crossed her legs at the ankle. "Your office is down the hall? Then you must be—"

"In insurance—Rossman Life and Liability. We've been in this building ten years, in existence for almost twenty. My wife and I started the business from scratch and worked together . . . until I lost her, that is."

Michelle brought her hand to her throat as Rossman coughed and averted his eyes. Maybe she'd been too quick to write him off. She'd begun to think that handsome, sensitive men could only be found in the pages of Nicholas Sparks novels.

Giving her visitor a moment to gain control of his emotions, Michelle lifted a framed photo of Olympia Densen-Jones from a box marked M's Office. Olympia still had hair in the picture, though it had gone silver from the first round of chemotherapy. By that time she had divorced Howard, retired to Tampa and left Michelle to run the Jones Personnel Agency. After Olympia's death, when Michelle had become part-owner of the business, Howard had been happy to buy her out.

With a sizable check and a shoe box filled with tacky tourist postcards from Olympia, Michelle followed her mentor's example and moved to Florida. Because the citizens of Tampa were more globally minded than those of Charleston, West Virginia, she established Tilson Corporate Careers with a new résumé and a broader vision.

Though half of her business existed only on paper and in exaggeration, in time her expanding operation required moving from a small strip mall to the Lark Tower. Michelle knew Olympia would be proud of her—she had learned to play the game, she had thrived in a man's world and she had never gone back to Bald Knob.

Now she took a deep breath and softened her smile. "I'm Tilson Corporate Careers," she told her visitor. "I'm a headhunter."

Parker Rossman gave her a lopsided grin. "Not a cannibal, I trust."

"I haven't eaten a client in months."

"But you do eat." He hesitated, one hand brushing his lapel. "Lunch, I mean."

"Sure I do." She spoke slowly, not sure if she wanted to go where he was leading. Perhaps he wasn't sure he wanted to lead, because his gaze had begun to rove over the bare walls, examining everything but her face.

Still . . . a businessman who'd been working in Tampa twenty years would know people. People with connections who wanted to change jobs.

"Since you eat lunch," he said, "maybe sometime—"

"Today would be great," she said, deciding for both of them. "I have to unpack a few boxes, but I should be free by twelve-thirty."

He grinned, then back-stepped toward the door, cocking his finger gunslinger style. "Great. I'll meet you here."

"It's a date," she said, smiling as he let himself out.

• • •

Michelle gapes at Gina across a sudden ringing silence. Parker is—what? Impossible; this has to be a case of mistaken identity. Parker isn't married, he couldn't be. He has given her names, dates and details. He still chokes up when he talks about how his wife died in a horrific car crash. Matt had been ten at the time, Amanda eight, and little Sam only six. Those poor children have been without a mother ever since, and Parker has worn himself to a frazzle trying to be father and mother and businessman.

If only he were here to clear this up. He isn't a cheater. Not a liar. Gina has to be deluded, maybe even a little crazy.

Gina's eyes light with fierce sparkling as she rises to her knees. "I should have known. Why else would you be on your way to the thirty-sixth floor?"

"I told you, my office is up there," Michelle says. "Dozens of people work on that floor." She presses her spinal column against the wall and slides one hand toward the shadows in the rear of the car. Can she count on Isabel for help? She tears her gaze from the gun for an instant, but the housekeeper is curled into a ball so tight not even her face is showing. She'll be no help at all if this madwoman starts shooting.

Meeting Gina's eye, Michelle speaks with deliberate firmness. "Parker has two boys and a girl—you said you have two girls and a boy. I'll admit it's a crazy coincidence, but you have to be mistaken."

"I didn't make a mistake." Gina's face has gone

deadly pale except for two garish roses, one blooming in each cheek. "You, however, made a big one when you went after my husband."

"Parker's boys," Michelle answers, careful not to make any threatening moves, "are Matt and Sam. His daughter is—"

"His only son," Gina interrupts, "is Matthew. His daughters are Mandi and Samantha. And that diamond bracelet he gave you? He paid for it with my children's inheritance."

Michelle exhales in a rush as relief avalanches over her. "Bracelet?" She holds up her arm, adorned with nothing but a simple watch. "I don't have a diamond bracelet. Parker has never given me anything like that."

Disbelief flickers in Gina's eyes, then steely determination returns to those fiery orbs. "So he hasn't given it to you yet. But he's going to, I know. It's not in his safe at the house."

With a shiver of vivid recollection, Michelle remembers Parker's parting words: *By the way, I ordered something special for you. . . .*

Realization strikes all at once, like a jolt of electricity to her spine. Parker didn't ask her to come downtown to give her an engagement ring; he wanted to give her a diamond bracelet. He isn't planning to propose . . . because he is already married.

To this outraged woman.

Michelle lifts her head to meet the eyes that seem intent on impaling her. "I didn't know."

265

You should have known."

"Maybe . . . I should have." Now she understands why Gina looks familiar—the striking green eyes that smile from the children's portrait in Parker's office are Gina's eyes. Amanda has this woman's chin, and Matt her nose.

And Sam is a girl. In the portrait, painted from a photograph of the kids playing at a ski resort, Sam is a short-haired, chubby-cheeked five-year-old in a snowsuit. Michelle had assumed Sam was a boy and Parker never corrected her assumption. Last year, when Sam's birthday rolled around, he even agreed with Michelle's gift suggestion of a baseball glove.

Just as he acted on her idea to buy Amanda a ring last December.

"Did your husband—" she struggles to keep the sound of stunned disbelief from her voice "—give Amanda a ring last Christmas? A band made from Black Hills gold?"

When a tide of hurt washes through Gina's eyes, Michelle has her answer.

She turns her head, unable to monitor her reeling thoughts and the gun only inches from her face. This is insane. Any moment now she will wake up and console herself with knowing that her life, her love and her secrets are still intact—

But there is the gun, and above it, the steely eyes of a wronged wife. Parker Rossman, the father of her child, is a complex man, not easy to know intimately, but she knows him . . . or does she? If he lied about having a wife and two sons, did he lie about his feelings for Michelle? Has he ever told her anything true?

With the gun steady in her right hand, Gina sinks back to the floor. That ring! She and Mandi had marveled over the intricate design of pink and green leaves; she had been impressed with Sonny's taste and thoughtfulness.

Yet Sonny deserved none of the credit—his mistress had been responsible for everything. He had allowed this stranger's influence to touch his daughter at Christmas, a time when families participate in the exchange of gifts. How could Sonny have allowed this woman to infringe on such an intimate occasion?

The determination that drove her to this building now has a sharper spur.

"I should have recognized you," she says, punctuating her words with jerks of the gun. "Tall, slim, young—I have a picture of you walking on my husband's arm. He's looking at you like you're the cream in his coffee."

From the corner of her eye, Gina sees the maid cross herself. "I didn't know," Michelle says again, a catch in her voice. "He told me his wife was dead."

"Maybe to him, I am." Gina laces every word with venom. "Maybe he thinks of his children as dead, too."

"He loves his kids. He talks about them all the time."

"Really?" She swallows a hysterical surge of incredulous laughter. "Tell me—did he introduce you to my children as his mistress, or did he pass you off as a client? How many times has he lied to them about you?"

Tears slide from beneath the younger woman's closed lids, glittering like silver in the dim light. "He never let me meet the kids. He was so protective . . . I thought he didn't want to risk them getting attached to me . . . you know, if things didn't work out."

Gina feels the corner of her mouth twist. Something inside her is relieved to hear that Sonny didn't expose the children to this woman, but she doubted he had the kids' best interests in mind. Matthew might be taken in by a pretty face and Samantha could be gullible, but Mandi is sharp; she'd sense anything that wasn't right and she'd tell.

No, Sonny wasn't thinking about guarding the kids. He kept the children from this woman to protect his own sorry rear end.

Across the elevator, Michelle opens her hands in a gesture of entreaty. "I don't know what to say. I would never go out with a married man—I would never want to break up a family. I'm sorry."

"Shut up." Gina lifts her free hand and massages her pounding temple. "I need a few minutes to think."

This morning she had tried to plan for every possible scenario, but she could never have imagined Sonny getting off scot-free while she sweat in a metal box with his pregnant mistress and a gutsy Mexican girl. The best-laid plans of mice and men have done more than go awry; they have doubled back to snare her.

But she can think herself out of this mess. She has time. She has courage enough to do whatever it takes to protect her children.

When she lowers her hand, she finds that her thoughts have crystallized. Though the mistress's baby is an unexpected wrinkle, her plans for Sonny don't have to change.

Still, children always complicate things. When Gina's sister divorced her gutless husband, he got custody of the kids, child support and alimony because Marion had established a medical practice while he'd sat on his tush watching soaps and football on TV.

Gina won't allow anything like that to happen in her situation. When they get out of this elevator, she is not going to let anyone set aside part of the estate to provide for this woman's child.

With newfound determination, she lowers the gun to her lap and looks the mistress in the eye. "I hate to break it to you, Michelle, but my husband is not going to be thrilled about that baby you're carrying. He has to pay for three college educations, so don't count on him for child support. I won't let him spend a penny on an illegitimate brat."

Michelle shifts the focus of her gaze from some interior field of vision to the gun in Gina's lap. All traces of good humor vanish from the curve of her mouth and her eyes. "You know, you caught me off guard when you pulled that thing out, but now I understand—you came here to kill Parker."

Gina doesn't flinch. "I told you—I came here to ask for a divorce. I brought the gun because I thought I might run into looters."

Icy contempt flashes in Michelle's eyes. "You were

planning to shoot Parker and leave him up there until after the hurricane passed. We all saw what happened during Katrina—it's possible no one would find him for days—"

"You've got quite an imagination." Gina smiles without humor and crosses her arms, moving the pistol to her left side. "Why would I kill Sonny? He's the guilty party in our broken marriage, so I'm sure my lawyers can devise several ways to empty his pockets. He'll be ruined when I force him to buy out my share of the business—I own half the company, you know. Rossman Life and Liability wouldn't exist without me."

Depleted by the waning of her adrenaline rush, Gina sets the Rohrbaugh on the floor and stretches her cramping fingers. "I'll admit I wanted to scare Sonny," she says, idly studying her nails, "just like I wanted to scare you. But I could never shoot him. I wouldn't."

She glances up, looking for some sign that her lie has been believed, but Michelle's expression remains grim. Perhaps it doesn't matter. When they escape this stifling cage, she will have to tell the police that Gina said the gun was a bluff.

Leaving the gun at her side, Gina swipes a hand through her hair and finds herself yearning for a cigarette. She hasn't smoked in years, but right now she'd happily commit armed robbery for a lighter and a pack of Kents. Her hands need something to keep them occupied . . . like a length of piano wire and Sonny's neck.

What is that Kipling quote? Something about pairs—

ah, yes: *For the sin ye do by two and two, ye must pay for one by one.*

Sonny still deserves to die, but her kids shouldn't have to suffer. She left the house early so she could take care of things without involving the children, but now they're alone and probably frantic. If chaos theory has its way with this elevator . . .

As water drips from the open hatch in an arrhythmic patter, Gina's anxiety shifts to a deeper and more urgent fear. She can't bear the thought of her children being orphaned. Her will names her sister as their guardian, but Marion is more doctor than mother; family lies at the bottom of her priority list.

Gina concentrates on taking steady breaths as another alarming thought rises—if Michelle's baby is born, the truth will come out. People will want to know who the child's father is, and Michelle won't hesitate to tell them. Though most of society doesn't even blink at infidelity these days, Sonny's crowd prides itself on discretion. If his reputation is soiled, Gina's children will pay a price.

Even if Sonny's in the grave, his family won't escape ridicule.

How will Matthew get references for a profitable part-time job if the old stodgies at the club learn about Sonny's philandering? None of them are saints, but they keep their skeletons locked in the closet. Sonny, on the other hand, has brazenly paraded his mistress through Tampa and may have even squired her to one of his Gasparilla Krewe meetings. The elite may have winked at those outings, but they won't be as forgiving if Michelle shows up at a Gasparilla ball with Sonny's child in tow.

Gina lifts her head as a cacophony assaults her ear—a screech of metal, the yowl of the wind, a brief rip that reminds her of shuffled playing cards. How apt—in the same hour that trauma is shattering her world, a hurricane is destroying her shelter.

But she's not alone . . . and perhaps she's looking at this from the wrong perspective. She's been so busy smarting as the wounded wife, she's forgotten that Sonny has wounded someone else.

She peers at Michelle, who looks pale and spent in the glow of the emergency light. Perhaps the woman is upset enough to terminate her pregnancy.

Gina gently clears her throat. "Have you," she says, reaching for the pearls at her neck, "carefully considered your situation? Would you want a man who has lied to you? Would you want to have his baby?"

Michelle's face empties of expression and locks. "You want me to have an abortion."

"No one would expect you to carry the child of a man who took advantage of you—"

"Killing's your answer to everything, isn't it?" Michelle draws her lips into a tight smile. "Think back, Gina, to what you told me a while ago—you said the birth of your son was the most incredible thing that ever happened to you."

"My situation was different. I had a husband. We had planned for the baby—"

"Maybe I won't have a husband, maybe I won't feel the same way. But if we get out of here, I'm giving this baby a chance."

Gina lifts her hands in a gesture of surrender. All right, so Michelle's hearing the tick of her biological clock. Now that she knows the truth about Sonny, she'll probably use the little darling to her own advantage, trading her injury for sympathy as she parades Sonny Rossman's abandoned love child through downtown Tampa.

Only one option remains, then. At some point Michelle has to die . . . along with the maid, who would otherwise be a witness.

Gina closes her eyes to focus her thoughts. The Mexican girl has a sufficiently shady past. She could have found the Rohrbaugh in Sonny's office and slipped it into her pocket, shooting Michelle before Gina managed to wrest the gun away and fire in self-defense. But she'd need a motive.

Gina opens one eye to peer at the brunette's wrist, where a watch dangles from a gold chain. Not expensive, but nice enough. The maid shoots Michelle for the watch; Gina struggles to take the weapon and kills the maid in the process. Two dead bodies, two bullet casings on the floor, gunpowder residue on everyone in these close quarters. Gina could place Isabel's prints on the weapon, then drop it in the center of the car.

It's not the most carefully thought-out scenario, but in the aftermath of a devastating hurricane, no one is likely to spend much time on the case. The authorities will be occupied with more pressing matters.

Gina swallows hard, grips the gun and stands, boldly meeting the brunette's gaze. "I'm sorry," she says, lifting her chin. "But I can't allow you to leave this elevator."

CHAPTER 21

Isabel feels herself falling. Black emptiness rushes up like the bottom of a dark lake and she will drown if she cannot breathe. . .

She snatches a breath when a moment passes and the red-haired woman does not fire the gun. The woman glares at Michelle with burning, reproachful eyes, but she does not pull the trigger.

Isabel brings her hands together and tries to pray: *Holy Mary, mother of God, pray for us sinners now and at the hour of our death. . . .*

The words that usually bring comfort do nothing to ease the torment in her soul. When she closes her eyes, instead of the light of God she sees Rodrigo's blue and lifeless body; instead of warm comfort, she feels death's chilly breath.

What is she to do? She has brought this horror upon them. The fire in the older woman's eye should be directed at Isabel; she is to blame for everything. She ought to confess, but Michelle and Gina see only each other.

Like so many times before, Isabel has become invisible . . . but she should not be forgotten. May God have mercy, she should not.

• • •

Michelle blinks as surprise siphons the blood from her head. She knew Gina was furious, but could she really be so calculating?

She scrambles to her feet, leaning on the wall as she pushes herself up. "I think we should take a few minutes to calm ourselves," she says, lifting her voice to be heard above the rising wind. "You don't want to do this, Gina."

"Yes, I do." The redhead's voice rings with finality. "To protect my children, I have to kill yours."

"Not so fast." Michelle raises her hand, then brings it to her forehead as dozens of objections jostle and shove in her brain. Choosing the most obvious, she meets Gina's eye. "You know I didn't get pregnant on purpose. I had no idea Sonny was married."

"Maybe you should learn more about your men before you sleep with them."

"I thought I knew him, I thought I could trust him—" A surge of remorse catches Michelle unawares and blocks the words that have risen like a sob.

How could this have happened? Her relationship with Parker, a bond she had thought as strong as iron, is only an illusion. She had believed him when he said he cherished and adored her. She had felt herself blossom in his affection; she had allowed herself to soften to the point where she felt comfortable revealing her vulnerabilities.

She had told him about her work; he knew what Tilson Corporate Careers did and did not do.

She had almost told him about Bald Knob, her mother and her humiliations.

She had allowed him to plant a baby within her . . . and she had trusted him to be around when the child needed a father.

She looks away, holding one hand up like a shield, until her roiling emotions have calmed.

"You're right," she admits, meeting Gina's gaze as tears trickle from the corners of her eyes. "I should have known him better. I should have asked around before I went out with him. But I was flattered when he noticed me, and I was interested in his connections. He knew everyone, and I thought he'd be good for my business. So I went out with him . . . for selfish reasons, at first. Maybe I've been with him for selfish reasons all along."

A wry smile curls on Gina's lips. "So you're as big a fake as Sonny is."

"Maybe . . . I suppose I am." With that admission, the cool balm of relief assuages the rawness of Michelle's alarm. "You're so right, I am a fraud. It's been years since I've been completely honest with anybody."

She draws a deep breath and braces for the impact of a bullet, but instead hears a question: "What do you mean?"

She lifts her head to find Gina watching her, one brow arched. The gun is still pointed at Michelle's chest, but interest, not fury, fires those green eyes.

With a rueful smile, Michelle shakes her head. Why should she explain herself to this woman? Her plans to marry Parker have crumbled; the love of her life has proven to be no love at all. She is pregnant with a child who will demand her time and energy, yet she won't be able to walk away from her business as she'd hoped. If by some miracle Gina doesn't kill her and they escape this creaking box, she will still have to endure a breakup with Parker, raise his child, and deal with that dirt-seeking reporter, Greg Owens. . . .

But it felt good to admit her reasons for first going out with Parker, and she was planning to neutralize the reporter's threat with honesty. What better place to come clean than in this unlikely confessional?

She hauls her gaze from the floor and returns her attention to Gina. "When I first met Parker, I told him I was an executive headhunter, and that's what my business is supposed to be. A few months ago, I told him the rest of the story, about how we don't process even half the applications we accept. We charge large fees to write up résumés, then we send our clients to conventions and Web sites and job fairs where they can attract attention. The thing is, they could do all those things without our help."

Gina's pale face shows no more than mild interest, but her eyes remain alert as she leans one shoulder against the wall. "So you're running a scam. And Sonny knew it."

"It's not quite a scam, but I'm not what people think I am. Everyone in Tampa thinks I'm Michelle Tilson, an MBA from Harvard. Not even Parker knows that I'm really Shelly Tills from Bald Knob, West Virginia, and I never even went to college. All the academic credits on my résumé are . . . invented."

Michelle's heart is squeezed so tight she can barely draw breath, but she forces herself to make one final admission. "That's another reason I had to come up here today. A newspaper columnist has been snooping around the agency, so I came to get his file in order to make some legitimate inquiries on his behalf." She looks at Isabel, whose eyes are as wide and blank as bare windows. "Actually, none of that seems very important now."

An unexpected crash rocks the elevator, overpowering Michelle's last words. The car dips to the left, upsetting Gina's balance and triggering a frightened squeal from Isabel.

Michelle catches her balance and considers grabbing for the gun, but Gina might fire, accidentally or on purpose. Though the woman brims with understandable outrage, Michelle doesn't think she's a killer at heart.

When the car returns to a stable position, Gina braces herself against the wall while her gun hand wavers. "What was that?" she asks, her voice strangled.

Michelle glances toward the ceiling, then looks at the pistol. "I don't know," she says, "and as long as you're pointing that thing at me, I'm in no position to speculate. So if you're going to kill me, do it now."

Gina says nothing, but her eyes appear to be at risk of dropping out of her face.

"Why are you waiting?" Michelle spreads her hands and steps toward Gina, moving forward until the gun grazes the knot of sorrow at her middle. "Go ahead and shoot, Mrs. Rossman. I deserve to be punished and your kids deserve justice. If you kill me now, you'll spare me the trouble of riding out this hurricane."

Gina's squint tightens. Michelle is convinced the woman will shoot until a bloodcurdling scream cuts through the howling wind. She and Gina turn to Isabel, who dissolves in a torrent of tears.

"*Silencio!*" the girl shrieks, her hands against her ears. "I cannot listen—I cannot let you talk like this."

Gina stares at the housekeeper in dazed exasperation. "What is your problem?"

"How can I expect God to hear my prayers when I have done a terrible thing today? I cannot keep silent. Let me confess—let them put me on trial. They can even send me back to *México*—"

Gina waves the pistol in a dismissive gesture. "Will you shut up about Mexico? If you're married to an American citizen, they can't send you back."

"Wait a minute." Obeying a hunch, Michelle crouches before Isabel and peers into the girl's face. "What is this terrible thing you've done?"

Color drains from Isabel's complexion as she lowers her hands. "I was in Mr. Rossman's office."

A change comes over Gina's features, a sudden shock of realization. "What happened in Sonny's office?"

In the pale light of the emergency lamp, Isabel speaks in a barely audible whisper. "They will arrest me because of Mr. Rossman. Because he surprised me

and I did not want him to call security. Because I found
. . . this."

Isabel's hand drops to her sweater pocket, then with-draws a bracelet that shimmers with the light of a hundred stars. When Gina utters an oath, Isabel breaks into frantic sobs. "I didn't mean to take it! I was trying to clean up, so I picked up my dusting cloth, a paper on the floor and this. I was not thinking when I put this in my pocket. I have no use for it, I do not want it, I did not mean to take it. I would put it back if I could—I would have put it back when I went again to Mr. Rossman's office except I do not want to go there, not now. Not since what happened to him."

The unspoken implication strikes the center of Michelle's chest with the force of a blow. Gina must have experienced a similar response, because she slowly lowers the gun.

"You saw Parker this morning?" Michelle glances at Gina. "Today?"

Gina stares blandly at the cleaning woman, but a twitch of one eye reveals her anxiety. "What happened to Sonny?"

"*Señor* Rossman—" Isabel's voice breaks in a rattling gurgle "—this morning. I didn't mean to, but he caught me and I pushed him and now he is . . . *muerto*."

Gina's eyes blaze into Michelle's with an extraordinary expression of alarm. "*Muerto?*"

"Dead," Michelle answers. She sinks back to her corner as the housekeeper presses her hand to her mouth and yields to a deluge of hot and noisy tears.

• • •

"Who are you and what are you doing here?"

Speechless, Isabel dropped the bracelet. "*Señor* Rossman!"

After her fumbling fingers released the hook at her neck, the fur jacket slid from her shoulders as if it were relieved to be free of her. A flood of words bubbled from her lips as she tried to fold it properly. "*¡Lo siento!* I didn't mean to hurt anything."

The man strode toward the desk, his jaw set and his eyes narrow. "I'm calling security."

"Please, no, I am only the housekeeper, not a thief. I wasn't hurting anything."

The man would not listen; he was dialing the phone. He would call security and they would file a report with Mr. Jones, the custodial supervisor. Jones had no patience for mistakes; he would fire her. He might even report her to the police, the authorities. Isabel did not think she could be deported, but immigration laws were changing and her neighbors were terrified of the possibility. . . .

Her fingers fluttered to her chest when she remembered the attorney general. That powerful man had an office in this building. He would find out that she had been snooping in the offices. If he or one of his people clicked on their computers and discovered that she'd disappeared after coming from *México* with a belly full of cocaine, they would make her stand trial. She'd have to leave Rafael and Carlos. She would go to jail and news of her trial would reach Ernesto, who would come to America and find a way to kill her as he had killed Rodrigo.

Isabel trembled as terror blew down the back of her neck. Parker Rossman could not report her.

"No, *señor, por favor,*" she said, panic firing her veins. "Please, *un momento.*" She moved toward him, intending to kneel and beg for his pardon, but he turned with the phone still in his hand. Startled by his forward movement, she stumbled and fell against him, then saw him lift his arms as if he could not bear to touch someone so ill-mannered and vile.

Rossman took a hasty half step back, planting one foot on a sheet of paper that had fallen to the floor, then slipped and tumbled toward the window in a clumsy spraddle of arms and legs. Isabel retreated, watching in horror as his head hit the edge of the desk before he dropped the phone and collapsed on the floor.

She pressed her hand to her mouth, resisting the scream that clawed at her throat. In a moment Rossman would open his eyes and then he would be truly furious. If she ran, he would call the security officers to track her down. But she could not stand and do nothing while she waited for him to wake up.

She took three running steps toward the door, then hesitated at the threshold. What if he needed help? She could not leave an injured man alone. Perhaps his temper would cool if he found a cold compress on his head when he woke. He might not even remember what had happened.

After another quick glance at the man's motionless

form, she hurried to the bathroom and pulled a hand towel from the rack. She ran it through a stream of cold water, then squeezed out the excess liquid and crept to Parker Rossman's side.

The blood had faded from the man's face, leaving him pale against the brown carpet. She stood above him, transferring the wet towel from one hand to the other while she studied the businessman's waxy complexion, then bent low to listen for the quiet inhalation of breathing.

She heard nothing.

Biting her lip, she placed trembling fingers on the side of Rossman's neck. The flesh felt cold beneath her fingertips, and though she probed in several different places, she found no pulse.

She crossed herself and gulped back a sob. She was looking at a dead man.

4:00 P.M.

CHAPTER 22

Michelle sits perfectly still, her mind and body benumbed by Isabel's revelation. How could the man who kissed her last night be dead today?

"Are you sure?" She hears her voice ask the question, though the words seem to come from far away.

Isabel balls her hand into a fist. "*¡Sí!* He was *muerto*. I pushed him, he hit his head, he fell. He was not breathing and I will be arrested." She looks at her other hand, which is still holding the bracelet, then flings it across the car. "I wish I had never seen Mr. Rossman's office!"

Michelle turns to Gina, whose face has gone pale and slack. Her hands hang at her side, her fingers limp.

When the gun clatters to the floor, Gina doesn't seem to notice.

More concerned about the gun than about Isabel's hysteria, Michelle slowly extends her arm and hooks a finger around the trigger guard, then slides the weapon toward the wall. When she feels the impact of metal against metal, she removes her hand and leans back, covering the pistol with her body.

The redhead makes no attempt to retrieve the weapon, but looks down at Isabel with glassy eyes. "Sonny is dead," she says, a quaver in her voice. "How ironic is that?"

Michelle glances at Isabel, who cowers at the back of the car with her arms wrapped around her knees. For a hysterical woman, she's awfully quiet and grim.

"Why don't you sit down, Gina?" Michelle extends her hand. "You have to be worn out."

Gina stiffens at the suggestion, then takes an unsteady breath and collapses like a marionette whose strings have been cut. Looking at the woman, Michelle can't decide whether to pity or despise her.

Her mind skates away from that unsolvable dilemma. She looks again at the housekeeper and forces herself to smile. "Isabel, I'm sure you thought Parker was dead—"

"He is dead." The maid speaks in a flat, inflectionless tone and does not meet Michelle's eyes. "I know death when I see it."

Michelle looks at Gina, silently urging her to contradict the girl, but Gina has gone deathly pale.

As pale as a widow.

As pale as the lilies that covered Michelle's father's casket.

The image surprises her, steals her breath for a moment. She blinks the vision of the past away, then breathes in the truth: Isabel has no reason to lie. Parker is gone.

Though the elevator does not move, Michelle feels the floor shift beneath her body. She reaches out, bracing herself against the wall and the door, and closes her eyes until her equilibrium returns.

Her unborn child is already fatherless. Michelle only knew her daddy ten short years, but her child will not know Parker a single day.

How can she raise a child alone?

How can she live . . . without Parker?

She tunnels her hand through her hair and tries to grip this unexpected revelation. She needs time for herself, time to fit this awful news into the other truths she has learned today. Parker will never ask her to marry him. The man she has loved and misled has lied to her . . . and now he is gone.

How is she supposed to confront and confess to a dead man?

She turns to face the wall and drops her head to the

top of her bent knees. What has happened to her life? When the world can upend in a fraction of a minute, why should she care about anything?

Maybe a strong wind will blow in from the Gulf and rip the top off the Lark Tower. The destruction has obviously begun; whatever rocked the elevator a moment ago must have come from the roof or one of the upper floors. One quick snap, a sudden fall, and her troubles would be over. One brief life, lived on a false foundation.

Maybe she and the others are already as good as dead. Maybe these hours of entrapment have been a gift, a chance to review their lives and prepare for the inevitable. Parker didn't have that benefit—if the housekeeper's story is true, he didn't have an inkling of warning.

Surely death, like everything else, is easier to manage if you've prepared for it. Michelle hasn't thought much about the end of her life, hasn't made a will or funeral plans. How could she think about such things when her calendar was so filled with *living?*

Because I could not stop for Death, he kindly stopped for me. . . . Gina closes her eyes, trying to set the Dickinson poem aside, but it insists on replaying inside her head.

Sonny is dead. The man she has loved and lived with for more than twenty years is gone. She will never again hear his key in the lock, his footstep in the foyer or his voice on the phone. The clothes in the laundry room will never be worn again; the muddy sneakers on the back porch will have to be thrown out. The sweaters she picked up at Dillard's will never be a Christmas gift; the anger burning a hole in her heart will never be vented in his presence.

Her fury and hurt have been doused by a cold dash of reality, and she has been numbed by an unexpected and chilly paralysis.

Sonny is dead and she didn't kill him. The arms that once held her lie motionless upstairs; the lips that caressed her neck are silent, stilled by a quirk of fate and cruel happenstance.

She presses her hand to her mouth as her blood soars with unbidden memories: her hand on his shoulder as they drove for hours on their family vacation to Arizona, Sonny's pale face and trembling voice during their wedding ceremony, his tender care for her after Matthew's birth. The man had his flaws, but in the early years he had been a good father and a good husband. What came between him and his family?

Perhaps the business was to blame. The company demanded more of his time as time went by, and Gina's focus naturally shifted from the office to the children. Sonny worked longer hours with every passing year while Gina concentrated on the kids. Wasn't that what every wife did? Wasn't that her duty?

From a place far beyond logic and reason, she dredges up a reluctant admission: Her all-consuming love for her children might have made Sonny feel unappreciated. Sonny might have gone looking for love because he was starving for it.

She covers her eyes with her hand, shielding her soul from other prying gazes. *Why, Sonny, did you have to be so unbelievably needy? I loved you, you fool. I always will.*

Sonny is dead . . . and though she was angry enough to shoot him, until this moment she has never thought about living without him.

Tucked into her corner, Michelle has run out of illusions. Despite the shadows in this dimly lit car, the hard light of reality is blazing into every sector of her life. She is in this elevator, facing death, because she wanted to save her business from an investigation and convince her lover to marry her. Neither situation was worth dying for because neither situation was *honest.*

Her mind thumbs through the names and images of people she has loved, and she'd like to believe she'd give her life for any of them. But this is not an exchange of life for life; no profound statement will be made if she and Gina and Isabel check out in this elevator. People will say it was an unfortunate accident. Their deaths will have no more significance than a man who runs a red light and expires because he didn't want to be late for a dentist appointment.

Like Gina and Isabel, a few hours ago she ignored the threat of a hurricane and came to this building. She traded safety for an opportunity to save her career and deliver an ultimatum. She has gambled not only with her life, but with her unborn child's and for what? She'll find no payoff here. No reward.

Once she switched a set of price tags so she could walk out of Maxim's with treasures disguised as bargains. In the intervening years, has she sold her soul for bargains while undervaluing treasures?

Isabel, curled into the darkness at the back of the car, has never known wealth or success, but she has a beautiful son and a husband who adores her. Though she is as shy as a mouse, she has displayed remarkable courage in some dire situations . . . including this one.

Michelle looks at Gina, whose eyes and mouth are bracketed with deep lines of strain. "Isabel didn't mean to hurt him." She touches Gina's bent knee. It was an accident."

"What will I tell the kids?" A frown line eases between Gina's brows. "How in the world do I tell them their father died because a Mexican maid pushed him? None of this makes sense."

"Housekeeper," Michelle corrects her, recognizing a glimmer of hysteria in the way Gina's green eyes erase her. "Maybe life's not supposed to make sense . . . not today, anyway." She reaches behind her back, making sure the pistol is safely tucked away.

Gina has not completely detached; she notices the gesture. "Don't worry," she says, absently smoothing her hair behind her ears. "I've had my fill of death, haven't you?"

Michelle peers across the space between them, wondering if the woman's new passivity is genuine. Gina might be hoping to catch her off guard, but for what reason?

The redhead covers her mouth and sits without moving for a long moment, then lowers her head and fills the car with laughter that shifts to a hollow, broken sobbing. Michelle stirs uncomfortably, not knowing how to comfort the woman, but after a long moment Gina wipes her cheeks with the backs of her hands.

"I didn't know," she says when she catches her breath, "that I'd miss Sonny. I don't think I realized how much I'll miss him until a moment ago."

Michelle brings her knees to her chest and looks toward the closed doors. The widow is entitled to her hysterics and grief, but what is she supposed to do? If Parker had died yesterday, she would have mourned for him like a wife. She would have expected to sit in the front pew at his funeral, listening with damp eyes as his associates and friends talked about what a great guy he was and how generously he supported various charities. But that man, the honorable widower who fathered her child, was as false as her own facade.

If she dies in this elevator, who will mourn her? A few clients and employees will attend the memorial service and make perfunctory comments about Michelle Tilson, but no one will speak of Shelly Tills. No one, not even Lauren, knows her.

Perhaps it's time they made her acquaintance.

"I lied," Michelle says, and at the sound of those two words, Gina's blood runs cold.

The woman lied? About what? About Sonny?

She stares at the woman across the car until the brunette crosses her arms atop her bent knees. "I lied about my happiest moment," she says, the back of her head thumping against the elevator wall. "It didn't have a thing to do with hanging out my shingle. My real happiest moment happened a long time ago, back in my childhood. I think all my happiest moments took place when I was a kid."

Gina's throat is too constricted to speak, but apparently the Mexican girl is ready to carry her share of the conversation. "Does this . . . do you miss your *mamá?*"

Michelle blinks, then chuffs out a laugh. "Ha! My folks weren't exactly PTA material, but I spent a lot of weekends with my grandmother. She took me to church, and though I usually slept through the worship service, I remember leaning against her shoulder and watching the sunlight slant through the windows."

The woman's face bears an inward look; whatever she'd seen, she is seeing it again. "When the preacher said Jesus was the light of the world, I thought he lived in those sunbeams."

"Nice thought," Gina manages to croak. She glances at the maid, who is listening with rapt attention.

Michelle's eyes fill with a curious longing. "That church had these Kentucky Fried Chicken buckets they passed around right before the sermon. When Grandma said that putting money in the bucket was the way we gave to God, I couldn't understand what she meant. I mean, why would an invisible person need money? Then I heard the preacher mention something about burnt offerings, so I figured that after church the ushers took the money outside and burned it up. The smoke reached God in heaven, and everybody was happy. So I went home, took a ten-dollar bill from Grandma's purse, and burned it in the driveway. Needless to say, nobody was happy with me that day."

Silence fills the car until Isabel snorts and covers her mouth with her hand.

"You think that's funny?" Michelle peers at the maid over the top of her glasses. "I believed a lot of crazy things in my childhood. But I really wanted God to live in the sunlight because it was everywhere and covered everything." Her voice softens. "I guess I wanted an everywhere-God to take care of me."

Gina frowns, unable to understand the point of Michelle's story. What sort of church passes a paper bucket for donations? Probably one of those sects that handle snakes after the sermon, which is the last place she'd expect to find a woman who could attract Sonny Rossman.

She gives Michelle an unconvinced smile. "You don't seem like the church-going type."

Michelle brushes a hank of sweat-soaked hair from her forehead. "I'm not religious now. As a kid there were lots of times I wanted God's help and didn't get it, so I stopped going to church when my grandmother died. Still, I'll never forget that feeling of being safe and warm. Sometimes I think I'd do almost anything to feel that way again." She tips her head back and studies the ceiling. "Especially now."

• • •

Isabel presses her lips together and watches the two women at the front of the elevator. The wife is no longer crying, though her eyes are red and her chin still wobbles. The younger woman wears a blank face, but beneath the smooth surface Isabel can see a suggestion of movement and flowing, as though a hidden spring is trying to break through.

They must hate her. They are calm now, each woman grappling with her thoughts and feelings, but they will turn on her after they are rescued. The wife will tell the authorities that Isabel stole the bracelet and murdered her husband; the younger woman will say Isabel killed her unborn baby's father. The authorities will believe them, because they are rich and American, and they will take Isabel and lock her away forever.

She glances up at the ceiling, where the large opening looms overhead. If she could, she'd climb up to the roof and jump off the car. But she can't climb alone, nor can she push her way to the front and try to open the doors. The *gringas* guard the door, and they are strong. They will want her to pay for her crime, to die for murdering the rich American businessman.

The old feelings of terror surface in Isabel's consciousness; like a powerful rip current they pull her into the deep well of memory and loss. She lost Rodrigo because she tried to refuse Ernesto; she had to walk away from her mother because she did not heed *Mamá's* warning. And now, because she came to work when Carlos urged her to stay at home, she will lose him and Rafael. . . .

She eyes the dark line at the front of the elevator. The younger woman was not able to open the doors earlier, but she is not as strong as Isabel. If she applies all her strength, she might be able to break through the latch holding the doors together. She could jump into the lobby and roll backward, sparing Carlos and Rafael from all the terrible things that will happen once the world knows what she has done.

She bites her lip, then stands on wobbly legs, hesitating only an instant before rushing the doors. The younger *gringa* automatically moves her legs out of the way, but gasps when Isabel slides her fingers into the space between the bronze panels.

"What are you doing?"

Isabel doesn't answer. A gap as wide as her hand appears, but it will not widen. She keeps pulling, convinced she can break whatever is holding the doors in place, while Michelle continues to yell. "Isabel! Stop it!"

"She's snapped," the older woman says. "She's gone crazy."

Hands fall upon Isabel's shoulders, strong hands that tug her away from the front of the elevator and turn her around to face brown eyes that are troubled, compassionate and still. Isabel searches those eyes, looking for signs of condemnation, but finds only understanding.

Suddenly she is caught in an embrace, and she and Michelle are sinking to the floor in a flood of tears and whispered comforts.

When Isabel has calmed down, Michelle offers the girl another tissue from her purse, then folds her hands. "What were you trying to do?"

Isabel blows her nose, then crumples the tissue in her fist and lowers her gaze. "I don't know."

"I think I know," Michelle answers. "You wanted out—but what you had in mind is not the way out, Isabel. You heard what Eddie said."

Reluctantly, Isabel looks up. Michelle meets her gaze and smiles, determined to prove that she understands what neither of them wants to say.

"Listen—" she grips Isabel's hands "—when we get out of here, I will go with you to report what happened upstairs this morning."

Isabel swallows hard. "To report . . . don't they already know?"

"Why would they know?"

"Because of the computers. Ernesto told me that American offices and buildings are filled with computers and cameras that see and hear everything. He said they would watch me, that they would always see me, and it would only be a matter of time before the authorities found me and put me in prison."

Michelle listens with rising bewilderment. "Oh, Isabel, no! Those were lies, all lies! Yes, there are some cameras in this country, but you have nothing to fear. You were the victim of a criminal. If you tell the police what happened and how they can find Ernesto, they'll probably give you a medal. They will keep you safe."

Isabel's eyes widen. "I cannot go to the police. I am too afraid—I am a coward. They will see my tears and know I have done something terrible—"

You are not a coward." Michelle squeezes Isabel's hands with each word. "Were you a coward when you hid from the drug dealers in the airport? Even if you were afraid, Isabel, you did the right thing and that takes courage." She smiles, finding comfort in her own advice. "I think you may be the bravest woman I know."

Isabel pulls away, murmuring something about getting some rest, and Michelle allows her to go. From her corner, Gina says nothing, but sits with her knees bent and her hands over her face. Michelle can't tell if the woman is mourning her husband or exulting in his demise.

She leans against the wall and closes her eyes. A wave of pity threatens to engulf her, but she pushes it back.

She will not feel sorry for herself or her baby. Instead, she will take the advice she offered Isabel—starting today, she will live an honest life. She will come clean about her past and when this ordeal is over, she will go through her accounts and offer a refund to any client who was not happy with the performance of Tilson Corporate Careers.

A new life waits outside this elevator . . . if she can claim it. She shivers as a gust blows down the shaft, bringing a touch of rain in its breath.

"More windows have blown out," Gina says, wiping

moisture from her face. "The outer offices must be totally ruined." She picks up the diamond bracelet, a shining jumble on the floor, and absently drapes it over her wrist. "So much for the perk of having an office with a view."

Michelle turns toward Isabel. "Would you turn on the radio? Just for a minute, so we can hear what's happening out there."

Isabel smoothes her wet hair, then pulls the pink CD player from her pocket and slides the earbuds into her ears. After turning the dial she halts, her eyes focusing on nothing as she listens with an intent expression on her face.

"The man says Felix is seventy-five miles away. Waves are high, the bay bridges are underwater." Concern and confusion mingle in her eyes. "How can the bridges be under water? The hurricane is not yet here."

"Storm surge," Michelle explains. "The wind pushes waves ahead of the hurricane, so the inland waterways fill up and overflow. I know they were worried about—"

"MacDill Air Force Base," Isabel interrupts, lifting her hand, "is almost underwater. The barrier islands are submerged. Pinellas County is an island."

Michelle meets Gina's wide eyes. More than nine hundred thousand people live on the Pinellas peninsula. Thousands of the residents are retirees who've come to Florida to enjoy mild winters and escape a state income tax.

Eddie Vaughn, Michelle remembers, lived in Pinellas

County. If he hadn't come to rescue them, he'd be safe, but now he's at the bottom of the shaft and his poor dog is roaming through a dangerous building.

"Never," Gina whispers, her hand at her throat. "I've lived here all my life and never expected anything like this to happen."

"In downtown Tampa," Isabel continues, a thread of panic in her voice, "water is over the seawalls and in the streets. No cars can get in, no rescue trucks—"

"So no help is coming." Gina hugs her knees, then lets her head fall against the wall. "We're going to be here for a while. Several days, probably. Maybe forever."

Michelle rests her hand on Isabel's arm. "Maybe you should turn the radio off so we can save the battery."

Gina looks at Michelle with eyes that have dulled under a film of indifference. "What does it matter? You were foolish to hope your mechanic could get us out. If we're lucky and the storm doesn't snap the cables holding us up, it'll be days before we're rescued. If we're rescued."

"We're going to be okay," Michelle insists, struggling to resist the spirit of pessimism that has invaded the car. "We have to keep our spirits up."

Gina folds her hands in a pose of weary dignity. " 'Because I could not stop for Death, he kindly stopped for me; the carriage held but just ourselves and Immortality.' "

Michelle listens through a vague sense of unreality. Gina has given up. The fiery, determined woman who wasn't afraid to threaten her husband like Dirty Harry no longer cares if she lives or dies.

She must have loved him and his faults . . . which is more than Michelle can say about Parker.

Michelle glances at Isabel, then gives Gina a grim smile. "Thanks for the poetic moment, but I'm not ready to die today. I'm not going to sit here and hope somebody comes to rescue us."

Isabel lifts her head. "What are you going to do?"

"I'm not sure," Michelle says, standing. "But you know what? Eddie Vaughn gave his life to save ours, so I can't ignore his sacrifice. I'm not dying today."

CHAPTER 23

Her eyes are brown, the shade of milk chocolate. Eddie notices the color despite the shadows around that perfect face, probably because those eyes are smiling up at him as if he just finished hanging the moon.

"We're snug," she says, the corners of her mouth lifting. "Snug as bugs in a rug."

Heaven help him, he's smiling, too. Not a good thing to do, no sir, not today, maybe not ever. He hasn't time to smile at brown-eyed women today, no matter how appealing they might be, because he has to do something important . . . but what was it?

He lifts his heavy eyelids and blinks, then stares into darkness and tries to grip something solid in this sea of confusion. He inhales, then winces as a stabbing pain attacks his rib cage. He is lying on his right side atop something solid, something hard. He raises his left arm and moves it in an arc, then his fingers encounter a metal beam behind his body. It is smooth and square, cold and wet beneath his fingertips.

A crosshead. He's on a rain-spattered elevator, so the ridge beneath his right elbow must be the handle of a hatch cover.

How in the world did he land here?

His senses are slowly recovering, but anxiety runs at the front of the pack. Forcing himself to be calm, he retraces his steps: he had driven to Tampa, climbed stairs and found the elevator. He'd climbed onto the roof and opened the cover; he'd tossed his harness down to the women (stupid move!). They'd heard a noise and he'd stood to check things out. And then—

The wind. A maelstrom had roared across the landing, tossing chairs and plants and prying pictures from the walls.

His breath catches in his lungs. He's been blown down the shaft.

Eddie presses his hand to his forehead as comprehension seeps through his shock. He's alive. He's on the top of an elevator cab. So the missile that knocked him from his perch must have pushed him aside, allowing him to fall onto the adjacent car.

He takes another deep breath, winces at another stab in the chest. Broken ribs, probably. Maybe a concussion, too. He wriggles his fingers, feels both hands respond. His left arm is mobile, so he reaches for the sturdy beam of the crosshead and wraps his arm around it.

So far, so good. He bites his lower lip and struggles to pull himself up. Pain strikes his midsection, sending a shower of needles through his gut, but he doesn't stop until he is leaning against the cross beam and his lip tastes of blood.

He steels himself for the pain at his ribs, then gulps air into his lungs. He needs oxygen; he needs to think. The elevators in this shaft are express cars; they only open to the lower parking levels and the upper floors. If he can stand—

"Arrrrgh!" He lowers his hand to his right leg as pain rips along his calf and slices at his knee. His nerve endings are snapping at each other, an unrivaled agony that resulted from the simple act of trying to turn his foot.

Okay, then, he'll sit for a while. He grits his teeth. A broken leg bone—the tibia, if his memory can be trusted—is not so good when a man is facing a walk of a thousand stairs, but at least he has the use of both arms.

He props his left elbow on the crosshead and peers upward. Nothing but thick darkness above and to the left, but a thin gray gleam to the right.

Many feet up and to the right.

He sags against the steel beam as reality crashes into his consciousness. He'd been working with the women near the twenty-eighth floor. The first openings in the express shafts are on the twenty-fifth. Which means he fell at least thirty feet, maybe more.

Please, God, don't let it be more than that.

Taking care not to move his right leg any more than necessary, Eddie grips the crosshead with both hands and faces the front of the car, then waits for his eyes to adjust to the darkness.

Is that a door in the wall? He blinks, then leans forward until the pressure proves too much for his injured ribs. He can see a rectangular shape, so perhaps this is the twenty-fifth-floor landing.

Stepping over the crosshead would ordinarily be a simple matter, but he can't risk the maneuver with a broken leg. Summoning all his strength, Eddie ducks under the wide beam and drags himself toward the front of the car. On his belly, he spits dust from his lips—somebody's not keeping their cars clean—and crawls forward. Pain rises inside him like a wave, sending streamers of agony in every direction, but he perseveres until he's within reach of the dark rectangle.

The surface is rough beneath his fingers, not smooth. Concrete, not metal. The shadows have played tricks on him.

Gasping, he rolls onto his back and stares up at the concrete slab, part of the shaft that entombs him. He clamps his jaw against the insistent pain while his breath comes through his nostrils with a faint whistling sound.

"Get a grip, Ed. Sadie's waiting for you." Ms. Brown Eyes is waiting, too, but he can't say that aloud, not even here. He wipes perspiration from his forehead with the heel of his hand, then forces himself to focus.

The power is still off. He can't rappel down without a line and harness, and he can't cut through the wall without tools. He can't manually pick the elevator brake because it's in the machine room on the roof of the building, which, in his current condition, is about as reachable as Saturn. He could slide down the cables . . . no, he couldn't. Not without gloves, and not in his condition.

He groans and sits up, then reaches under the crosshead to the emergency hatch, where the thick dust is damp with a layer of his sweat. He could open the exit cover, lower himself into this car, and try to use the phone, but what good would that do? He's probably the only elevator tech working in a three-county radius. And if he enters this cab, he'll be as trapped as the women . . . without anyone to help him out.

The idea persists until he realizes that a drop would force him to land on an already-broken bone. That thought, combined with the pain blazing a trail down the length of his leg, is enough to make him lie back on the rooftop and close his eyes.

Maybe he has finally finished paying for his mistakes.

Michelle feels the expectant pressure of the others' eyes as she examines the opening in the ceiling. "I know none of us wants to think about Eddie right now," she says, dropping her hands to her hips, "but he came out and made a way for us to escape. I think we ought to try and take it."

Isabel gapes at her while Gina laughs. "You want us to climb up to the roof? How are we supposed to do that?"

"The same way we were going to climb up when Eddie was here. Look." She bends and scoops up the tangled harness. "This is still attached to something up there, so you can't fall if you put it on. Two of us will boost one up—that one will wait on the roof and help the second one. Then we'll lower the harness again and the two of us will pull the third one up and out."

Gina closes her eyes so tightly her face seems about to fold in on itself. "I'm not getting on top of this car. We all know what happened to that man, and conditions are even worse now."

"Eddie was caught by surprise," Michelle says. "We'll know to hang on. Sure, the wind's blowing, but everything that can fly through those doors is probably long gone."

"What about the roof?" Gina interrupts. "The roof is blowing off, and who knows what will fall down this shaft."

Michelle ignores Gina and gives Isabel a bright smile. "We'll climb out, we'll hang on to each other, and we'll go to the stairwell, like Eddie said. We can ride out the storm there."

Gina refuses to open her eyes, but a faint line appears between Isabel's brows. "You think we will be okay?"

Michelle softens her voice. "I don't know anything for sure. But I don't think we can be comfortable here without food or water, and Gina's right about the roof being vulnerable. The cables might hold the elevator, but they might not. Besides—" she smiles "—I would appreciate access to a bathroom. So I'm climbing out."

Isabel glances at Gina, then shakes her head. "I am not sure."

"What a fool," Gina whispers. She opens her eyes and jerks her chin toward the ceiling. "What if the power comes back on while you're walking around on the top of this thing?"

"Eddie said the car wouldn't move as long as the cover's off the hatch." Michelle picks up the harness and tries to make sense of the loops. "How do you get into this getup?"

"You should stay put." Gina crosses her arms. "That's what I tell my kids—if you're lost, frightened or in trouble, get someplace safe and stay put."

"You think this car is safe?" Michelle lowers the harness and meets Gina's gaze head-on. "Look, I know this has been a day none of us will want to remember. I know we're upset because Parker and Eddie are dead and we're probably alone in this building. But before we lost him, Eddie said the way out was through that opening in the ceiling. I choose to believe he knew what he was talking about."

Gina's brows rise, graceful wings of scorn. "You'd trust a man who couldn't even save himself?"

"Absolutely." Michelle bends to pick up her purse, then glances over her shoulder. "Isabel, last chance. Are you coming with me?"

The cleaning woman's face clouds with worry, then she nods. "*Sí*. I must think of Carlos and Rafael."

"If you love them, you'll stay put." Gina's creditable attempt at confidence is marred only by the unsteadiness of her voice. "Someone will come to rescue us eventually. By now my kids have realized that Sonny and I are missing. They'll call someone to find us as soon as the roads are passable again." She reaches for Isabel's arm and clings to it with surprising desperation. "Sonny and I are important people. The authorities will come for us right away."

Isabel glances from Gina to Michelle, then lifts her gaze to the opening that leads to freedom. "I am going up."

When Gina's lower lip quivers, her fear becomes visible—brittle in her cheekbones and haunting in her eyes. Michelle stares at the woman across the car and realizes that Parker's wife is terrified of being left alone. She is hard, but she is not strong. Not without her husband.

"Gina—" Michelle softens her voice "—would you please reconsider?"

Despite her fear, Gina has apparently withdrawn into a place no one can reach. "I'm not moving," she says, crossing her arms. "I'm staying here . . . where I know I'll be safe."

Michelle swallows hard. "Will you at least help us out?"

The redhead hesitates only a moment, then she pushes herself up from the floor. "Let it be noted," she says, woodenly stepping to Isabel's side, "that I predicted you would kill yourselves within the hour."

Eddie opens his eyes. He's not dead . . . so he must not have outlived his expiration date.

"Why not?" he asks the darkness. "Why not take me now? This storm is probably going to usher a lot of people into eternity, so why not add me to the guest list? You haven't left me with a lot of other options."

He listens, but hears only the sound of the bawling wind and the flutter of debris outside the shaft.

So. . .the Almighty is going to hold his tongue today. This is going to be one of those work-it-out ventures. One of those experiences his grandfather would have called *soul-strengthening*—

Eddie groans and brings his hand to his forehead. At this moment, his soul needs strengthening about as much as a pig needs a manicure. What he needs is a way out and the strength to rescue the women whose quandary brought him to this place.

Because gray light is coming through the open doors at the twenty-eighth floor, his eyes adjust to the gloom. The thin light outlines the women's car first, then touches the back wall before creeping almost imperceptibly across the hoistway. There it blends with the murk of the yawning shaft overhead and submits to the greater darkness of the depths.

But it is enough. Eddie draws a deep breath and stares at the rail at the side of the car. The vertical beam, which runs from the basement to the building's highest floor, is one of a pair designed to steady the elevator cab. With its twin, located on the opposite side of the car, the rail prevents any horizontal movement. A divider beam near every landing extends from the front wall to the back, anchoring the rails.

He's never climbed up a rail before, but he's heard stories of other elevator mechanics who were forced to scale them in order to escape a hoistway. In none of those daring tales, however, were any of the heroes suffering from cracked ribs and a broken leg.

Eddie wipes the dust and moisture from his palms, then grips the vertical steel beam at his side. He can't remember the last time he tried to do pull-ups, but he figures he can do at least thirty before his arms give out. If necessary, he can pause to catch his breath on the horizontal divider beams positioned about every ten feet throughout the shaft.

If he can climb thirty feet, he can reach the narrow divider beam at the twenty-fifth floor. From there he can cross the steel rail and reach the hoistway sill, where he can stand on tiptoe and cling to the wall while he unlocks the doors.

Theoretically, it's a credible plan. Any Olympic gymnast could manage it.

Eddie tugs on the beam, then struggles to get his good leg under his weight. He manages to place his left foot squarely on the cab, but when he strains to pull himself up, the broken bone of his right leg scrapes across the bent edge of the crosshead at the center of the car.

He cries out in dazzled agony as a flashbulb explodes behind his eyes. His strength fails as his body sings with pain, then he folds gently at the waist and crumples onto the dusty rooftop, letting the darkness claim him.

Gina runs her hand down her throat as she watches Michelle slip into the nylon harness. Though it's a hard truth to admit, she can now see why Sonny desired the younger woman. Michelle tackles challenges with capable confidence, yet she disarms people with friendliness. This beautiful young woman must have swept Sonny off his feet, binding him to her with smiles and laughter and an absolute refusal to make demands.

When he was with her, he must have felt as free as an eagle.

Yet Gina knows her husband, and, given complete information, she has always been able to predict his behavior. If Michelle had told him about the baby and insisted that he marry her, he would have refused. He would have broken off the relationship, and probably come clean about his existing marriage.

So perhaps this elevator mishap has been a mercy. Now Michelle will never have to know the sting of Sonny's rejection or the pain of his betrayal. And though earlier Gina told the woman that Sonny would never accept another child, now she would like to recall those words. Not for Sonny's sake . . . but for Michelle's.

Sonny Rossman was a lout . . . but he was also much loved. In fact, some still-functioning part of Gina's brain marvels that his mistress could even think about climbing out of this elevator to rejoin the world. She ought to be bowed with grief and stunned by loss.

She couldn't have loved him, not really. If she had, she wouldn't be able to imagine a world without Sonny.

Michelle snaps the buckle across her chest, then tugs on the line that dangles through the opening. "Okay, it's secure." She absently pats the pockets of her jeans, then her gaze falls on her purse. She crouches, pulls out the cell phone and her keys, and slips them into her pockets. "I guess I'm ready."

Gina bends her knees and catches a breath as Michelle places a sneakered foot in her locked hands. Isabel whispers something in Spanish—a prayer?— while Michelle leans on their shoulders.

"Okay," she says. "I know this is the hard part, but I need you to straighten and lift me as high as you can. I don't think I'm strong enough to pull myself up other-wise."

Gina catches Isabel's eye. "Ready?"

The maid nods and Gina counts: "One, two, three!" They stand and launch Michelle upward. The effort requires less strength than Gina imagined, and she blinks when Michelle catches something beyond the opening and pulls herself onto the top of the car.

Gina steps back, impressed. The girl is stronger than she looks.

"Wow," Michelle calls, her voice like an echo from an empty tomb. "It's creepy up here. And dirty." She dusts her hands, then looks down at Isabel. "Want me to give you the harness?"

Isabel considers the question, then shakes her head. Apparently she'd rather fall than repeat her previous experience.

Gina retreats to her corner by the door. Those two young women have more energy than brains. They may climb out of the shaft, but this is a tall building and at any corner they could be blindsided by a piece of flying shrapnel or accosted by a crazed homeless person. She, on the other hand, might spend another forty-eight hours in this car, but she'll be safe when the hurricane is over. When power is restored she'll ride the elevator to wherever it lands, then step onto a solid structure, alive and well.

But alone.

A new sound catches her ear, a hum that seems to come from overhead. She frowns. "You hear that?"

Beside her, Isabel stiffens. "The wind?"

"I don't think so."

From somewhere above them, Michelle calls, "Hang on. I see a toolbox—"

The overhead lights come on, blinding Gina with sudden brightness, but though she can hear the sounds of movement in the shaft, their car does not rise. She reaches for the railing, bracing for a delayed reaction, but the elevator refuses to budge.

She looks toward the escape hatch, which looks far less promising in the light. Of course! The mechanic said the elevator wouldn't move if the hatch—

Before she can finish her thought, darkness over-takes the car again. An instant later, the emergency light flickers and begins to glow.

The bulb, however, seems less bright than before. Is it dying, too?

5:00 P.M.

CHAPTER 24

Eddie dreams of bees. They surround him in an angry swarm, stinging his chest, his leg and his ankles as they carry him off. He feels the breath of movement on his face and swats at the buzzing creatures, but not until he strikes his breastbone does a dart of pain bring him back to reality.

He's still on the elevator, and it's moving. Startled, he reaches for the solidity of the crosshead, then he laughs, not at all surprised to hear a note of hysteria in his voice.

Whoever decided to bury Tampa's downtown power lines deserves a medal. Despite the fury of this storm, electricity is flowing and the elevator is descending. After so many outages, the controller has undoubtedly lost its awareness of the cab's position so, like the others, this cab will descend to the lobby to reestablish the connection.

Eddie's laughter halts as suddenly as the elevator. The electric hum ceases, the car stops, and the brakes clamp down, holding the car firmly in position. Eddie pushes himself up and studies the front wall of the shaft. His brief ride carried him in the wrong direction, so now he'll have to climb sixty feet, not thirty.

But he will climb . . . because apparently his arms, legs and soul need a vigorous workout.

Before turning again to the rail, he leans across the car and hits the Stop button—no sense in risking any further movement of the car. He reaches for the guide rail with both arms and pulls himself upright, ignoring the shaft of pain that rips through his wounded leg. Hopping on his left foot, he swipes his damp hands on his jeans, then grips the rail again.

"I'm comin', Sades."

He lifts his gaze to the horizontal divider beam a few feet above his head and pulls himself upward. His broken tibia protests, but he braces himself against the pain and tries to remember how good it felt to finally reach the top of the rope in his middle-school gymnasium.

Ten strong pulls should take him to the first resting place in this concrete crypt. Ten individual efforts, then he can swing his good leg onto the beam. The broken bone will hurt like a mule's kick every time it strikes the rail, but at least he'll be able to use the muscles of his thigh on the climb. And his ribs—well, he has to breathe. His lungs will have to withstand the pain.

He climbs until the muscles of his arms and thighs burn, then he reaches the divider beam. His ribs stab at his lungs with every gasping breath, but he manages to shift his weight to his good leg and cling to the vertical rail with one hand, allowing the other arm to rest.

Despite the warm humidity of the shaft, a chilling thought threatens to freeze his scalp to his skull. This climb may be the most difficult ordeal of his life. Once he reaches the twenty-fifth floor, he will have to maneuver along a horizontal beam crowded with vertical hoistway ducts. It'd be a tricky maneuver under the best of circumstances, but he'll be exhausted, wounded and wet from the trickle of rainwater that persists in falling from above.

Eddie closes his eyes and lets his forehead fall to the steel in front of his face. It'd be so easy to let go. A quick plunge down the shaft would bring an end to this agony and might even earn him some kind of posthumous award for service beyond the call of duty. A plunge to the bottom of the shaft would end everything—his regrets about his marriage, his guilt about Panama City and his doubts about the future.

But this life . . . is not his to throw away. He didn't create it, and despite a desperate willingness to hand it back, he's still here.

The drowned boy, the women in the elevator, even himself . . . how presumptuous to think he could wield the power of life or death over any of them.

He can only commit to his present task and do the best he can. The Creator of life, and storms, and seas, will have to do the rest.

So he won't give up. Sadie's out there waiting for him, along with three women who shouldn't be in the building, but are. Because one of them looked up at him with trust and confidence shining in her eyes, he will keep climbing.

Maybe she needs her soul strengthened, too.

Michelle is trying to untangle the lanyard from a beam at the top of the car when a new sound causes her to freeze—could that be the whoosh and hum of a moving elevator? Beneath her, the car brightens and for an instant her soul floods with hope, then she remembers what Eddie said: as long as the escape hatch remains open, their car isn't going anywhere.

When the lights go out and the electrical hum fades into the hurricane howl, she leans toward the opening in the roof. "Isabel? You ready?"

The corners of the housekeeper's mouth are tight, but she nods and moves beneath the hatch. She shoots a timid glance at Gina, who stands next to the elevator panel, the emergency light sparking in her red hair.

"Gina, if you can boost Isabel to the railing, it'll support her weight until I can pull her up."

When the redhead compresses her mouth into a thin line, Michelle is afraid the woman will refuse to help. She has no real reason to balk, but no one wants to be left alone.

But Gina squares her shoulders and moves forward, bending her knees as she laces her fingers together. "I still think you're making a mistake," she says.

A flicker of uncertainty creeps into Isabel's expression, but she places one foot into Gina's linked hands.

"This is going to be a little tricky, but we can do it," Michelle says, straddling the sturdy crossbeam. In front of her dangle a half dozen cables as thick as a man's fingers. The hatch lies to her right, but to her left, a pair of open doors lead to the twenty-eighth floor and freedom.

Eddie's pet, she realizes with mixed feelings, has apparently given up its vigil at the doorway. Though Michelle has never had a single sympathetic feeling for a canine, she finds herself admiring the dog. The animal has exhibited more courage than she has, because she can't bring herself to look down the shaft that claimed Eddie.

With the lanyard and one leg hooked around the cross-beam, she bends at the waist and extends her right arm into the opening. "Ready when you are."

Isabel nods, her countenance immobile, and Gina yells, "Now!" Isabel stretches upward; Michelle clasps the girl's wrist and Gina staggers beneath the cleaning woman's weight. Michelle pulls, straining until nearly every bone in her body feels out of joint.

Somehow, Isabel gets both arms out of the car and braces them on the edge of the hatch. Michelle helps the girl hoist one leg onto the roof, then Isabel rolls against the center beam and stares up at the collection of cables that stretch into the darkness like some kind of industrial-age beanstalk.

The girl's eyes are wet when they meet Michelle's.

"Muchas gracias."

"Don't thank me yet." Michelle steps over the housekeeper and peers at Gina, who has retreated to the pool of light cast by the emergency bulb. "Won't you come? You're thin—the two of us can pull you out."

Gina edges closer to the control panel. "I'm not breaking my neck up there."

"But Eddie was right—it's only a small step down to the landing. After all this, getting to the stairwell will be a cakewalk."

For a brief instant Gina's face seems to open. Michelle sees uncertainty, a quick flicker of fear, then the return of stubborn inflexibility. "I'm staying," Gina says. "I'm safe here."

"You're in a box hanging by a few cables. You know that rocking we felt? There are rails out here, and one of them is bent. That's why this car's not stable."

"Maybe I'm used to this car." A smile spooks over the woman's lips, fading almost as soon as it appears. She jerks her chin upward. "You girls go ahead and fight the wind and rain. Get smacked around by debris. Take your chances with looters. I'll be fine, and heaven help anyone who tries to bother me."

The comment makes no sense until Michelle glances at Gina's hand. She's holding the gun, which shines dully next to the glitter of the diamond bracelet.

"Michelle? Look!"

Michelle turns toward Isabel, who has stepped closer to the landing. Eddie's dog, a white-muzzled golden retriever, is standing near the open doorway, her nails clicking on the threshold as she covers Isabel's bare knees with kisses.

It's a beast, but it looks friendly. More important, the beast was Eddie's.

"Keep it away from the shaft," she calls. "I'll be with you in a minute."

Michelle leans down to give Gina one last chance. "Are you sure you won't come with us?"

"Quite sure."

"Have it your way, then. If we make it down first, we'll send someone up to help you."

"I doubt I'll need your assistance, but thank you, all the same. Now, would you please close that hatch? When the power comes on, I want this car to move."

"Whatever you say." Michelle touches her forehead in a mock salute, then lifts the hinged cover and drops it back into place.

With Gina's words ringing in her ears, Michelle steps over the center beam and picks up the flashlight Eddie left beside his toolbox. She is about to duck under the edge of the doorway and step onto the landing when she hears a cry—a sound that is definitely human.

Eddie?

A thin blade of foreboding slices into her heart as she turns to face the darkness of the shaft. Is Eddie in agony somewhere below? She can't bear the thought of his suffering, but she's no nurse and she has no way to reach him. Still, she can't leave him alone, not after what he did for them.

"Eddie?" She wipes her damp hand on her jeans, then clings to the sturdy beam on the top of the car and shines the flashlight over the sides. The back wall is only a few feet away, but the shaft is wider than she expected, with darkness stretching to the left and right. "Eddie, is that you?"

The frenzied wind screeches an answer, punctuated by pounding rain, and then, barely audible, she hears another reply that sounds like *hello.* . . .

"Eddie?"

From a distance, a weary and broken voice: "Still here."

A flush of relief rises to Michelle's face. "Are you all right?"

She strains to hear a ripple of broken laughter. "I've been better . . . but I'm still hanging around."

For a moment, she cannot speak. She presses her hand to her chest and feels her heart thump against her palm. This situation is not hopeless. Against all odds, Eddie Vaughn is alive.

Somehow, Someone has seen them and answered Isabel's prayers.

She shines the flashlight into the open space. "Can you tell me where you are?"

The incessant roar of the storm obscures his reply, but it is enough to know he is alive. Michelle feels suddenly light on her feet, as if she could fly down the stairs without any effort at all.

"Eddie—" she releases the crossbeam to cup a hand around her mouth "—Isabel and I are out of the elevator. We're heading to the stairwell. We'll look for you, okay?"

She listens intently as the building stretches and groans. "Eddie?"

No answer, but a roaring bedlam rips through the air, freezing Michelle's skin like the howl of a banshee. Despite her relief at Eddie's survival, the voice of the storm reminds her they are not safe yet.

Before joining Isabel at the landing, she stares into the darkness one last time and, emboldened by the girl's example, whispers a prayer for Eddie Vaughn.

At first, Eddie thought he was hearing angels. His grandmother, according to family legend, sat straight up on her deathbed, stared at the red-and-white flowered curtains, and announced that angels had arrived on a golden ladder, so she was ready to go home. Then she lay down, closed her eyes and committed her soul to Jesus.

The voice he'd heard, however, belonged to one of the women. He wasn't sure which woman had called to him, but he definitely had his preferences. Her high voice had cut through the noise of the storm, but he wasn't sure she'd heard his replies.

He clings to a vertical rail and smiles, glad to know at least two of them are out of the elevator. If he doesn't climb another foot, the results will have been worth the struggle.

He draws a deep breath, peers into the inky darkness below, then lifts his face to the upper portion of the shaft. Rainwater is falling more steadily now, so the wind has definitely taken out a few more windows.

Might as well climb while he still can.

• • •

Though Felix is officially still two hours away, the wind has already uprooted a landscape of carpet and smashed the window at the end of the landing. Michelle feels its blows to the side of her head as she crunches shards beneath her sneakers and maneuvers around a pair of toppled chairs that have blown into the center of the hallway.

The stairwell has to be right around the corner. She yells at Isabel, urging her to follow, but the wind snatches her words and leaves her as silent as a mime. She makes a come-on gesture and runs, hoping the housekeeper will follow.

She turns the corner and skids to a halt on the wet floor. A soft-drink machine, dark and without power, lies on its side in front of the door that leads to the stairs. Michelle stares stupidly until she feels a nudge on her arm. Isabel stands beside her, her wet hair plastered to her face, her eyes as wide as platters. Gooseflesh has prickled her arms and a trickle of blood runs from her lip. "What do we do?"

The wind catches Isabel's words, too, but Michelle understands her meaning. She makes a shoving motion, then pushes at the vending machine, but her strength is no match for its weight. Even in the trailer park, when kids routinely rocked the machines in a search for spare quarters, she had never been able to budge the behemoths.

She looks around and in a barely comprehendible flash she realizes that rain is falling in the hallway.

These slashing raindrops aren't coming from the sky, however; they're falling horizontally and coming from an open window.

But this is not the time to marvel at Mother Nature. She pushes wet hair out of her eyes and flinches when something touches her leg. The dog, its fur tufted and dripping, has crept to her side.

Ignoring the animal, she yells above the ripping wind. "Do you see anything we can use to push this out of the way?"

Isabel glances over her shoulder, where a potted ficus has begun to scoot over the wet carpet. She holds up a finger, then lowers her head and runs toward an unmarked door. Taking a clutch of keys from a pocket of her sweater, she unlocks the lock.

Michelle smiles as understanding dawns. A custodial closet might have tools. Isabel appears a moment later, a mop in one hand and a broom in the other. For an insane instant Michelle is afraid the woman wants to clean the hallway, then she realizes that the industrial mop and broom are mounted on steel poles.

The girl is brilliant.

Michelle sets the flashlight on top of the soda machine, then takes the broom from Isabel and insinuates the tip of the pole into the gap between the vending machine and the door to the stairwell. Beside her, Isabel does the same thing with the mop, then both women brace their poles against the edge of the machine and push. Michelle's broom slips on the wet surface, but Isabel's mop finds purchase, enough to slide the vending machine forward an inch.

Michelle twirls her finger in the air. "Change positions!"

Approaching the machine from the side, the women again shove the handles of their tools between the heavy metal box and the door frame, then they push again. The steel poles groan and their veneers of paint crack and flake away, but the machine slides over the wet rug until the edge encounters a clump of carpeting.

Michelle drops her broom, pleased to see that they've created a passageway large enough for them to squeeze through. She motions Isabel forward, then she claps for the dog. The animal crouches on all fours and barks, refusing to follow.

Isabel shouts from the doorway, but Michelle can't understand what she's saying. She creeps closer to the dog. "Come on, pup, we need to go now."

The dog continues to bark, its big feet splashing the wet carpet in some strange doggy dance. Michelle chews her lip. She can't do this. She doesn't like dogs; she's never had one; she doesn't speak their language. How can she help the animal if it won't come when she calls?

She turns, about to follow Isabel, but the retriever's frantic barking pricks at her conscience. She can't leave Eddie's pet. If he cared so much for this creature that he wouldn't leave it alone with the storm approaching, she can't abandon it in a dangerous skyscraper with the worst weather yet to come.

Despite the blood pounding in her ears, she kneels on the carpet and tries to hold the dog's attention. "Come on, nice puppy. Come with me and we'll get you out of this wind and rain."

The dog looks at her, then runs in a tight circle before stopping to bark again. The sound arouses a memory that swims up through the years. *Dogs know when you're scared of 'em. When they smell your fear, they'll attack 'cause they know they can take you down.*

CHAPTER 25

Sweat pours from Eddie's face as he pulls himself upward, then swings his left foot onto the horizontal beam across from the twenty-fifth floor. He stops to catch his breath, then eyes the vertical duct that stands between him and the landing doors.

What's the old saying? So close, and yet so far away. If not for the vertical duct, he could sit on the horizontal divider beam and slide toward the doors, letting his broken leg hang free. Standing would be a challenge, but what's one more?

Rain—or sweat—runs a trickling finger down the back of his neck as Eddie pulls in several quick breaths. Along with the pain of his injured ribs, a sludge of nausea churns in his belly. He can't look down. His eyes cling to the duct as he pulls his weight onto his arms and swings his good leg toward the landing. There! Because he's off balance, he shifts his weight onto his left leg, then removes his left hand from the rail and reaches for the duct. His eyes close when his fingers contact its smooth surface.

After a moment of quiet self-congratulation, he releases the rail entirely and curls his left arm around the four-sided duct, letting it help support his weight while he struggles to hop on his good leg. He shouts with every excruciating movement, his voice blending with the clamor of the storm, until he embraces the duct and repeats his swinging maneuver around the obstacle in his path.

Clinging to the duct like a wet towel to a nail, he lowers his forehead to the metal and shivers with fatigue. He's not sure he can manage the remaining distance because his lungs are burning and his arms are . . . like gelatin.

Gelatinous, ten letters, like gelatin, rubbery. Semisolid.

In spite of the pain, he laughs when another word occurs to him: *manumit,* a seven-letter word meaning *to free.* He can't give up if he wants to complete his manumission and finish that stupid puzzle.

He lifts his head and looks toward the landing. Nothing much to cling to over there, only a one-inch door frame and a steel strut. But at least there's something.

All right, then. Another journey across emptiness, a few more painful hops and all the screams he can muster. He draws the deepest breath he can and stretches for the door frame.

When he finally reaches the sill, he gingerly eases his

left foot onto the narrow strip, allowing himself the freedom to bellow like a bull gator when his broken limb strikes the surface of the door. His right hand is fastened to the strut with a clawlike grip; his left hand must release the rollers above the door.

Mindful of the yawning black emptiness at his back, Eddie closes his eyes and listens intently for angelic voices. When he hears nothing, he presses his chest against the smooth metal and hobbles sideways until his fingers find the locks at the top of the frame. He presses the release, then smiles when he hears a soft click. He slips his hands between the doors and exhales as they slide open with the smooth precision of well-maintained machinery.

Struggling to maintain her fragile control, Michelle crawls forward, speaking nonsense in a low voice. The skittish animal dances before her, alternately retreating and advancing, and Michelle's heart leaps into her throat when she finally lunges forward and hooks the dog's collar. She freezes, holding the animal at arm's length, but it doesn't snarl or try to bite her.

She smiles, hoping the dog understands that her intentions are friendly, and uses her free hand to stroke the dog's chest. "Nice doggy."

Under her palm, she feels a heart pounding as fast as her own.

"You're scared? So am I, but we're gonna get out of here." She moves forward and attempts to lift the animal, but the dog is heavier than it appears. She manages to pull the retriever onto her knees, but when she tries to stand, her feet slip and both of them fall onto the floor.

"Can't you cooperate?" Michelle's voice breaks as she releases the animal. "Please, sweetheart. I don't want to leave you, but you're too big to carry."

The dog whimpers, then licks her face. From the door, Isabel calls another indecipherable warning.

"Okay, then." Michelle pulls off her belt, slips the end through the buckle, and makes a loop. "Come on, sweetie," she says, slipping the circle over the dog's head. "Like it or not, you have to come with me."

She tugs on the belt, intending to use it as a leash, but the dog lies down, then rolls onto her side. Michelle pulls again, hoping the dog will understand, but pressure from the taut noose is forcing the animal to wheeze. The dog's tongue lolls from her mouth as terror enters her eyes.

Good grief, she's killing Eddie's dog.

Frustrated, Michelle turns toward the stairwell door, where Isabel is watching with obvious alarm. *"Vamos! Prisa!"*

A rise of panic threatens to choke Michelle, but she can't leave the dog, not after what Eddie did for them. What did he call the animal? Lady? Sally? No—Sadie.

"Sadie?" Tamping down her fear, she kneels to release the pressure on her belt. "Sadie, we're going home."

The dog lifts its head, its ears pricked forward.

"Sadie, come!" To reinforce her good intentions,

Michelle drops the belt and lifts her hands. The retriever watches as she retrieves her flashlight, then the dog rolls to her feet and trots forward.

"Good girl!" When they have passed through the stairwell doorway, Michelle gives the animal a tentative pat on the head.

She turns on the flashlight as the door closes behind them. Eddie was right—it is quieter here. Though the wind continues to howl, the lack of windows and the reinforced walls have created a safe haven. Only dim exit lights brighten the space, but Michelle doesn't expect any surprises in the stairwell—only concrete steps, two sets per floor, with handrails along each wall.

She walks to the metal railing and shines the light over the steps. The lobby lies twenty-eight flights below, but from the eighth-floor Pierpoint Restaurant they'll be able to survey the street and most of the downtown area.

Before heading down, though, she turns and looks at the steps that lead up. Her office lies at the top of those stairs, and Greg Owens's file waits on her secretary's desk. She could leave Isabel and the dog, run up four flights, grab the file and be back in ten minutes . . . but somewhere below, Eddie Vaughn needs help.

In the glow of an exit light, she gives Isabel a tremulous smile. "Are you ready?"

Isabel's look of confusion melts into understanding. "*Sí.*"

"Then let's go to the Pierpoint. We'll look for Eddie on the way down."

Isabel places one hand on a stair rail and the other on the dog's head. "It is a good plan."

They are halfway down the first set of steps when the fluorescent lights along the concrete walls hum and flicker. A moment later the stairwell is as bright as a new day.

Michelle clicks off her flashlight and laughs. "Gina may reach the lobby before us after all."

Gina catches her breath as the overhead lights burst into bloom. The car shudders faintly as a machine begins to hum. She reaches for the railing, then presses a hand to her chest.

The elevator is operating; the lights are burning steadily. The car is moving downward, not in a free fall, but at a stately and relaxed pace.

Twenty-seven, twenty-six, twenty-five . . .

She stares at the control panel, mentally counting the passing floors even though there are no landings at the express elevators. Her heart races, her fingers flutter, but surely she has no reason for concern. A fall would feel much swifter than this, wouldn't it?

Twenty-two, twenty-one, twenty . . .

At this rate she'll be downstairs long before Michelle and Isabel. She covers her mouth to restrain a nervous giggle. What did that foolish girl say about the storm ripping the roof off the building? Who cares if it does? She'll be safe downstairs, tucked into one of those nice leather chairs near the grand piano in the Pierpoint's lounge. Right across from the lovely restrooms.

Eighteen, seventeen, sixteen . . .

Perhaps there are others in the building—people who found themselves trapped in their offices or in the other elevators. They've probably taken refuge in the restaurant, too, or in the lobby. She might step onto a marble landing and discover the attorney general or one of his lawyers. If they're stranded here, rescue won't take long. As soon as the hurricane passes, they'll be barking orders on their cell phones. She'll have one of them call the children so they'll know she's all right.

Fourteen, thirteen, twelve . . .

Gina glances at the panel, realizing she's forgotten to select a floor. She presses the eight, but the button doesn't light.

A prickle of unease nips at the back of her legs, but surely everything is fine. Perhaps the elevator is in maintenance mode or some such thing. What did that young man say? Something about when an elevator starts up again, it will return to the lowest floor to pick up its programming. Fine, but she wants to go up to the Pierpoint. The restaurant will be a much more comfortable spot to wait for rescue.

Gina picks up her trench coat and the gun, then drops the weapon into her coat pocket. When it strikes something with a metallic chink, she sighs and remembers her car keys. She won't be able to drive out for a while, but she can wait.

Ten, nine, eight . . .

What is she to do about Sonny? Instinct warns

against mentioning his name, but he's gone and she had nothing to do with his death. Though her mind can't quite accept the idea, she is a widow.

The Mexican girl should go to the police . . . and if she doesn't, Gina will follow up. The kids will never need to know about Sonny's infidelity. The family reputation will be safe, along with the estate. Michelle Tilson is still carrying Sonny's child, but Gina saw the look in the younger woman's eye when she realized the truth. Her romantic illusions died with Sonny, so she's not likely to be bragging about her child's paternity.

As a matter of insurance, though, Gina might send the woman a check, accompanied by a suggestion that Tilson Corporate Careers relocate as soon as possible. Ten thousand ought to cover it. With the rates her company charges, she could deposit that amount in her business account and no one would be the wiser.

Five, four, three . . .

With a soft sigh, the elevator approaches its berth on the ground floor. Only as the tension leaves Gina's shoulders does she realize how overwrought she's been. She laughs softly at her anxieties, and smiles at the overhead lights.

Still burning, bright and strong.

The elevator shivers beneath her feet, halting with a distinct splash.

What the—

Almost immediately, water invades the lower edges of the car, coating the floor in a slick shine. Gina presses the eight on the elevator panel. The button lights beneath her fingertip, but before she can lift her hand, water begins to trickle from the rubber strips at the bottom of the elevator doors.

She steps closer and jabs the Close Door button. In the distance, a motor hums, the car vibrates . . . and the mechanical hum stops. The car is sinking; she can feel it moving beneath her feet as liquid seeps through the seams of her loafers.

This cannot be happening.

The trickle increases to a torrent that appears to climb the door like flame. A rising stream spatters her legs and contains a coldness she has never experienced in Florida waters.

"No!" She slams her fist against the control panel, but even though the overhead lights are still burning, the buttons have gone dark. This isn't a power outage, it's an elevator malfunction.

She drops her coat and steps toward the doors, then stops. If she tries to open them, she will only let more water into the car. The only way out . . . is up.

She lifts her gaze to the ceiling, where the exit hatch cover sits squarely in place . . . at her request. A hatch that can only be opened from the outside.

Because I could not stop for Death—

She trembles as her mind approaches an undeniable and dreadful understanding—

He kindly stopped for me.

In the hollow of her back, a single drop of perspiration traces the column of her spine. Shivering, she moves to the rear wall and as the water rises she hears herself repeating syllables as if she has been stricken by a spontaneous case of stuttering and will spend the rest of her life unable to stop speaking a single name: "Sonny!"

6:00 P.M.

CHAPTER 26

I know why you risk your neck . . . because you're afraid to risk your heart.

Through a haze of pain and exhaustion, Eddie keeps hearing his sister's voice. She speaks in the ripping wind, in the steady patter of rain dripping from a sagging ceiling tile, and in the fluttering rustle of papers blowing from an open doorway. He has collapsed in a leather chair that must have rolled from some secretarial desk; there's a definite nail-polish stain on the armrest. It is a lovely chair, one he would happily occupy for at least a week, but three women are still in the building and he needs to help them.

He forces his heavy eyelids open and squints toward the hallway. The stairwell has to be around the corner. All he has to do is pull himself out of this seat and walk, a feat that won't be impossible, even in his condition. After all, he just climbed sixty feet with a broken leg.

Incredulous: eleven letters; doubtful, skeptical, unconvinced.

How the other techs will react when they hear his story.

Michelle figures they have reached the twenty-sixth floor when Isabel hesitates on the landing. "I hope Mrs. Rossman made it downstairs."

Michelle laughs. "She's probably pacing in the lobby, wondering why the Tampa police aren't rushing to rescue her." She winces as a twinge of guilt strikes. "I shouldn't have said that. She went through a lot in that elevator."

They have just turned a corner when darkness engulfs the stairwell, an inky black broken only by the exit lights above each door.

"We'd better hurry," Michelle says, switching on the flashlight. "I don't know how long the backup generators will last."

Together the women and the retriever start down yet another flight of stairs. As they walk, Michelle shines the light over the concrete walls around them. Despite the roar and rip of the storm, the stairwell has held firm.

Isabel hesitates on the landing. "You think the hurricane is almost over?"

Michelle checks her watch. "Why don't you turn on the radio? Let's see what's happening out there."

Isabel pulls the CD player from her pocket and presses it into Michelle's hand. "You will better understand."

Michelle stops walking long enough to adjust the dial and slip the earbuds into her ears. A moment later the scratchy voice of an announcer fills her head. "St.

Petersburg is cut off from the rest of the state," he intones in a voice that strikes Michelle as oddly triumphant, "and police estimate that downtown Tampa is under eighteen feet of water. The West Shore area is completely flooded."

The news strums a shiver from Michelle. She stops on the stairs. "Isabel?"

"Yes?"

"How do you feel about vending-machine food? I have a feeling we may be here a while."

A shy smile crosses the girl's face. "I have a key to the Pierpoint Restaurant. Crackers, drinks, soup and canned goods—I know where they are kept."

"You're a wonderful woman, Isabel."

They have just turned another corner when Sadie stops, her nose vibrating, her tail rising like a plume. Michelle steps back and elbows Isabel. "What does that mean?"

"She is not growling. Maybe she hears a rat?"

Before Michelle can speak to the dog, Sadie takes off, bounding down the steps. Michelle leans over the railing, searching the dim depths, but she can't see anything.

An instant later she hears a bark, an astonished cry and a yelp of pain—a yelp that sounds strangely human.

She looks at Isabel. "Could that be—"

She doesn't wait for an answer.

Eddie isn't sure if he's more pleased to see Sadie or the women. The dog throttles him with her welcoming jump, and the brunette does as much damage when she throws her arms around him.

Though he tries not to groan, he can't help releasing a restrained *ooof* when she squeezes his ribs. "Are you—" She pulls away. "Oh, my goodness, you're hurt!"

He attempts a smile, knowing that his expression probably looks more like a grimace with teeth in it. "I'm alive, and that's what counts." He is about to congratulate them on their escape when a sudden thought strikes. "What happened to the other lady?"

The air around them vibrates with dread, then the brunette answers, "She stayed in the elevator."

"So she's still up there?"

"I don't think so." The woman's voice vacillates between confidence and uneasiness. "She had us close the hatch so the elevator would move if the power came back on. And it did—we had lights for a while, maybe twenty minutes."

Eddie closes his eyes, trying to imagine what might have happened. The car would probably descend to the first floor, where it would get in step with the controller. With power, it would operate normally unless something shorted out the circuits. . . .

"Mrs. Rossman is okay, no?"

Eddie looks up to answer the housekeeper's question. "I hope so."

"We tried to get her to come with us," the brunette says, her words coming in a rush. "But she wouldn't budge."

The housekeeper averts her eyes, unwilling to join the

conversation. The gesture arouses Eddie's curiosity, but this is not the time or place for an interview.

The brunette, who has retained control even in this situation, backs up and plays the flashlight over his face and the push broom he's been using for a crutch. "Hold still a minute—let us have a look at you."

Eddie leans on the railing, unable to resist a rising feeling of gratitude. This corporate woman might be bossy and light-years out of his league, but at the moment it feels good to let someone look after him.

"Good grief." Her voice, coming from behind the flashlight, is flat with disbelief. "You're as bruised as a hockey goalie."

Eddie squints into the light. "That doesn't sound good."

"How are you even walking around?"

He extends his hand to block the bright beam. "There's no drug like adrenaline."

The woman turns the light to the wall, leaving him momentarily blind, then her shoulder slides under his arm. "Throw that broom aside and lean on me, Mr. Eddie. Isabel and I are going to fix you up."

He tips his head back to study her face. "You know anything about setting broken bones?"

For an instant confusion and fear mingle in her eyes, then a smile trembles over her lips. "Back in the holler, I fell out of a tree and broke my arm. I watched my daddy set the bone, so I know exactly what to do."

He snatches a wincing breath. "Who are you, lady?"

"You," she says, her breath warm on his neck, "can call me Shelly."

Michelle loses count of how many doorways they pass. With Sadie leading the way, she and Isabel drape Eddie's arms over their shoulders and carry him down the steps. Adrenaline might have fueled his escape from the elevator shaft, but he feels more like dead weight with every passing floor.

"Here," Isabel finally says, nodding. "The eighth floor."

"About time."

Michelle supports Eddie while Isabel opens the door, then together they lead him to the lush lounge outside the Pierpoint Restaurant. A grand piano occupies the central space, but a leather sofa stretches against the wall and a thick carpet covers the floor . . . a carpet, Michelle notices, that is still dry.

She moves her watch into the flashlight's beam. Nearly seven o'clock, so the storm is probably swirling around them now.

While Isabel leads Eddie to the sofa, Michelle shines the flashlight over the area. No windows, which is good, but no lights, either. The restaurant, however, has small candle lamps on each dining table. She and Isabel can gather enough to light this sheltered space.

"We need lamps," she tells Isabel. "We need to take a look at Eddie's broken leg."

"Shouldn't we wait?" Isabel rubs her arms. "There are big windows in the restaurant, so if we go in there to get lamps—"

"The glass ought to hold," Michelle assures her. "I remember when they redesigned the place, they put in windows that are supposed to be hurricane-proof. So we need to get the lamps and take care of Eddie's leg before the bone starts to die."

A groan rises from the sofa as Isabel takes the flashlight and moves away. "Die?" Eddie asks. Are you kidding?"

Michelle turns in the darkness, hoping her voice will convey a confidence she doesn't quite feel. "Isabel has a key to the restaurant, so we're going to get lights, a cutting board and plastic wrap. I'm going to make sure the bone is straight, bracing it against the cutting board if I have to set it, then we'll secure it with napkins and plastic wrap—"

"And I'm supposed to live through this?"

Michelle allows herself to laugh softly. "Don't worry, Eddie. I'm also going to fetch a big bottle of brandy. You won't feel a thing."

SUNDAY, SEPTEMBER 16
11:00 A.M.

CHAPTER 27

Michelle dips a kitchen towel into a bucket of murky water and wishes someone in the Lark Tower had thought to fill a couple of bathtubs. She isn't sure the building *has* any bathtubs, but right now she'd give her entire 401(k) for a cold bubble bath to relieve the sticky heat of this enclosed space.

She presses the wet towel to the back of her sweaty neck and tries not to think about the bacteria that may be breeding in it. Isabel filled the bucket in the stairwell, happily reporting that the water level had dropped several feet during the night. "The only water remaining is probably the water that can't get out," Eddie answered, lifting his bottle in a salute. "Someone's going to have to pump it out of the basement."

Michelle hopes they won't be around to watch the pumping crews.

After falling into an exhausted sleep last night, they woke to a changed world. Isabel awakened first and scoured the kitchen for supplies, returning with bread, crackers, cheese, batteries and bottled water. Over that fine breakfast, Eddie, looking even more battered than he had the night before, turned on the radio and repeated the news for Isabel and Michelle.

Tampa had experienced a direct hit by a category-four hurricane. One-hundred-fifty-mile-per-hour winds had ravaged buildings up and down the coast. Tides had risen over twenty-three feet, flooding the downtown district, the international airport and the military base. More than a million people had safely evacuated and were waiting to hear from those who remained behind.

Several fishing piers in Pinellas County had been washed away. Scattered looting had been reported in Tampa, Clearwater and St. Petersburg. Electrical power and telephones—landlines and cellular service—were out almost everywhere, and trees blocked many roads, hampering rescue efforts. Numerous tornadoes, spawned by the storm, wreaked peripheral damage in Lakeland, Plant City and Winter Haven.

The Port of Tampa, the sole source of gasoline for Florida's west coast, would be out of commission for several weeks. Due to the prolonged power outage, Hillsborough County's eight hundred pumping stations had shut down, causing sewage to bubble up into city streets.

Tampa General and St. Joseph's hospitals, both of which had been built to withstand one-hundred-twenty-five-mile-per-hour winds, had been demolished. Downtown, the mayor's office, city and county government centers, police headquarters, and the state and federal court buildings were all presumed uninhabitable.

A helicopter flying over the downtown area reported mounds of shattered glass and asphalt on roads chewed up by the receding storm surge. Officials estimated that the sixty-six thousand people who worked in the downtown area would be out of work for months. "Things are pretty bad downtown," the pilot reported. "We hope the area was evacuated, because we didn't see any survivors down there."

"Not all the news is bad," Eddie added, smiling. "The county tax collector recently added a concrete bunker, an emergency generator and steel shutters to his office. He's happy to report that all local tax records have been safely preserved."

Michelle brushed bread crumbs from her hands, then tossed her last crust to Sadie. "I guess we need to hang a flag or something out a window to let them know we're here."

"Might be easier to wade down to the tax collector's office." Grinning, Eddie pulled the earbuds from his ears, then handed the radio back to Isabel. "We have supplies, so we'll be luckier than a lot of people. Until they send someone down here, we can make like we're at Scout camp or something."

Michelle noticed Isabel's blank expression and smiled. "I don't think I'm the only one who never went to Scout camp."

"No?" Eddie straightened and grimaced, revealing the pain he tried to hide. "Well, it's all about survival and keeping a positive outlook. You search for the things you need, see if you can't use whatever you have at hand, and make the most of what you have. Simple stuff "The corner of his mouth dipped slightly when he looked at Michelle. "I've got to admit, at first I thought a woman like you wouldn't know much about roughing it—"

"Surprised you, didn't I?" Michelle lifted her chin. "I think I've surprised myself."

She waited for him to come back with a smart-aleck retort, but he only smiled, winking the dimple in his left cheek. "I reckon you have."

Now she sits on a chair in the restaurant, trying to cool off as she looks through a gaping window at what used to be a bustling business district. The newscaster was right—a river of water swirls up what used to be Tampa Street, but the level is several feet below the waterline on adjacent buildings.

She turns her head at the sound of a creak—Eddie is coming her way, supported on two push-broom crutches, the bristles under his arm thoughtfully cushioned with linen napkins Isabel found in a closet. Sadie follows him, as devoted as ever.

Michelle smiles, then points at the road below. "My car's gone. I parked it right down there, and it's vanished."

"Probably swept away." With an effort, Eddie sinks into a chair, drops his makeshift crutches onto the floor and surveys the damage with a rueful expression.

Michelle nods. "I know. It's . . . unbelievable." Though she has lived in Florida for years, she has never imagined seeing anything like this. The moving water below is filled with debris—bits of plants, broken glass, wooden planks and police barricades— but no bodies, praise God.

At least, not yet.

She brings her hand to her mouth as the thought unsettles her stomach. As long as they remain in this building, they can't escape the specter of death.

As soon as Eddie woke this morning, he insisted that she help him to the eighth-floor elevator landing. Gina might still be trapped, he said, and by now she ought to be desperate to climb out of the car.

Using a special tool from his pocket, he opened the doors to the center express shaft and searched for the car that had held them prisoner for so long.

He finally spotted it far below. Covered with water.

No one has mentioned Gina or Parker since that grim discovery, but thoughts of them haunt every conversation and memory. Death lives in this building, and Michelle can't wait to leave.

Eddie watches her, his face displaying an uncanny awareness. "You feeling okay?"

"It's . . . morning sickness."

He looks toward the window. "I see."

"I don't think you can . . . understand." Michelle closes her eyes, assaulted by mixed emotions and a deep sense of shame. "Let's just say that my past . . . Well, when we get out of here, I'm starting over."

Eddie nods, then hooks his arm over the back of his chair. "I've started over before. It takes time, but things do begin to look better."

She looks away, embarrassed by the relief his words give her. She scarcely knows this man, but she owes him her life. She bullied him into coming to Tampa, to an area that isn't even his territory, and yet he's still willing to sit here and comfort her.

She turns, suddenly curious. "I was wondering."

"Yeah?"

She studies his face another moment, then shakes her head. "Why'd you come for us, Eddie? You didn't have to. We shouldn't have been here, but you risked everything—"

She stops when a dusky red tide advances up his neck. For a moment he says nothing, then he clears his throat. "I thought I came because I owed a debt . . . but in that shaft, I realized the debt I owe can never be repaid. My life, your life . . . we really don't control the big picture, do we?"

She turns the thought over in her mind. "So . . . you came here for nothing?"

When Eddie's gaze moves into hers, his eyes are compassionate, tender and understanding. "I wouldn't say that. I came for you."

OCTOBER 29
9:00 A.M.

~✕~

CHAPTER 28

Wrapped in the remnants of a dream, Michelle opens her eyes and stares at the ceiling until she remembers what day it is. She reaches for the remote on the nightstand and powers on the television, tuned to the local news channel. A somber-faced young man appears before the Lark Tower, which still bears the scars of Hurricane Felix.

Not needing to be reminded of the storm, she turns down the volume, then drops the remote and eases out from under the comforter. In bare feet she pads toward the bathroom, where she knows she'll find a shower and sink and toilet, all of which will run with blessedly clean water.

After showering and drying her hair, she slips into

a loose-fitting dress and calls a cab.

When the taxi drops her at her destination, she pauses to knit the raveled fabric of her nerve before exiting the vehicle. She hasn't been to this part of the city since a rescue boat pulled her from the Tower three days after the storm struck.

Even now, memories of the elevator haunt her dreams.

Her therapist says it's only natural that she should be experiencing an emotional roller coaster. On one fateful day, she faced several earth-shattering revelations and bonded with strangers, one of whom died in a macabre accident. In time, the therapist keeps promising, life will return to normal.

Michelle isn't sure she wants *normal*. She knows she doesn't want the life she had. In the elevator she chose to trust Eddie Vaughn; now she's choosing to trust the Savior her grandmother had talked so much about.

And she is keeping the baby.

She steps out of the cab, smoothes her jacket over the slight bulge of her tummy and hooks her purse over her shoulder. The asphalt is cracked in several places and the live oaks are gone, but the city's landmarks are still recognizable. From across the street she scans the Lark Tower and notices that nearly all the upper-floor windows are covered with plywood. According to her claims adjuster, her office suite, along with Parker Rossman's and several of the attorney general's, is a ruined shell. Her company's files and papers—those that haven't disintegrated or been washed into the bay—are drifting in the currents of the Hillsborough River.

She accepted his assessment without argument because she's in no hurry to return to any elevator in the Lark Tower.

She swallows hard, her nerves at a full stretch, but as the cab pulls away she sees a man waiting on the opposite curb. At the sight of his crutches, she quickens her step. Sadie stands by his side, joined to him by a pink-and-purple leash.

The glow of the man's smile overcomes the slight October chill.

"Hello, Eddie." She enfolds the man in a gentle embrace, then bends to fondle the dog's ears. "Hi, Sadie. Love the new leash."

Eddie chuckles. "I would never have bought any-thing with pink in it, but you convinced me she needs a little more pizzazz in her life."

"She deserves it." Michelle wipes her hand on her skirt. "So—how's rehab going?"

"Fine." He looks down at his leg and bends his knee. "The doctor said you did a great job of setting that bone."

"Beginner's luck, I think."

"Give yourself a little credit. It was more than luck."

"Well . . ." Michelle tilts her head toward the building. "You ready to go inside?"

"I was waiting for you. Isabel and Carlos are already in the lobby."

"Any news on Isabel's situation?"

Eddie shifts his weight on the crutches. "She and Carlos went to the police and explained what happened. The detectives took her statement, but they're not going to file charges because there's no evidence to prove Parker's death was anything but an accident. They did place a call to the DEA, who alerted the Mexican authorities to Ernesto Fuentes and his operation. He won't make it over the border again."

"That's a relief."

Michelle adjusts her step to match Eddie's as they walk toward the revolving doors that lead into the first-floor lobby.

"I hear—" she brightens her voice "—that the mayor wants to present your award. I threatened to arm-wrestle her for the honor, of course."

Eddie scowls. "I still think this is all a waste of time. I wouldn't have come at all, except—"

"Except what?"

He stops in midstep, his eyes searching her face. "I had to see how you girls were doing."

Michelle lifts her chin. A few weeks ago she would have bristled if anyone described her as a girl, but from Eddie's lips the term feels . . . flattering.

He hesitates. "Did you go to any of the funerals?"

"I went to the Rossmans' service, more for Gina's sake than Parker's. It was hard to see them be buried. I felt horrible about the way she died. I should have forced her to come with us."

"That lady was determined," Eddie answers. "And she probably thought she made the right decision. I heard that the medical examiner's office found no signs of a struggle, apart from a few bruises on her hands. She drowned, pure and simple."

They take several steps in that special silence in which difficult words are sought and carefully linked together. "I heard," Michelle finally says, "that Gina's sister took a leave of absence from her medical practice and has come to live with the kids. They're still adjusting, but I hear she's committed to sticking around for a while."

"That's good."

"I thought so, too. Change can be beneficial. That's why I'm moving my business."

Is that a flash of disappointment in his eyes?

"Not far," she hastens to add, "but to a smaller office in a shopping plaza not far from here. I thought I might downsize, see what I could do to find real jobs for real people."

"Aren't CEOs real people?"

She laughs. "Sure they are. But they don't need as much help as other people do."

A trace of unguarded tenderness lingers in Eddie's eyes when he smiles at her. "I've missed you. I guess you can't spend seventy-two hours with someone and not get to know them well."

Not quite ready to share her hero with the world, Michelle stops on the sidewalk and looks into the face she'll never forget. "I've missed you, too."

"So. . .you won't mind if Sadie and I drop by for a visit? Or take you out to a movie?"

She looks at him, her heart brimming with a feeling she had thought long dead. Eddie is so unlike Parker and the other men she's known. He is . . . sweet.

"In Bald Knob," she says, grinning up at him, "we call it the picture show. So sure, you can take me to the show as long as you're okay—" she runs her hand over the bulge at her belly "—with everything."

He looks at her, his gaze as soft as a caress. "I'm okay with you, Shelly."

Unspeakably grateful for this reassurance, she places her hand tight against his cheek, then thrills when he turns his face into her palm and kisses it.

He might have kissed her again, but the revolving doors are turning, spilling a wave of photographers, cameramen and reporters. A dark-haired couple sweeps out with the crowd, and at first Michelle doesn't recognize the attractive woman in a tailored pantsuit. But when the man next to her lifts an adorable dark-haired toddler into his arms, the pieces fall into place.

"Isabel!" Michelle hurries forward to embrace the Suarez family.

The four survivors exchange greetings, then Carlos wraps his arm around his wife and together they move into the marble lobby.

ACKNOWLEDGMENTS

No novelist writes alone, and I had lots of help with this book. First, thank you to my blog readers, who helped me fill Michelle's purse.

I owe a huge debt to my agent, Danielle Egan-Miller, and to Steeple Hill editors Joan Marlow Golan and Krista Stroever for their great enthusiasm for a one-paragraph synopsis.

A deep and abiding thank-you to the two elevator technicians I met at the Imperial Swan Hotel in Lakeland. When I asked for their names, they said I could simply thank the "two handsome gentlemen" who gave me a guided tour of the inner (and outer) workings of an elevator and let me peer into the shaft. Gentlemen, my hat's off to you.

Thank you to fellow novelist Randy Singer, who introduced me to Michael Garner, who not only answered dozens of e-mailed questions, but seemed to enjoy doing so despite the story's high estrogen level. Thanks, also, to Michael's friend P.J., otherwise known as Paul G. McGrath, who answered queries from Michael, who then passed the answers along to me. Gentlemen, this book would not be complete without you.

Hugs and *muchas gracias* to Vasthi Acosta and Veronica Beard, who helped me with Isabel's Spanish. Any lingering errors are mine alone.

Center Point Publishing
600 Brooks Road ● PO Box 1
Thorndike ME 04986-0001 USA

(207) 568-3717

US & Canada:
1 800 929-9108
www.centerpointlargeprint.com